HOTEL LIVING

"Ioannis Pappos's *Hotel Living* could be *The Great Gatsby* reincarnated in a contemporary hell beyond even F. Scott Fitzgerald's imagination. It's harrowing. It's smart and sexy; it's funny and tragic. It is, in short, a great and terrible beauty of a book."
—Michael Cunningham, Pulitzer Prize winner and *New York Times* bestselling author of *The Snow Queen* and *The Hours*

"If Trollope were alive today and he wanted to write *The Way We Live Now* about New York's élite consultants, he would have written *Hotel Living*. Really a terrific book."   —Edmund White

"I read *Hotel Living* in an evening. Pappos is a first-rate storyteller and keen observer of our current moment. The prose here shimmers, and the narration drives hard like the hard-living lives in these pages. It's a smart book that also happens to be entertaining and a damn bit of fun to read. I can't wait for his next book."
—Anthony Swofford, *New York Times* bestselling author of *Jarhead*

"What do you feel when somebody with no writing track record you know of hands you a manuscript? Profound misgivings? Right! Ioannis Pappos had asked me to read just a chapter of *Hotel Living*. My misgiving vamoosed on page one. Pappos delivers a fast-moving narrative set in the new model world of the international business culture. The sexual and social mores of a wired world are well and truly captured through sharp conversations and vivid vignettes that get you feeling, Well, yes. Of course! These are the ways of our world."

—Anthony Haden-Guest, author of *The Last Party, Studio 54, Disco,* and *The Culture of the Night*

"Like a cross between *The Wolf of Wall Street* and Edith Wharton, Ioannis Pappos gets all the details right in this insider's look at love and money in NYC in the postmillennial age. Pappos is such a good writer, it's hard to believe he leads a double life in the trenches of Wall Street; but it is that combination that gives this moving story both its punch and density."

—Ira Sachs, writer and director of *The Delta, Keep the Lights On,* and *Love Is Strange*

"Ioannis Pappos may be the F. Scott Fitzgerald of the wired postmillennial age. *Hotel Living* is an unforgettable debut—an all-night party, a race around the world, a dangerous high-stakes game played in the violently competitive world of international business. The novel's urgent pulse, no-holds-barred pace, and heartbreakingly honest narrator will thrust you into a captivating story that is, all at once, about love, sex, class, greed, and the search for one's humanity against the blinding light of the American Dream." —Julia Fierro, author of *Cutting Teeth*

"Ioannis Pappos's *Hotel Living* is a social novel of remarkable breadth and depth. His command of narrative and his complex characters make for a fast-paced yet thoughtful story of one man's experience in the rough-and-tumble world of high finance and the rougher world of failed love. Not only does Pappos make us understand, he makes us feel. This may be Pappos's first novel but it reads like the work of a seasoned writer."

—Pablo Medina, author of *Cubop City Blues*

"As he romps through the highs and lows of the global economy, Ioannis Pappos will make you laugh even as he lays bare the very real human costs of our recent—and current—economic troubles. Hilarious and heartbreaking, *Hotel Living* captures perfectly our own interesting times." —Scott Lasser, author of *All I Could Get*

"From the caverns of New York finance, first-time writer Ioannis Pappos bursts out with a fast-paced tale of an unblushing Greek Gatsby living the high life, a party skidding toward destruction. The pleasures are quick and voyeuristic, the bedroom cold, the banter knowing. His protagonist is diffident yet accessible, bold but aware, an unbruised stranger grappling with a world of little consequence until the bright nights turn bittersweet."
—Edie Meidav, author of *Lola, California*

"In *Hotel Living*, Pappos delivers room service at its best and most corrupting. A searing and smart indictment of the players at the helm of today's global economy, *Hotel Living* is also sexy and fun, as Stathis, the son of a Greek fisherman, navigates waters replete with treacherous men and women swimming or drowning and not knowing the difference."
—Pamela Painter, author of *Wouldn't You Like to Know*

"In between the words, sliding out into the margins and slipping into our consciousness, Ioannis Pappos's devastating and engaging book *Hotel Living* reveals the dominant forces that have shaped the new millennium. Bold and insistent, this book is a creative response challenging us not to blindly accept the world around us as it appears but to see beyond the glib facade and discover what is real. With a sharp eye and inimitable worldview, Pappos has given us a work animated by the spirits of Bolaño through Pasolini to Edmund White. Blending clever prose with piercing socio-political investigation, this book draws the line, ultimately asking each of us if we embrace the spectacle (what separates) or choose society (what connects)."

—Antonino D'Ambrosio, author of *Let Fury Have the Hour*

"I came to regard each and every character as if they were real people, who deserved and provoked real emotional responses. Pappos's quicksilver touch of the New World is never convoluted or heavy-handed, even when describing love in its most complicated manifestations. There is a penetrating sweetness even in the most bitter regret, and a handling of Greekness reminiscent of Eugenides in *Middlesex*: something at once looming at arm's length and painfully unattainable. *Hotel Living* is nothing short of a masterpiece. It moved me and will continue to do so in more ways than I could imagine possible for a story told with such disarming clarity and plainness. Rest assured that we'll be talking *Hotel Living* for years, as will its overawed readers and reviewers."

—Auguste Corteau, author of *The Book of Katherine*

"Whew! I need to check into rehab for a week. I just finished reading Ioannis Pappos's bold, painfully intimate novel *Hotel Living*. All that booze! And blow! And unadulterated fucking! Yet rendered with such insight, and crafted with skill and compassion. Every decade or so a novel comes along that utterly captures the Zeitgeist of our benighted times. I think of *Less Than Zero*, *Bright Lights, Big City*, and now *Hotel Living*. Kudos for Pappos. This is a writer to reckon with." —Richard Stratton, author of *Altered States of America*

"We've read and watched depictions of the reckless excess of our recent gilded age, but rarely do we get a glimpse into the inner life of one of its players. *Hotel Living* is *The Wolf of Wall Street* with a heart." —Mike Albo, author of *The Junket*

HOTEL
LIVING

A novel

HOTEL LIVING

IOANNIS PAPPOS

HARPER ◉ PERENNIAL

NEW YORK • LONDON • TORONTO • SYDNEY • NEW DELHI • AUCKLAND

HARPER PERENNIAL

HOTEL LIVING. Copyright © 2015 by Ioannis Pappos. All rights reserved. Printed in the United States of America. No part of this book may be used or reproduced in any manner whatsoever without written permission except in the case of brief quotations embodied in critical articles and reviews. For information address HarperCollins Publishers, 195 Broadway, New York, NY 10007.

HarperCollins books may be purchased for educational, business, or sales promotional use. For information please e-mail the Special Markets Department at SPsales@harpercollins.com.

FIRST EDITION

Library of Congress Cataloging-in-Publication Data

Pappos, Ioannis
Hotel living / by Ioannis Pappos.—Trade paperback
pages cm
ISBN 978-0-06-237636-7 (trade pb)—ISBN 978-0-06-237637-4 (e-book)
1. Business consultants—United States—Fiction. 2. Single-room-occupancy hotels—United States—Fiction. 3. Luxuries—Morals and ethics—United States—Fiction. I. Title.
PS3616.A66H68 2015
813'.6—dc23

2014042023

15 16 17 18 19 OV/RRD 10 9 8 7 6 5 4 3 2 1

To my three brothers, Savvas, Alek, and Christos

PART I

Erik

ONE

I LEFT MY FISHING VILLAGE IN Greece because I was good at backgammon and ridiculously lucky. I was thirteen when a tourist saw me beating everyone in the village square and registered me for an aptitude test at a school in Athens. My mother cried when I left Trikeri. My father was out fishing, said he couldn't take the day off, but he wasn't the type for good-byes anyway. Ten years and two scholarships later, I graduated from the physics department of Stanford and got a programming job in Silicon Valley.

After rural Greek tempers and Stanford egos, engineers from India were damn fine people to work with. They were fantastically intelligent, possessed a discreet charm, and didn't question authority. They worked as if they reported to someone higher. Married with mortgages, they exemplified the Bay Area's civic, complacent order. They lived as if they would never leave.

I, however, did not. I was still curious; Northern California was not a destination. With the dot-com meltdown, my Silicon Valley enthusiasm fizzled out. I was getting more and more unsatisfied.

WHEN I TOLD MY COLLEAGUES that I was about to start an MBA in France, they were amused.

"Stathis, I didn't know you spoke *French!*"

"France has *business* schools?" a Java programmer said, snorting a laugh.

"The Greek will take a wine course!"

But I was excited. Late that summer of 2002, I caught myself with a permanent smile at work. I drove around the Bay Area, windows down, nasty rap rock from that summer's blockbuster sound track blasting from the stereo's speakers. I would miss my exit and keep going down the highway, to Half Moon Bay, to ride a wave or two.

At my farewell lunch in Redwood City at a fancy Chinese restaurant, my colleagues grinned and wobbled. Someone squeezed my shoulder. Sure, it was my day, but after two rounds of layoffs—the payback from the tech bubble— everyone was cheering a legit departure. I leaned back in my chair and looked around the table. We all had something in common: we were educated immigrants who'd lacked opportunities back home. Some of us had had rough childhoods.

At first, an MBA was my plan B—insurance in case I wasn't caught up in something bigger, like a business-technology job in Europe. But a couple of months into my applications, some MBA virus infected me. Brochures assured "the amalgamation of strategy, finance, and organizational behavior" (whatever *that* meant), but all I read was an understory, some buzz about "being there." My interviews with alumni revealed a sky's-the-limit optimism that took success for granted:

" . . . become an unscripted leader . . ."

" . . . the helicopter view of the corporate world . . ."

" . . . bonus culture, which is *not* about the money!"

"EBS is the best business school in the world. EBS is *the* business school of the world," a McKinsey executive and European Business School graduate told me at the end of my interview. "You'll be at the right place at the right time," he said as I entered the elevator.

They got me.

I gave away my IKEA furniture, sold my Honda Civic to my boss's daughter, and bought a one-way ticket to Paris. I boarded the plane, beaming. Once again, I was eager, Greek.

THE FIRST THING I NOTICED on campus was that everyone in my class had been around. Everyone spoke at least three languages—one of the school's requirements—while *via* was the way to answer the "Where are you from?" question. Italians came "via the States and South America." Brits came from "Cambridge via McKinsey." People rarely asked where you grew up; it was where you'd worked and studied that mattered.

"From Greece, via Silicon Valley!" I'd say.

A forty-five-minute drive from Paris, the EBS campus was in the center of the Fontainebleau Forest next to a fifteenth-century palace. Most of the students lived in nearby châteaus maintained, barely, by once-wealthy, now in-decline counts who lived in the garden houses on their properties and collect-ed rent from us who stayed in their crumbling grand courts.

I traded my one-bedroom apartment in a cookie-cutter San Mateo complex for the Château de Montmelian, a disin-tegrating four-hundred-year old mansion with Münchausen-esque roofs with gables and chimneys, all of it piled on thirty acres of thickly wooded land hiding abandoned nurser-ies, tennis courts, statues, and peacocks. Once unpacked, I realized I had stepped onto an Italian movie set, a stage for diversions—not in the least conducive to homework—while my class smelled of testosterone.

"MANAGEMENT CONSULTING IS RIDICULOUSLY OVERRATED," said my classmate Paul, the balding son of a European prime minis-ter, at a recruiting event that fall. He handed me a brochure for a consulting firm called Command.

I browsed the glossy leaflet. "You don't care for 'value inno-vation'? You don't want to be a 'game changer'?" I smiled, mocking the brochure, but Paul was distracted.

"Value my ass," he mumbled. "Want to change the game? Go into private equity."

"Yeah, hmm, I skipped school the day they handed out job offers," I joked, but Paul was gazing around. He had brokered a fourthhand Renault for me that had belonged to a friend of his, a recent graduate, and I was getting uncomfortable about driving a car I still had not paid for—Paul was always "too busy" to pass me the money-wiring instructions.

"Yes. Next week. Promise. I promise," Paul said when I mentioned something about writing him a check. He finally looked back at me. "This week is insanely busy. My mother is visiting. Which reminds me . . ." He paused and gave me a head-to-shoes look. "Stathis! You are Greek, *fine*. But this is a recruiting event, and you are wearing brown shoes."

I gave my Filene's Basement loafers a quick look. I used to wear sneakers to work on Fridays. "Uh, right," I mumbled.

"In London you can get fired for that."

"That'd first require *having* a job," I whispered, wondering what exactly it would take for me to make a go of it here: studying? Shopping? Sucking up to schoolmates' parents?

Paul placed his fist against my torso. "Just tell them your GPA, mate."

I laughed. "Gotta split. I need to pack. Alkis and I are moving tomorrow."

"*Excuse* me?"

"Montmelian got flooded."

"You are *joking*!" Paul's mouth stayed open. "The comte has totally dropped the ball. Really. Okay, let's have a moving party."

"Paul!"

"A moving lunch. Beer and takeout, simple. I'll bring the gang." Paul was excited. My loss was his excuse to get wasted.

"Great," I said flatly.

He gave me an apologetic look, as if to say: *This is a small price to pay to be one of us, Greek boy.*

THE NEXT DAY I MOVED with Alkis, my London Greek via Harvard, president of the student body, "château-mate," from Montmelian's main court to a freezing shed at the edge of the property. The entire shack was a thirty-by-thirty box split into three murky bedrooms and a mice-infested kitchen.

A crowd showed up, indeed, which turned the hut's extra bedroom into a falafel-and-cigarette-smelling living room. Slouched on a bed, Paul held court, describing our costumes for that evening's party. Halfway through Alkis's outfit he paused and picked up my hummus-crusted *Valuation* book, slowly, using only two fingers. "You might want to split these pages up before you get finger frostbite in this cabin," Paul said, and threw my finance book at a dusty nightstand.

Sitting on the bed opposite him, I looked at the crusted hummus on my book and realized how ridiculously cold it was to sleep through the night.

"Mr. President!" I shouted to Alkis in the kitchen. "How's fixing that heater coming along?"

But there was no reply.

Paul went on rolling a joint while planning his fiancée's visit from London. In the thick of his third campus fling, he was rehearsing his plea. He looked at me: "Sleeping pills take away REM. We *know* that," Paul said.

I just shrugged.

"When they didn't let rats have REM sleep, you know what they did?" Paul asked, but no one spoke. "They went into sex overdrive. A frenzy. They couldn't process it."

I heard Alkis laugh in the kitchen.

"We know that rats have, what?" Paul continued, passing me the joint. "Two, three percent DNA difference from us?" He couldn't be high yet; he had just lit the damn thing. "Sta-this, *you* know what I'm talking about."

I was about to burst out silly, but then I thought about how sometimes first class had few dealings with the real world. Extreme privilege could be surreal, but could also trigger funny social changes too. I took a hit and made an eyes-wide-open Paul-in-Wonderland yet brotherly face. "*Malaka*, listen," I said, but tools banged and dropped in the kitchen.

"Cunting *bugger*!" Alkis yelled.

"*Malaka!*"

"*Bastardo!*"

"*Cazzo!*" Curses to the Montemelian comte all around.

I got up and made it into the kitchen, to find Alkis still in the loosened black tie he had worn on his way back from London that morning. He was yelling into his cell phone. "*Yes!*" Alkis shouted. "I'm looking for a plan B for sleeping tonight. Our heater's a fucking *recycling* bin. Got a problem with that, *mate*?" He hung up. "Fat *fuck*!"

"Is this your moving tux?" I raised my eyebrows.

"Piss off, mate," Alkis said. "I had to red-eye Eurostar. And it's too bleeding freezing in this shithole to change."

"How can one red-eye Eurostar?" I asked.

Alkis thought for a moment. "Mate, thanks for packing my crap last night. You're my ace."

"Don't mention it," I slurred. "Listen, an American who studies journalism at Oxford is coming to EBS for a couple of days. He's writing an article on European business schools for his school paper in England. I think."

"And?" Alkis said, browsing through contacts on his cell.

"The Dubyas thought it would make a good impression if he stayed at Montmelian."

"Here?" He looked at me, annoyed. "Are they high?"

"LBS booked him at a Radisson, so we're trying to be different. It's only for a couple of nights," I said.

"Fine. And if we don't like his draft, we lock him indoors to die," Alkis grumbled. Then, on his cell phone: "Hey, it's me . . . your *president*?"

"I'll tell him to crash in our study-living room thing," I said, and turned to leave.

"Hold on, babe!" Alkis yelled into his phone, or to me. "Give the Dubya my room. I'm heading to Zurich on Sunday for job interviews. I'm not back until the middle of next week."

"Good," I said. "Gotta run."

Alkis looked at me suspiciously.

"I need to stop by the prof courts before training," I said.

"Hobnobbing with the faculty now, are we?"

My eyes drifted. Truth was, I felt at home around professors. There was something in them that I could not see in Paul, and even in Alkis. The faculty must already have grappled with career anxieties, and many of them, like me, had left their homelands to get ahead and make some money. "It's just rugby." I tried to dismiss Alkis. "Carpooling for training with—"

"Corporate Finance *rugbies*?" he laughed. "The twat's forty."

I was getting ready to counter him, but Alkis was back on his phone: "No, no. Not at all, baby. Of *course* not. Of *course* I'll be at your dinner." He put his thumb over the speaker of his cell phone. "When's the Al Jazeera dinner?" he distress-whispered to me.

"Whenever you want!" Paul said, marching into the kitchen in the black paramilitary hood—Ustaše badge pinned on—that he planned to wear at that evening's annual EBS S&M party at the largest château in the forest. He checked his reflection in the kitchen window, fixed the hood, and pulled a travel guidebook from his back pocket. I pretended not to notice him, but he began to read aloud:

"There is an end-of-the-world feel about this part of Pelio, as the road to Trikeri becomes more and more desolate. If you like taking one step farther even than those who have gotten away from it all, head for this little island with a year-round population of less than 150, just off the coast of the Pagasi-tikos Gulf. But the main pastime in Trikeri is explaining to locals why you're there—and then explaining to yourself why you're leaving."

Paul lifted his hood. "So, why did you leave?"

"'Cause I didn't wanna fish no more," I said calmly but shortly. "And I believe you read the word *desolate*." I exhaled and stood still. I hadn't been back home for a while, to avoid mandatory service in the Greek army, something that made me self-conscious even in front of half-Greeks like Alkis. I looked around. Paul was playing with the shoe box by the sink that served as our mousetrap, and Alkis was listening to voice mails.

"Cunt," Alkis said, and pressed 7 to delete the message.

"OUR CRUSH ON MANAGEMENT CONSULTING jobs comes from the Europeans' silliness," Paul told me at the campus bar after my training.

We were both sweaty, me from rugby, Paul from running around finishing nothing—from being Paul. I dried my face with the towel over my shoulders, but sweat kept dripping onto the bar.

"Silliness?" I asked.

"Europeans have this chip about money. We think that we're above it," Paul said, and downed his beer. "We act as if banking is not intellectually challenging enough. Like it's only good for Americans and emerging markets."

"What about entrepreneurship?"

He narrowed his eyes. "That's okay. For the Brits."

"I respect money," I said.

"Stathis, you respect money 'cause you don't have any. You grew up in a fishing village in Greece. Look around. People didn't come here to have a career or become rich. This is not Wharton. You get to play with classmates who *happen* to be royals. With me! You learn how to manage down school-mates from Japan and India, and how to dress up for balls and Michelin-starred restaurants in Barbizon. You're in a Fitzgerald camp for children." He pulled the towel from my shoulders and dried off his face and neck.

"Sounds exhausting," I said, glancing around awkwardly. The campus bar was getting busy. A guy from my finance group was staring at us. I wasn't sure how to deal with the bar, with EBS—with anything. Paul was deconstructing a world that I was trying to enter just by being there. I was probably a joke for him. Amusing. There could never be a real friendship between us. "I thought they taught us that managing and leading are different," I half joked.

He tossed the towel back at me. "You're full of shit—that's why *you* are here."

I took issue. Pollyanna or not, I'd left my village with some sense of responsibility. I'd taken out student loans for EBS, which meant that skills and career goals were vested there, and since its academic intensity was considered one of the highest in the world, I took EBS seriously.

Yet, proving Paul's point, half my class already had jobs lined up, which allowed for a campus hedonism of epidemic proportions: a final year of partying, of "don't-ask-but-please-do-tell" promiscuity mixed with sleeping pills, pills, driving drunk in the forest, and any other type of self-indulgence as long as you stayed cocky or "MBA-bohemian" about it. Each week was dedicated to a country, whose students hosted alcohol-soaked blowouts that built up to weekend wickedness. On top of that, there were "party playoffs": the Summer Ball, hosted either at the Château de Courances or at Versailles; the Winter Ball; the Montmelian Ball—all black tie—the Bois le Roi parties; the Farmers' party (planned around a cave); the "Crossover" party—for crossing the middle of the academic year—where guys wore girls' clothes and vice versa; and, of course, that evening's S&M party in the chambers of the Château de Fleury-en-Bière, an EBS tradition that sent students all the way to Pigalle sex shops to get outfits, and summed up all my campus disillusionments about Paul's play-for-future-network mantra. He was selling me indulgence as the first step toward old-world entitlement; a puzzling concept, but after three years of programming C++—and another ten of studying, working, and constantly proving myself—I didn't mind a sample. I mean, come on, I was in a French forest. I could play for a change. For a bit.

I finished my pint and hit the bar with my glass. "Are you bringing your fiancée to the S&M tonight?" I asked, trying to find out how deep his dirt went.

"That's where we met two years ago." Paul smiled teasingly. "So, what do you think?"

My curiosity had put me on the spot. "You said you wanted to work on your engagement," I said carefully. "So, I guess not?"

Paul gave my empty glass a once-over, almost reached for it, gave me a brother-handshake instead. I mirrored him tentatively, awkwardly—hand, arm, and shoulder, then hand again—guessing that I was being rewarded for my answer. He slowly stretched and disengaged our sweaty fingers. "Try again," Paul said. Once more, I looked around.

WHEN I GOT BACK TO the hut, there were no cars parked outside. The lights were on, but no one was there. A plastic bag was on my bed with a Post-it on it: "You know you want it." I peeked in: there was a toga, basically. A pair of leather sandals lay on top of what looked like blue drapes. Half a shower later—forest freezing water—I caught up with Alkis, my fellow Montmelian refugee, at one of the many S&M preparties held in houses around the forest. It would be hours before a bunch of us made it, drunk, to the Château de Fleury.

Under Paul's artistic direction, Alkis entered the château's dungeon in chains. The enslaved president was paraded around the floor to be auctioned for whipping, and I was too wasted to remember if, or for how much, I was supposed to bail him out. Still, Alkis was dressed on the Disney side, not as Mapplethorpe as others. I scanned the chamber and saw the chain hooks on the walls that the Nazis had used to torture prisoners some sixty years before. At the end of the catacomb, a snake was being passed around. I needed another drink to make sense of all this, so I was heading toward the bathtub that served as a beer cooler when two Argentineans with permanent suntans offered me a shot.

"Are you from Buenos Aires?" I asked the one with a lollipop in his mouth.

"Via London investment banking." He handed me another shot, though I was clearly still holding the first one.

His friend mumbled something about Chechen gunmen seizing a Moscow theater.

"Not if Paris Hilton's performing," the lollipop replied. "She should be on the cover of *The Economist*."

They were dressed in dark suits and sunglasses, and I couldn't tell what their costumes were. *Men in Black?* I didn't get it. I did both my shots and tried to read those Latin type A's—the lollipop, the lazy body language, their snubbing of the overachievers on the dance floor. "What are you dressed up as?" I asked.

"Investment banker," replied the investment banker.

I waited for my jolt to fade, contemplating whether his exotic confidence was expected of me too. I wondered if I wasn't meant to become a screw-you Greek guy with a success story that would make me a "game changer."

"I need a beer," I finally said, and walked to the massive tub. I reached for a bottle, but I was fought off by our Finance professor, who had showed up as Muammar Gaddafi.

"Yours." I let Muammar keep the disputed Stella.

"You should become a Muslim," Muammar yelled to a Swedish-Chinese Lara Croft by the tub.

"Can't teach old cats new tricks," she replied, with no trace of hesitation on her face.

"Bitch!" Muammar said. He turned to me: "I need to get some, man. My three-year-old is visiting from London next week."

"Bring her to campus. Could help," I said.

"Uh, you—you think so?" Muammar asked, wasted but dead serious.

"I'm kidding."

He looked lost. "Uh, they tell me you're good at backgammon."

"Rumor," I said.

"Rumors in this forest tend to be true." Muammar's sweat kept dripping down his medals and beer. "I know. Been stuck here five years now."

I pointed toward the end of the catacomb, where Alkis was posing with the snake. "I gotta go bid him up," I said, starting to make my way through Gomorrah, but Muammar grabbed my Spartan outfit.

"Hey!" he yelled.

I turned.

"Managing for . . . ?" Muammar asked.

"Value!" I pointed to him with my index finger.

"My Greek whiz! Teaching for . . . ?"

What? "Huh?"

"Pussy!"

"Well, maybe it is time you went back to Georgetown," I said. "For a bit."

"*Pussy!*" Muammar yelled, spitting an ice cube my way, taking a tumble, and hitting Paul, who was being trained as a dog by the two Argentineans. Before I realized what exactly was going on, Paul's collar had gotten stuck. He started hyperventilating. With no one around sober enough to unbutton him, Paul looked at me in red fright.

"There's an army knife in my car," I said, and Paul toppled behind me toward the dungeon's exit.

The three minutes to the parking lot felt like ten. I was numb under my costume's skirt. My feet, in tight open sandals, were needled by frozen grass. Paul was chasing me, cursing and moaning like a bitch: "Cut it now! I can't breathe!" he cried every five seconds.

I placed the knife between the collar and his neck, and felt his heart racing. I twisted the knife and Paul choked.

"Do it!" Paul ordered me after he stopped coughing. I pushed the knife hard, and vodka mixed with pieces of leather and sausage suddenly covered my feet.

"*Bastard!*" I yelled.

Paul bent, roaring, and a second burst landed inches from my sandals. He was shaking.

"You okay?" I said.

"I'm okay. Will you drive me home? Please?"

I was seriously drunk. Plus, I had to pick up this American dude, Erik, from the train station in a couple of hours and still hoped for a nap—a write-off, given where Paul lived.

"I'm fucking wasted, Paul," I said, feeling his vomit freeze on my toes. "Where the hell's your fiancée?"

Paul shook his head. "She stayed in London. Whore." Then he vomited again.

I looked away in disgust. "I'll take you home," I said.

Driving on icy lanes, I watched for trees, deer, and Paul's puke breath.

"I owe you one," Paul said before passing out next to a bag of pot and a bunch of blue pills that were spread on his bed. I lifted his stash to pocket a nibble and, beneath it, saw a photo of Paul with his family. He must have been twenty, still had his hair; his arm was linked with his father's. They were laughing, posing as if they had just dragged something big out of the sea. I thought of my father, working his fishing nets. His hands ran rhythmically, pulling and rowing. He never laughed.

"Don't worry about it," I said to no one. I put a pinch of Paul's pot in my underwear (no pockets in my Spartan outfit) and walked out.

By the time I got back to the hut, there were still no cars parked outside. I sat in my car for a moment, gearing myself up for another icy shower. Again, I thought of my father. "Your body's a fireplace in a cold mountain," he told me when, at twelve, I had to jump into the freezing Aegean to retrieve the cross our priest had thrown in for the baptism of Jesus.

Ten minutes later, drying off with my blanket—towels still packed—I felt wide-awake.

Halfway to the train station to pick up the American, I noticed that I had a couple of cigarettes' worth of time to kill. It was already light out, so I stopped at the boulders outside Barbizon in the middle of the forest. I got out of the car and climbed the least slippery–looking stone. The rock was icy and full of mist. Birds and squirrels were everywhere. My piss streamed twenty feet down, and the first sunlight through the oaks made my liquid sparkle. I rolled Paul's stuff, lit it, and squatted, and at that moment when I wasn't drunk anymore but not yet hungover either, in that false sense of calmness in the middle of my mess, my love-hate relationship with EBS seemed clear. The whole thing was simple, really. I was building a network by tucking wasted people into bed. Which would eventually mean money, opportunities, and all the buzzwords in the pamphlets. If that's what it takes, so be it. I was fitting in—piss off, Paul—and with school ties built on either attentiveness or arrogance, we had bonding-via-fuck-you privileges; we had entertainment. By my second smoke, I felt free. Like I'd just woken up from a lithium treatment in a magical, liberating forest. Free to offend and be offended. None of the California correctness, no filtering or tact whatsoever. No repercussions either—which made the American's French accent the first thing I noticed and made fun of as he struggled: "Ab*ie*ntot" to the schoolgirls who cheered him "Au revoir, Er*ik*!" at the train station.

"Bienvenue à Fontainebleau, Erik," I said in my Greekest accent. "Je m'appelle Stathis."

"Stathis is Greek," Erik said.

"Stathis *is* Greek. I'm Greek too," I smart-assed, stoned, drunk, and sleepless.

"Everything cool, brother?" Erik said in working-class talk. Did I catch some South Boston in there?

Six-two, lean, with a boxer's nose, black hair, and curved-down eyes, he was in a blue North Face jacket and jeans. No smile.

Driving us to Montmelian, I became the target of questions about everything around us. Granted, he was doing two master's, one in journalism and one in urban planning; however, he was far more curious about the region, its history, its "palatial solar system," than in EBS itself. "The region's Haussmannization," he explained, "which started centuries before Haussmann," and moved on to the roles of different monarchs, regimes, and wars in the area over the last four hundred years. He asked if I'd visited the palace.

"Once," I told him—for a recruiting dinner.

Did I know about the pope's imprisonment there, or Napoleon's role? Had I been to the White Horse Courtyard?

"The white *what?*" I asked, clearly irritated.

"La cour du Cheval Blanc," he answered seriously.

I reflexively laughed at his French again, wondering why my body language wasn't registering with him. Or was it just natural to pound a person with questions when first meeting them? As if discovering someone slowly was a luxury left for Greek villages, something gone extinct for the online, overeducated dicks in the Western world.

When he brought up the treaty of Fontainebleau, I casually said: "Which one?" hoping to end our harlequin of exchange. But that didn't work either. Erik asked me what sports I played, if I had a mountain bike, trekked, or climbed in some of the best rocks to do that.

"As a matter of fact," he said, "these are the rocks that named it Fontaine-la-Montagne during the French Revolution."

I did not laugh. I thought of the frosted rock I had just climbed and wanted to ask him why and where on earth he'd homeworked that crap. Haussmannization? In a Southie accent? Something did not square here, but with my hangover kicking in I just drove. Dreading a smoking spiel, I cracked open my window and lit up fast.

"We're about to get to Montmelian," was all I said, and we drove the last couple of miles in silence.

In the parking lot outside the hut, Erik beat me in getting his bag from the trunk. He paused at my Spartan sword and the butt plug that Paul had worn around his neck as a pacifier.

"It's not what you think," I said.

"I don't."

Our first legit exchange in the twenty minutes we'd known each other.

Walking toward the hut, his steps tracing mine, I was disturbed and relieved all at once.

DURING THE NEXT FORTY-EIGHT HOURS I only saw Erik in the background: jogging on the property, hanging out on the floor or by the fridge, drinking our French yogurts. Our interactions were logistical—where was this and what time was that—and brief.

"Aren't you cold?" I asked him when I saw him shirtless on Alkis's bed, reading a book and eating granola that he must have brought with him. You could have stored milk in the freaking room.

Erik shook his head while crunching his cereal.

"I have a class tomorrow at nine. Do you need a ride to campus?"

He didn't answer. He lifted his bowl and drank from it. As he cleaned his chin with his palm, an old scar on his upper arm became visible. "I was hoping to take Alkis's mountain bike there," he finally said.

"What are you reading?" I asked.

"Mike Davis. *Ecology of Fear.*"

"Nonfiction, I take it?"

"Always."

I went to bed without my T-shirt. Half an hour later, I put it on.

"ERIK DOESN'T MAKE ANY SENSE," I told Alkis the next day, walking into the campus bar.

Alkis smiled. "Apparently not. Look."

Erik was doing shots at the bar, flanked by Paul and Muammar. Muammar was talking to Paul, Paul was talking to Erik, and Erik was looking at us.

"A round." Alkis elbowed me. "Come on, I'm driving to Paris tonight. One for the road."

There was something about Erik's indifference, his casual confidence, that enervated me. Something I couldn't pinpoint yet. I hesitated. "I got a deadline," I swayed, but Paul spotted us, and we joined them in a round of bourbon shots.

"*Malaka!* You must read this." Paul waved a piece of paper my way. "It's a poll the Dubyas bounced by Erik before it hits our inboxes during the American week."

Paul and Muammar were fighting over the survey, grabbing it from each other's hands, reading questions out loud. "Its title—" Paul laughed. "'Why do they hate us so much?'"

Erik looked at me and bowed slightly. Then he turned to chat with our school's French bartender, and that bugged me enough—the way you feel weird the day before you get sick, and you don't know why or what's wrong—that I left.

The fourth and last day of Erik's visit, I ran into him outside the hut. It was six or seven a.m.; there was barely any light. I was back from a case-study group turned into dinner, drinks, all-night slouching, and smoking, with eggs and cheap champagne for breakfast. Erik was back from jogging—"training for the New York marathon," he said. It was zero Celsius and he was in shorts, a T-shirt, and my sneakers. He was about to say something, but I cut in.

"Any deer?" I asked.

"Just a couple of wild boars."

"Wanna get back to bed?"

"With you?" he half smiled. First time in four days.

I stayed put. "Yes, with me."

We fucked on Alkis' bed before I rushed into Finance late and red-eyed, so of course Muammar cold-called me. I couldn't remember shit about the case study—something about Chrysler's balance sheet before the Daimler acquisition—and I didn't even try to fake it. I'd never been unable to answer a question before. Paul turned and gave me a stunned, happy look, as though I had finally done something right.

"*What?*" I shrugged.

TEN DAYS LATER, ERIK'S ARTICLE showed up in one of Oxford's student newspapers. He took EBS head on:

"For the first couple of days, EBS seems liberated and open to pursuing its wishes, as opposed to US business schools, long ago sterilized by political correctness, no longer able to shortcut to ingenuity or enjoy themselves. Actually, and in spite of all the bright, beautiful worldsters, the democratized champagne flowing in the campus canteen, and the weekly balls in the impressionism-inspiring Fontainebleau villages, EBS is a devastating place full of old, decomposing souls and the children of unfulfilled industrials, bitter politicians, or indifferent parents, trapped between the American dream— glimpsed through cult and cliché movies like *The Player* and *Jerry Maguire*—and a European license to decadence, exploitation, and toxic private equity shrouded under energy, software, or real-estate project finance. It's unclear whether it's more dangerous or silly. As if colonialism had walked a mere hundred meters in three hundred years: from the courts of the François I palace to a campus down the street playing Studio 54 with McKinsey recruiters serving as bouncers."

If any of my classmates heard it as the voice of reason, they didn't speak up. I wasn't sure what intrigued me most: that a single paragraph gave my fascination with EBS a corrective slap, or that we had been exposed by a mere passerby. But it all became clear soon enough.

In the hut's freaking freezing extra bedroom, I was preparing for job interviews with Alkis. He was role-playing the recruiter, while I kept nodding without listening.

"Stathis, *mate!*" Alkis shouted. "I'm *talking* to you! You got into an early round with Bain, will you *fucking* concentrate?"

I was thinking of that crazy communist and his article, of his Southie accent and his dick; I was thinking of Erik, nonstop. I was falling in love.

TWO

WAS ABOUT TO E-MAIL IN my Decision Traps and Tools homework when Erik's handle showed up on my screen. I looked at his first and last names. Somehow they made more sense than the rest of the names in my in-box, as if the letters had been put together in a cubist structure that meant more than the sum of the letters.

I clicked on the e-mail and saw a one-line note in its body, which made me pause—was that all? I silently protested against this laconic sugar high of a next step. I gazed at the message in the unfocused way I looked at my classmates from the podium seconds before I presented my solution to a case study.

"Bro, I passed out on Eurostar and you're to blame for that . . . What are you doing next weekend? Wanna hang out in London? E."

ENDLESS DAYS LATER, I WALKED into a shabby neighborhood pub on Earls Court, dragging my carry-on. A couple of old-timers turned to give me a glance. Erik, against the bar, in an M79 army vest, was working on a pint and talking to the bartender. They looked deep in the middle of a joke.

"Hey! My man!" Erik threw his arm around my neck and eyebrowed my suitcase's high-tech wheels. "Nice bag."

"Good to see you," I said. "I'd have dropped my bag off if I had a hotel addy, but—" I smiled at his jacket—"it looks you were busy enlisting."

"Enough!" Erik made a cease-fire face. "This is my Greek mate, Stathis," he said to the bartender. "This is Ian," he said to me.

Ian reached for a glass from the bar's ceiling. The tattoo crawling up his arm looked like Jesus on the cross in a Manchester United outfit, or Madonna at a concert. "You're Greek, *malaka*?" Ian asked.

"Born and raised," I said.

"My first wife was Greek." He pushed a London Pride to me. "She liked *spanakorizo* and Telly Savalas."

"Who loves ya, baby?" I tried, but it came out more Greek than New York Kojak.

Ian pointed at our pints. "The house," he said, and disappeared into the kitchen.

"Don't get too cocky," Erik warned me. "He told me his second wife's from Boston."

"So he moved up in life."

Erik managed a grin. "Plus, we're staying at his place."

What? "Come again?" I said.

"He has rooms upstairs for thirty pounds," Erik said casually.

I had to restrain myself from looking around. Ian's pub was falling apart faster than Montmelian. "I'm in school debt and all, but, er, we have a bathroom, right?"

"Of course. There's a bathroom on our floor," Erik said, studying his pint.

Right, what was I thinking. "I spent two summers in a Greek camp. E. coli's a friend." I lifted my pint.

"Cheers, mate!" Erik faked an English accent. "I thought we better see the room after a drink."

"Or a few," I murmured.

"More fun getting naked drunk anyway," Erik said, his face unchanged. He didn't glance at me to check for a reaction; he took sex for granted.

"Maybe we stay that way. Be on the safe side," I double dared.

"Drunk or naked?"

"I'm Greek. What's the difference?"

He smiled. "It's my birthday. Will you suck my dick?"

Prick. "Need ID for that one."

FOUR PINTS, SIX SHOTS, AND two fucks later, we were lying naked at opposite ends of a smaller-than-double bed, needing a shower and a new set of sheets. All through the evening we could hear footsteps and coughing from our floor. Given the time they took to get from the elevator to their room, our neighbors had to be in their eighties, or obese.

As I came later for a third time, growling, I heard a walker being dragged outside our door. Erik put his hand over my mouth, an act that somehow tamed him, while in the hallway outside I heard fragile hinges clap. When they had gone, Erik went to use the bathroom down the hall, buck naked, without shoes, which threw my tame-Erik hypothesis out the window. I walked there only to see how flooded it was and U-turned back to our room, hoping I wouldn't have to use the bathroom for the rest of the weekend. I pissed in empty beer bottles in our room, something that Erik found hilarious and competitive. He tried it, but without my precision.

"It's a skill I got from driving around Pelio, in Greece," I said. "I can actually do it without stopping the car."

"Liar!"

"If I stopped for more than twenty seconds, the relanti would die. You had to pour gas straight into the engine to get the car going again."

"What did you do at traffic lights?"

"It's a mountain." I paused. "Only thing, you wanna make sure your bottles are stored right."

"You didn't, did you?"

"What? Spill?"

"Yeah."

"Nope," I said, remembering an old embarrassment. "But I did mix up the bottles once."

Erik was excited.

"Hey, I was drunk." I shrugged. "I kept extra gas in a bottle of Coke and I had pissed in a Sprite, thinking, green bottle, you know, less obvious, and easier to remember what's what."

"Fucker!" He went for my abs with his foot, but I grabbed it.

"I was wasted, I couldn't smell the difference. So the fucking Datsun doesn't start, and I keep pouring piss in the carburetor till the butterfly gets totally fucked," I said with a brief laugh. I lit a cigarette.

"Did you fuck up the car?"

"Not really." I let out my smoke. "But when I figured it out, I had to run and crawl two miles to make the last ferry to Trikeri."

"I have to run ten miles tomorrow," Erik said, waving away my smoke. Then he picked up my briefs from the floor and threw them on my sticky torso. "Fuck it! Let's stay drunk. And it's your turn to bring the juice, amigo."

IT WAS FRESH OUTSIDE. LONDON'S Friday evening was in full force. People in work clothes talked eagerly while cutting one another off on the sidewalk, their taxis waiting for them. It would have been a three-minute walk to the liquor store had I followed Ian's shortcuts, but I stayed on Earls Court Road, feeling slightly proud, like I owned part of this pavement. As I passed the Court Tavern—packed, EBS-loud—suddenly my last three months were thrown into a new light. Though hidden within the forest vignettes, I saw some good turns in my recent past, and I felt, this weekend, like I had become someone new. It was like I was a spy, as if I was sleeping with the enemy.

The moment I stepped into the clean liquor store, I strangely longed for Ian's pub, the very grime I'd detested growing up back home, which I was now "fortunate enough to be spared," as my sister kept reminding me over the phone.

"May I help you?" the clerk asked.

"I'm all right," I said, and picked up a bottle of Springbank and some Beck's. Then I asked him where they kept the champagne. He pointed to a bottle two pounds cheaper than our rent for the night.

ERIK WAS NAPPING NAKED ON his stomach under the pillows when I made it back to our room. I was about to pop the bottle when his head surfaced.

"Bro, I haven't had champagne since the summer of '95," he said sheepishly.

"Oh, yeah? What happened that spring?"

Erik looked at me, stunned. "The French resumed *nuke* tests?" He let his head fall back on the pillows. "I ain't fucking drinking it now," he said, muffled.

I stared at his jogger's ass and messed-up hair while sorting out whether he was joking. Actually, technically he was inaccurate; the French hadn't resume their tests until that September. I thought of bringing up the French yogurts he drank at Montmelian while I struggled not to laugh and to hold back the cork, a battle I lost. I filled a plastic cup.

"Happy birthday!" I cheered.

Erik grabbed my hand, pulling me to bed.

"I'm not having any, but my cock can," he said, and stuck the head of his half-hard dick into the cup. "Wanna suck me now?"

I looked at Don Quixote's dick in front of me and thought of the Pauls on campus, and Bain & Company. "Nuke the bastards," I said, and ripped my shirt off.

THERE WAS LITTLE HE WAS not: mountain climber, marathon runner, activist, savvy traveler, skier, writer—started two alternative papers at Yale—community and labor union coordinator in South Boston, Beacon Hill–raised, son of a gynecologist and a Democratic pundit. He was everything I wasn't.

After London, Erik's name in my in-box became the title of a favorite book, movie, or brand—the most popular adjective, verb, and noun on campus. I would wait for a lecture to end before I opened his one-liners ("What's up, Competitive Advantage? Cooking for Thanksgiving with the Dubyas on campus? E.") to stretch my high and replay London in my mind, hoping to break Erik's codes and understand what he saw in me and what I could become. Many a time, my speculations turned into doodles of possibility trees. In a Stats lecture once, I borrowed the regression model from the blackboard to build a quiz assessing the pace and depth of my falling for him. I used parameters such as "willingness to travel" and "sex initiation," plus "reading the other's mind," only to come up with a spooky correlation between poor mind reading and fast falling, something I hastily credited to sloppy math. I deleted my stats-*Cosmopolitan* algorithm just in time—Paul ready to license its interactive version for Bellinis on campus.

> "How is your 'tell me your strengths & weaknesses' season coming along? Any consultant bought your BS yet? E."

Job interviews started early. A couple of months into the program, investment banks and consulting firms stormed into the forest with presentations, schmoozing events, and drinks and dinners at Michelin-starred restaurants in Barbizon. In late November, the first round of interviews started in the thirty suffocating five-by-seven-foot rooms that EBS had built for the process.

"You are from Greece, how exciting!" the Senior Associate from Command Consulting called out as I entered their chamber.

He'd spent his honeymoon there. A lovely time. And which island was I from? "Please sit—oh, this is Andrea Farrugia, a VP from our New York office." He tried to introduce the late-thirties silk-wrapped woman who was sitting behind him, but she kept typing away on her laptop.

"It's nice to meet you," I said, standing up—trying to shake her hand, for all I knew.

"Do you think you'll be ready for the Olympics on time?" she asked without looking up or slowing her binge-typing.

THE FRIDAY BEFORE CHRISTMAS I walked into the Washington headquarters of Command for my final round of interviews. I was confident, smart. I nailed case studies and personality tests, thinking of my Christmas break with Erik in Bequia— "pronounced *Beck-Way*," he'd warned in his e-mail. By four p.m. I knew that Command would make me an offer. At six the next morning, I was on a two-stopover-flight-and-one-boat-ride journey to the Caribbean.

Erik had already been in the Grenadines for a whole month, part of "an eight-week Yale-Oxford off-site NGO-sponsored urban planning graduate credit project," he rambled over the phone.

I tried to translate this train of organizations and adjectives into a single CV bullet.

"But UNICEF paid for my flight," he punch-lined.

"Of course." I laughed.

The two-second silence that followed made me regret my sarcasm. I didn't backtrack. I didn't go: *I mean* . . . Petrified, I couldn't tell whether my silence grew or shrank my balls in Erik's mind.

That evening I saw the island of Bequia, black, getting

larger, from the deck of the ferry I'd boarded on St. Vincent.
The lights of Port Elizabeth sparkled as we headed straight
toward them, at the southern end of the Caribbean. There
was something familiar and definitive about our ride, the
way the ferries cruised confidently into the port of Trikeri
in Greece, sliding between adjacent fishing boats like they
didn't exist or matter, or simply knew their exact place in a
routine-reassured coexistence. I couldn't remember the last
time I was more tired, jet-lagged, and happy.

Erik was leaning on a semirusted Toyota truck that looked
like those death traps I used to drive around in Pelio. He was
parked twenty feet from the ferry, radio on, driver's door wide
open. He was tan, in a T-shirt and jeans. Barefoot.

"Hey, Feta!" Erik yelled. "*Kalos irthes.*"

"I thought I was your only coach in Greek," I said with a
grin.

He mussed my hair and pushed my head back. "The last
one didn't have a garment bag. So you must be better."

"Did he wear shoes?" I said, throwing my bag in the truck.
"My uncle had this car. It's a stick, you know."

"Nah, this one doesn't run on piss."

"Let's see if it runs at all," I said. I couldn't stop smiling.

"Careful. I'll put you in the back, and it's a bumpy ride to
the lodge."

Warm wind hit our faces as Erik drove past the port. The
sea, all dark, was eight feet from my right, often less, as Erik

strayed to avoid potholes, dogs, and large spiders. I was half-asleep when we arrived at Moonhole, on the very west end of the island. The truck's radio played Joy Division as we walked into a log cabin and collapsed in the dark.

The next morning I woke up alone, in a room within nature. There was no glass in the windows, nor a door separating the room from the patio, just holes in stone walls. Tree roots surfaced in the middle of the floor, and a bird's nest clung to a round opening in the ceiling. Still in bed, I pulled my flight itinerary from under my sneakers. Erik's handwritten note on it said: "Sleepy Greek, welcome to the Arch! There's coffee. Ask Jeevan down the steps if you need anything. Back at noon. E."

I couldn't really make sense of where I was, this unfinished, deserted, 1960s James Bond–meets–*National Geographic* eco-cabin. What arch?

I needed coffee badly. I walked out onto the patio and forgot about it. Loud birds circled in the sky. Below me, in front of me, everywhere, the big blue ocean spread out. To my right were rocks, with trees bulging above and between them. To my left were more cabins made of gray stone and mortar, arranged at different levels among the land formations. Their walls had no corners or edges, just sweeping forms, as if extensions of the hill. A chill—less of a where-am-I, more of a *when*-am-I—ran through me.

I found Jeevan under a tree outside a cave house on a hundred-foot-long beach. He was busy rolling a joint, ten feet from a rod with a rusty bell tied to a fishing line that disappeared into the water. "Lazy fishing," my father used to call that. There was no one else in sight.

My steps on the sand made Jeevan look up. "You Stathis?" He laughed. Late forties, skinny, years in the sun, he had more cloth in his hair than on his body.

"Yes, I'm Stathis. You must be Jeevan."

"Welcome to Moonhole, my brother." He lit the joint and offered it to me.

I paused. It must have been nine a.m., pre-coffee, pre-everything. Still, I was so mesmerized by the last-person-on-earth feel of the place that I wanted an in. I took a hit and felt it from my brain to my toes. I sat down under the tree, among tiny tortoises and what looked like broken whale bones. The breeze came in rushes, rotating the color of the sea from bright blue to darker to black. "Thank you, Jeevan." I passed back the joint. "Damn strong."

"See the moon?" He pointed to the sky. "In a couple of months we'll see it through the arch. I keep the good stuff for then," Jeevan said, scratching his sweaty armpit while having a puff. Then he got up and disappeared into the cave house.

I looked up to the fading moon. Everything seemed to be in a different orbit in this place, reversed or halted in yesteryear. The tortoises walked away from the water, and the whale bones were dark. I was trying to break one with a stone when Jeevan returned, holding a jar with something like fruit punch in it. "Erik's a friend of mine. He told me to take care of you," he said with a smile.

I looked at Jeevan and then at the jar.

"It's rum punch! The colony's drink!" he yelled.

I was ready to ask what the story was with the arch and the colony, to find out what on earth he was talking about, where the hell I was, but Jeevan took a sip and offered me the jar. I stared at it for a moment, wondering how long the punch had been sitting out. "Perfect," I heard myself whisper as the sea changed again.

By the time Erik came back, I was passed out in our cabin.

I SPENT MY MORNINGS SMOKING, having "breakfast" with Jeevan, and swimming off deserted cliffs at Moonhole. When the sun settled good and the sea stopped changing colors, I'd have a siesta. In the afternoon I would join Erik and his young local friends in saving baby turtles from "evil, bloody birds" at the turtle sanctuary in Park Bay. We weighed and fed the turtles, checked for trauma from birds, and moved them around the shallow nursing pools, following the park custodian's assessments on the turtles' "preferences and well-being." It was a skill I couldn't crack; as if one needed some tuning-in, some leveling with the silent turtles before one got to understand them.

Erik's entourage got bigger by the day. Kids kept showing up out of nowhere, while I couldn't work out how these ten-year-olds made it from Port Elizabeth to the turtle sanctuary with no bus, cars, or bikes in sight. When I asked, they'd just shrug. I tried to explain what I saw by a bay of a small island without letting go of rationality; my Greek rural instincts failing me. I went as far as conceptualizing an *HBR* case study around them, hypothesizing on the kids' timely appearances and disappearances, hoping to explain this mystery with a b-school operations principle that I thought I must be missing. They were unguarded, ubiquitous, screaming little monsters, splashing into the three-foot-deep pools, weight lifting the turtles, even throwing them to one another, ready to drop everything for a game of soccer on the beach. But the turtles were oblivious to their yells. They didn't swim away, hide, or bite, adding to my Cartesian angst, which had been making me a touch less Greek every day since I left home a decade ago.

Late in the afternoon on Christmas, I jumped into the water to rinse off an hour of soccer. After some strokes, I pushed my head back for an almost 360-degree view of the horizon. I could hear the kids' yells and the metallic sound of their footsteps on the sand, through the water. I closed my eyes and floated.

"Little punks! That was murder," Erik said, handing me a Carib when I got out. He sat next to me on the beach. "Jesus!"

I smiled. "We stood our ground. For a bit."

"Oh yeah?" He clung to my bottle, looked at me funny. "Last ten minutes I couldn't even get close to the ball."

I took a sip. "I couldn't *see* the ball," I said. "We started with twelve. I turn around and there are twenty-five, thirty. They kept popping up, like in a video game. Swapping sides, too. I didn't know who I was playing with or against."

"I know." Erik nodded. "We'll have to go shirts and skins next time."

"Oh, you *have* a shirt?"

"I was hoping you'd leave one or two behind. As long as they don't say EBS," Erik said with a wink.

"You still got my socks I left at Ian's."

"Oh, those." Erik smiled. "Those are at my dry cleaner's back home."

"You do own a suit, right?"

"*Now!*" He pointed a finger. "That's irrelevant."

"Tell you what," I said. "You beat me one-on-one—okay, two-on-two, I get Learie, you get Gokul—and I'll leave behind my polo shirt. If we kick your asses, we take Jeevan's dinghy out to Tobago Cays on Sunday."

"Feta, Jeevan's *bell*'s gonna ring before you beat me in soccer," Erik said. All Southie.

"The planet calls it football. You kick the ball with your feet. Noticed?"

Erik shook his head and burped. "*Right.* Forgot you're the first Greek who crossed the Atlantic. By the way, I'm Olympiakos."

"*Excuse* me?"

"Sorry, the French don't burp?"

"Fuck you, and *excuse* me?"

"You heard me. And you look like a Panathinaikos."

"Dude!" I almost stood up. "Stop fucking with me. You speak Greek?"

"That's about it," Erik said.

I prompted him with a wave. "Spill the beans. Now."

"I had this summer job in Hyannis, I must have been twelve, thirteen. A Greek dude there, Constantine, great guy, was teaching sailing during school breaks. He and my brother put together a soccer team. We stayed in touch till he dropped out of school, broke up with his fiancée, and went to Afghanistan to fight with the tribes. I've only seen him—"

"I'm sorry." I had to wiseass: "There's yelling in the background and I thought you said that a Greek went to fight in Afghanistan."

Erik's tone changed, his eyes fixed way out on the sea. "Maybe you come from different parts of Greece," he muttered seriously.

I was lost. Did I just make fun of someone who was to be taken seriously? A Greek hero? *His* hero? I wanted to bargain, undo if necessary, but Erik was already up, looking far into the sea. I was ready to call a time-out when I saw a flock of birds three hundred feet out near the opening of the reef, free-falling into the water from fifty feet up. The children were already calling Erik, pointing at the birds and shouting, pushing a dinghy into the water, robbing me of my own turf.

JEEVAN NEVER LOOKED AT ME without laughing or smiling. He didn't ask me any questions or say that he wanted to visit Greece, like unguarded people do the moment they meet me. In fact, he didn't care about any travel that didn't involve his dinghy. And yet I couldn't see anything self-absorbed about him. There was something reassuring in his lack of curiosity and ambition: a consistency, a finality in accepting his life and whereabouts that reminded me of my father in Trikeri.

Jeevan was ten when his family joined Moonhole's "colony," a self-sustaining community founded in the '60s by an architect and his wife. The couple built their home from stone, wood, and whale bones under a natural arch of rock overlooking the sea. The first time I saw their house from Jeevan's dinghy, I thought I was looking at a *Robinson Crusoe* version of the Treasury in Petra. It was a deserted, multilevel domicile carved into the landscape, looking all mystical and sacred, humble and natural. The day before my last on the island, I talked Jeevan into climbing it with me.

He hadn't been inside for years, he told me. He gave me the tour, smoking, laughing, and talking about the natural ideals of the free spirit and sharing that had run the community, "the *colectiva*," in the early years, before rocks fell from the arch and most of the houses were abandoned.

"We never sold out. Maybe we never had the chance."

"Where did the people go?"

"We're good ghosts," Jeevan said, laughing, and passed me the joint. "There's still no electricity. Just kerosene and propane."

Right then and there I knew I'd miss Bequia. And yet, at the tip of this small island, I couldn't relax. I kept speculating, unsure why Erik went for me. I was trying to find an algorithm and clone it—isn't that what people do? Work on things? I knew I was good at interviews, at first impressions. I put people at ease. I was good at making peace with anything, but I couldn't get my head around Erik.

Jeevan lit one more joint in the roofless attic of the house under the arch. He'd never asked about Erik and me, as if he understood the whole thing but wasn't the least interested or surprised. We sat there for a while, looking at the archipelago below us, and then I caught myself murmuring Ian Hunter's ballad "I Wish I Was Your Mother":

> *And then I would have seen you, would*
> *have been you as a child*
> *Played houses with your sisters*
> *And wrestled with all your brothers*
> *And then who knows, I might have felt a family for a while.*

ERIK GRABBED THE TREE BRANCH above him and started doing pull-ups, half in the air, half floating on the sea, counting lifts in Greek. The trees above us filtered the sun. To our right and left, rocks held us, kept the green waters calm, forming a natural harbor within the sea. I saw small fish cruising against white and black pebbles at the bottom, and each time Erik pulled up, a bit less of his cock rose above the water till I couldn't see it at all.

"What happened to your dick?" I yelled.

He let go of the branch and splashed into the sea-pool. "Go back to Greece!" he said when he got up. He spit seawater in my face.

"Thought I was there for a moment. The sea, you counting in Greek . . ." I spit back but missed him.

"Have you heard yourself speaking English?"

"I try not to speak," I answered.

"When was the last time you were back home?" Erik asked, reaching for the branch again.

I felt my fleeing-the-army insecurity rising, my Greek manhood threatened. "It's been a while. Almost two years."

Erik glanced my way, pulling up.

I didn't say anything either, so he looked at me again.

"I can't go back. It's just stupid, really," I tried, casually. "I haven't served in the Greek army."

Erik smiled. "And how does that make you feel?"

"Educated," I groaned.

He did two more lifts before he let his body fall into the water again.

"Well, you're not the only Greek who skipped that one."

"Let me guess . . . Constantine!" I smiled.

"Nope. His mother's English. He didn't have to. Dual citizenship or something."

"I guess he and I are from different hoods, after all."

"We got a chip there, island boy?"

"Hell yeah," I said. "And I can still join Uncle Sam, track him down in Afghanistan, and kick his Harvard ass."

Erik laughed. "I never said he went to Harvard, you punk!" He swam onto me and tried to push my head underwater, but I slipped to his side.

"Island boy!" I said, raising my eyebrows. "How come you're not in Beacon Hill for Christmas?" I asked.

I caught his grin before he looked the other way. " 'Cause I'm here with you," Erik said, and I got jitters. The island laws I grew up with took compliments as shameful. A weakness for givers and receivers alike.

"Or in the West Village, writing articles about the West Side Stadium?" I pressed on, pretending I missed his compliment, unable to handle what I wanted the moment it arrived.

"You spend too much time online," Erik said.

I wanted an instant replay—*I like being with you* is what I wanted to say. But we rarely get a second go at anything, so I marched on, dragged down by sunk cost, betting on offense and hoping to recover by holding on to some principle I might not even have believed in. "Do I, now?" I said. "I read your article on EBS. 'Sterilized'? 'Ingenuity'? Not a Southie. You're from Beacon Hill, so what's up with the accent?"

"You're stereotyping me, Feta."

"Oh yeah? Did you pick up the talk during your Boston-I-Care outing?"

"My pad's in Roxbury, *brother*!" He grabbed my leg, pulling me closer. "Unlike the Greeks, I don't live with Mom and Dad anymore."

"WASP-trash."

He laughed and lost his grip. I pushed his head under.

"Greek prick!" he shouted, surfacing. "My article was work, just like hanging out with you."

"Urban planning in Bequia . . . Cut me some slack. I didn't even know the island existed," I said, and swam closer. "So, how're things coming along?"

"Slowly," he said with a grimace.

"I guess you haven't gotten the kids eBay accounts yet?"

"No, but I can put you on Craigslist. And by the way, it's urban *and* regional planning. We're a full-service program." Erik spit, and dived to mock-suck me.

I saw his saliva on the water's surface slowly diluting. I reached for it, tried to hold it together, but Erik touched my belly button, which made me ticklish. I grabbed his armpits and lifted him up.

"Fuck, bro! Is your Greek dick ever not hard?"

"I thought you didn't stereotype." I saw Erik's full smile. "When you get close to me, I'm wood. Mathematics," I said, and Erik kissed me.

LATER, AT THE CABIN, AS I shot my come over his torso, I tasted the sea salt on Erik's chin and fell backward, crashing into his arm with my shoulder. I tried to lift it, but Erik held me there.

"We all deserve a pause after coming," he said.

"Even Saddam?"

"Even Bush."

I lit a cigarette, took a drag, and looked at the bird's nest on the ceiling. It was made from dirt and broken shells, perfectly curved, with a funnel-like entrance, holding on to nothing at the opening of the roof. Its acrobatic knack disturbed me; I saw our fragility in it. Erik and I were compatriots in leaving our upbringings. He was born in privilege but had a taste for discomfort and poverty. I was born with a talent for adapting. I tested well and left my backwater for good schools and jobs on his side of the world. Narcissistically, maybe, I saw us mirroring each other. He showed me how I should have grown up in Greece, taught me how I could have lived in Pelio, with no money, happy; how beautiful I used to be without knowing it. But then, I wasn't poor anymore. I couldn't go back in time; I couldn't even go back to Greece, which had turned Bequia into a familiar parallel universe. I reached and kissed Erik to share the homesick sea-salt taste in my mouth.

THE YEAR I MET ERIK, 2002, was the year I started writing everything down. In my e-mail I stored my homework, cover letters, and application memos, my travel plans and party invites. E-mail covered our lives and made us all actors in a kind of reality theater. Composing them, we got to flesh out arguments and—pre–instant messaging—deliver our punch lines. We had the luxury of making up different personalities. We got to be funny, sarcastic, caring; we even *xoxo*-ed people we wouldn't stop to say hello to on campus.

Except Erik. He had none of that. His e-mails were to the point, factual. Journalistic. He ignored notes with any "contextual or personality agenda"—from "real-life cowards," from "e-lames."

I one-upped him, of course. I treated e-mail as a bore that needed containment. I used a PowerPoint-like writing mode, skipping verbs or nouns while scrutinizing his notes for any hidden signs of affection. I'd get an e-mail saying: "I think it's time we hit the road again," and I'd microanalyze every word. I'd see an us-against-the-world camaraderie in *we hit*. I'd romanticize *the road*.

After Erik went back to Oxford, we began meeting at off-season places on our free weekends. Worked for me. There was a quiet luxury to those foggy beaches, an antidote to the busy bar and amphitheaters on campus. We walked on a pier in Normandy on a freezing night, the only ones at the boardwalk's canteen. In Maincy, the echo of Erik's voice through the rooms of the Vaux le Vicomte was the only sound. He couldn't stop making comparisons. He argued about how much better life is in Brittany than Kansas. He defended the woman at the Vendée museum's ticket counter for being five minutes late: "Why shouldn't she have lunch at the same time as the rest of us?" he snapped to the complaining peacoated family from Seattle.

By then our school days were reaching an end. Early that spring, both Alkis and I had accepted Associate positions at Command. Alkis would be in the London office; I was assigned to San Francisco. Paul broke up with his fiancée and decided to travel the world to "re-find" himself, and Erik finished his two master's degrees at Oxford, in journalism and urban planning. Come July he'd be the manager of a *west side*—he was specific on that—community board in New York and would freelance for *The Nation*. He'd make a fifth of my base.

I pictured Erik in two-dollar-pint dives with his mates in Manhattan and I got it: I loved Erik as a man, as a gentleman. He came from privilege, but there was an outcast within him. His was the ultimate intimacy that I had always craved. Erik was a city kid, running off in the summer to hang with the underdogs, breaking into the village church to steal oil and gas for the boat, speaking up for us when we were busted in whorehouses in Volos. True, times had changed. I'd be an Associate soon. I'd made my own choices and might even have deserved some credit. And yet I wanted Erik to see the childish way I wanted him, and for him to want me too, in that island camaraderie that was still haunting my mind.

"I'M NOT COMING TO YOUR *prom*!" Erik said, checking his Eurostar ticket on the Sunday of our last weekend away in France.

"The ball's in Versailles," I appealed. "They have some kick-ass gardens there. May come in handy when you plan your west side park."

"You'll e-mail me the photos," Erik grumbled, still shuffling tickets.

"Right." I looked at his bag and the Gare du Nord ticket booth. I checked for my keys, my hands in and out of my pockets, making the seconds register, making more of them. My Finance exam, in twelve hours, flashed before my eyes. A nod from him, just a fucking *I know*, and everything would be okay.

"So, later," he said, and punched me on the shoulder.

"Sure."

I saw the back of his North Face jacket as he sped toward security.

Driving back to Fontainebleau, radio off, throat sore, I kept policing my mind to stay in rejection-denial. Brainwashing myself that we were locked in a prisoner's dilemma, in some sort of emotional inarticulation, though feelings were mutual.

Monday, dry-mouthed with fever, staring at the exam sheet in front of me, unable to calculate the weighted average cost of capital, I was reflecting on Erik's sobriety against the EBS audacities around me—surely a trigger for falling for him—when it came to me that, a master's later, I was heading back to the Bay Area with a better salary, everything else pretty much equal. I failed.

THREE

AT COMMAND WE CAN'T HAVE fun without learning," the head of human resources had told me over the phone after I accepted the offer. I thought she was kidding, sharing an office joke, but training was a fixation at Command: formal, informal, on the road, at client sites, "on the beach" (i.e., while waiting for client work), even during vacation at half-expensed "bettering retreats." It never stopped.

In July 2003, Command's annual orientation was held outside Washington.

"You are management consultants now," a senior-senior Partner christened us. "The new Beaujolais. The new Associates. Within weeks, leaders of major corporations will start paying lots and lots of money for *you* to tell them how to run their businesses. Simple as that." He looked around the auditorium, nodding to show how pleased he was with what he saw. "Who wouldn't want your job?" he said. "Congratulations! You made it to Command!" he cheered. A nothing-can-go-wrong two-week fiesta was launched. A party of rising self-esteem.

VPs kept stressing to us that we would approach corporate challenges in "dramatically better ways than our competitors." That there were "no dead ends for Commanders." All we needed to do was "trust the fundamentals, the frameworks that create shareholder value: the markets, the brands, the *leadership* of your colleagues."

Senior Associates put on superhero costumes to explain the "abundance paradigm."

"There are no circles," they said. "No cutting the cake, no zero-sum perspectives on resources. Just spirals of growth."

Propaganda, sure, but I was attracted to the promise of making money. This was the pudding for ten years of studying, scholarships, and immigration forms. "Arriving"? Belonging to "the club"? Of course. But what intrigued me most was Command's credo that brainwashing a group of consultants—corporate observers and analysts, really; advisers, at best—about the sustainability of economic euphoria might in fact contribute to materializing it. As if the real economy was a state of mind: monitor it, believe in it, and it will keep growing. The paradoxical monitor-equals-influence law of quantum physics that I remembered from college had just gotten a tick. I saw myself as part of an experiment, about to walk a bridge that linked theory with business, and on the other side, the market's dividends might even exonerate me for fleeing my family and Greece.

I wasn't alone. Everyone nodded along. My class rarely if ever challenged the partners. They were the legitimate source. Command's perpetual-spirals-of-growth theory—seen as solid and joyful—was taken as a given. As a matter of fact, we rationalized it, and then some. We got into make-mine-a-double mode: "Fee-based consulting is old-school," Alkis told me over dinner on Cape Cod during our end-of-training weekend retreat.

"Come again?" I said.

"Actually, consulting *itself* is just a stepping-stone," he said, pausing to read my expression. "Don't get me wrong, mate," he hurried. "I'll enjoy building brands as much as the next Commander, but I don't see any reason that we should be loyal to either partners *or* clients." He was drinking champagne, red wine, and a latte.

"Alkis, we haven't even started working yet," I said. "And won't you need favors from ex-clients in order to build your fund, or whatever you plan to do after you leave Command?"

Alkis's eyes softened, the way they had at EBS when he thought he was about to teach me something. "It's our *right* to keep nexting, Stathis."

"*Nexting*? Excuse me?"

"Clients will approach us with some real opportunities." He leaned closer. "Clients will keep courting us to participate in their ventures. If you don't like this one, you jump ship at the next one."

"What are you talking about?" I asked skeptically.

"I'm not talking about consulting. I'm talking equity. Listen, new brands will be made, whether we take advantage of it or not. Someone will. So think of your job like a computer game that keeps throwing cele-brands your way."

I nodded along, speculating about how many more words like *nexting* and fucking *cele-brands* Alkis was going to come up with during dinner.

"Actually, it's even sexier than that," he smirked. "The markets will assess the brands that we'll build, but *pervasive* brands will become markets *themselves*."

I finished my red and let him finish.

"*Of course they will.* Strong market players will become market makers. Look around: Craig Venter, Google, Elon Musk, Abby Cohen, Miramax. I can go on and on. Even juveniles like Tyler Brûlé, they're all Oprah-positioning fads and teams. Cele-brands today are both goods *and* markets."

"Stop saying *cele-brands*," I said seriously.

But Alkis went on. "Once you're endorsed by a cele-brand, you pick up or license anything. You recognize what skill set you lack and you just go out there and buy it, or hire it." He made a peace sign to our waiter and then gestured toward my glass.

Who was Tyler Brûlé? Was Elon Musk a perfume? I was disturbed by Alkis's charade, and distracted by my glass and the surfer-looking waiter. See, after a year of living in Alkis's shadow on campus, at times beneath his scolding eye, I wanted to understand what it was about his Mediterranean looks and English accent that allowed him to father me. Where did he get the balls? I tried to grasp him. The thing with Alkis was that he had no apparent flaws. You couldn't find the bad stuff mixed with the good, like we see in people's personalities and we have to accept or sometimes just tolerate—a C++ programming genius, say, who is also a nerd. When it came to Alkis, there were no tradeoffs. Much like our classmates had at school, Commanders gathered around him for both work and play.

"When you mix market playing with market making, you get unfair advantages," I protested. "You let the winner take everything. You *know* that."

"So?" Alkis shrugged, and the tattoo by the collar of his white shirt—a handgun—flickered. "Today, taking all, being ubiquitous, is more important than being correct or effective," he said. "Being everywhere *is* being effective. Which is exactly what makes globalization our tribe's high-end problem. I love this place." He raised his glass.

I mimicked him, not sure to whom exactly he referred as "our tribe." Greeks? MBAs? Consultants? Bankers? And what did he love? The restaurant? Command? Cape Cod? I looked at the boats at the far end of the restaurant's patio, off the boardwalk, and thought of Erik, who had spent his summers here as a child with his family and his hero, Constantine.

I hadn't e-mailed Erik. I didn't want to legitimize his "later," his illegit good-bye. Behind my ego was, of course, my fear of closure—Erik's official rejection. Just like my mother in Trikeri, who refused to see doctors, I felt that not knowing was better than facing the facts. Ten years later and in a different part of the world, my demented choice to avoid closure with Erik was still a rural denial, a disillusioned ray of hope. Theoretically, technically, anything could still happen.

Alkis had moved on to "the anti-Western bias in Reuters's Middle East coverage," and I pretended to listen, wondering what I would do if Erik walked into the restaurant right at that moment. Or if I ran into him back at the hotel in Chatham—how would we react? We hadn't communicated in six weeks. As far as I knew, he might have been in Cape Cod that very weekend. A scary thought, although at this particular time it played out as a happy encounter. " . . . until a bus blows up in central Jerusalem," Alkis said, bringing me out of my zone. Then he waved "peace" to our waiter again, exposing his handgun tattoo again, and the world of juxtapositions we lived in which permitted me one more—one last, I promised myself—escape into Erikland. Had I said or done something better, the outcome might have been different with Erik. My what-if scenarios were all over the place—from sucking his dick better to meeting him before my "toxic MBA." My magical endings varied wildly too: a fishing life with Erik and Jeevan in the Caribbean, building schools in South Boston, producing olive oil in Greece and exporting it to Manhattan restaurants for Alkis and his friends.

"Do you party these days?" Alkis asked as he massaged his shoulder, where the gun was.

A WEEK AFTER TRAINING, I signed a lease for a one-bedroom apartment in San Francisco. The following week, I got my first client, my first project—an hour's drive north of Chicago.

"Your hotel will be the Deer Path Inn in Lake Forest," Command's in-house travel agent e-mailed me. "A historic property with stone fireplaces, antiques & artifacts. A landmark!" he elaborated in bold and italicized letters before requesting my confirmation so he could make the reservation.

"Is it a business hotel?" I replied.

"It's the only game in town," the agent responded.

Late on Sunday night, I checked in at the Deer Path Inn. The manager explained that half their rooms were suites. "Including the Mrs. Frederick, where you will be staying," he said.

"That's great." I faked interest.

"Your suite is named after a hundred-year-old lady who lived with us for thirty years," my porter later said, helping me to my room.

With *us*? Was he born in the hotel? He looked like he was fourteen. I checked my watch. It was approaching midnight. "I'm not afraid of ghosts," I said, handing him a ten.

For the next three months I was expected to "live" on the nearby campus of the client, a major pharmaceutical, and help managers there shape up the research and development strategy for their anti-infectives franchise.

Command protocol had it that I, the Associate, should never leave the client's premises before my project leader

did, and, "it goes without saying, never, *ever* before partners."
Once in a blue moon one of them would drop by.

"What about the client?" I asked my project leader.

"Oh, don't worry about them," he said. "They're home by
six. That's when we start the real work."

I didn't care if it was a 24–7 job. Lake Forest was beyond
sleepy. It was a don't-wake-me-up suburb. On the weekends
I ran, just to have something to do, which exposed me to a
suburban *Children of Men* dystopia: it looked as though Lake
Forest had been hit by mass infertility from the 1960s till the
late '80s. And yet everyone there was still jogging away hap-
pily. The young ones performed synchronized runs in groups
of four or five. Their positions were choreographed, forming
some version of a Greek phalanx to keep them at a minimum
distance of ten feet from any fifteen-mile-per-hour cruising
Grand Cherokee. They always greeted me, all of them at
once, even if I was running in the opposite direction on the
other side of the street.

"Good seeing you too!" I paused and yelled the first time,
assuming that, in spite of their age, they were interning at the
client.

After two runs it became obvious that the typical Lake
Forest house was the size of the forty-room Inn, and equally sedated. "Oh, it's a *wonderful* community," the Russian
midtwenties Deer Path Inn receptionist told me.

By my third weekend, the quietness was intolerable; the
sounds of wind and cardinals outside Mrs. Frederick's

window stirred up déjà vu of wanting to escape from my village. "Fuck this cemetery. Got to get out of here," I said to her portrait and headed out for a sprint. Forty-five minutes later, my runner's high bolstered me enough to e-mail Erik. By then we had had no contact for almost three months.

"What the hell," I began. After five deleted drafts, I simply asked if he was still alive.

He responded immediately, which filled me with joy and speculation. "Feta! Good to hear from you. How's the West Coast treating you?"

Was he casual? Indifferent? Opportunistic, even?

We went on exchanging weekly notes on work and Donald Rumsfeld until, a few Sundays later, Erik asked me if I'd be in New York "anytime soon." I pressed the New E-mail button instinctively and requested a meeting that Friday with Andrea Farrugia, the VP who'd interviewed me at EBS; the only VP I knew at our New York office. "To get your perspective on the competitiveness of macrolides and quinolones," I typed.

Andrea replied at midnight:

"I don't consider myself an anti-infectives expert, but I'm happy to share my thoughts. I'm only available for lunch after a meeting at the Sloan Kettering Institute. How is noon at Sant Ambroeus on Madison? Andrea."

I responded immediately, "Perfect."

IT WAS THE LONGEST WEEK in Lake Forest yet. On Thursday at lunchtime I fled the client's headquarters "to spend three and a half days with Erik in New York," I bragged to Alkis over the phone while driving to O'Hare. "He said I could *totally* crash at his place . . . Mate? You there?"

"Is that your cell phone? Or do I spot some Southie in your accent?"

"You're funny," I said.

I heard Alkis exhale. "Have fun. But remember, don't overcompensate. The Dubya's got nothing on you."

I didn't react. This was a compliment; I didn't know how to react.

"We don't tell you this often, but you're not a shabby guy, Stathis. So just be yourself."

"I'm always myself."

"Really? 'Cause Erik thinks you're going to New York for work. And based on your e-mail, Andrea thinks you're going there for your project."

"Well . . . Sure, the project too. Two birds with—"

"You're not the kid who stole gas to push the boat out anymore. Get it together, *mate*."

"Cops. Gotta go!" I lied, and tossed the phone into the passenger seat.

I'd be in New York soon. I smiled.

ERIK'S OFFICE WAS IN THE McGraw-Hill Building, a depressing bluish-green art deco giant overlooking West Forty-Second Street. The second I entered the lobby I got the sense that I should take this skyscraper quite seriously, like it was a landmark or something. After what seemed to be a five-minute elevator ride, I found Erik in his two-room office on the twenty-sixth floor overlooking the Port Authority and the rest of Manhattan. Freshly shaved, in a blue oxford shirt and chinos, he was comfortable, his feet on his desk. Brown loafers—really. The other two people there, a young woman and a man, were typing in Hotmail accounts. Neither seemed older than twenty, and neither acknowledged me.

I walked over and offered my hand for him to shake, thrown by the J.Crew look.

Erik laughed, pushed my hand away, and said: "Good to see you, Feta. Here are the keys. I'll see you at home." Then he dismissed me with a wink.

When I reached his office door, I hesitated and looked back. He was already typing away again on his laptop, his feet again up on the desk. *Give Stathis keys—check.* Like I was a piece of admin.

Leaning back in my cab seat, I felt his keys in my pocket. I took them out and looked at them, two sorry yellow keys in a locksmith bangle, and replayed in my mind the ease with which Erik had granted me access to his pad, as though my impressions of and reactions to his place and stuff had little substance or were taken as a given.

My cab ride seemed shorter than the one in the elevator, and the driver handed me six back from a ten. I kept four and stepped out in front of Erik's building, off Tenth Avenue in the west Twenties, adjacent to an abandoned elevated railroad that crossed his neighborhood and ran along the southwest side of Manhattan.

I entered Erik's street-level studio, and there was practically nowhere to step. I was faced with a dilemma. I could either stand there or sit on his grimy futon, surrounded by high-tech lights, duct-taped cables, two bikes and locks, heating pipes, and musty Yellow Pages piled with keyboards wired to computer screens that never stopped flickering. Everything made the 250-square-foot space look like evidence of a future-gone-grim pad from *Brazil*. A four-foot-high storage loft above the kitchenette was his bedroom.

I moved a pair of smelly sneakers out of the way and sat on the futon. The screensaver on the computer facing me slide-showed beaches in Mozambique, soccer games in Africa, World Cup finals, deforestation, boxy Jeeps, Erik at the pyramids with his brother. All around me, equipment lights bleeped in abstract synchronicity, like a Xenakis mathematical concert. Erik's place looked like it was perfectly lived-in, like a machine god had come down and paused life in an ideal chaos. I wanted to touch everything, like a schoolgirl nosing around. I made up rules to check myself: don't log into my e-mail from his desktop; don't look for photographs and notes, or for a second toothbrush in his bathroom. *How about I watch some TV,* I thought, but of course there was no set in sight. My mind was working up a headache. Maybe I could find some Advil by his bedside table or in his drawers. I got up, opened the door, and strolled down Tenth Avenue. Bought *Nature via Nurture* at 192 Books and ended up at the Empire Diner.

Four chapters later, Erik was finishing my burger at our booth. "I put my TV on the pavement when Bush got elected," he said, stuffing French fries into his mouth.

"You killed your TV?" I joked.

"I needed a hiatus," he mumbled with a full mouth. "For a bit. But it didn't really work. I watch news online now, streaming."

"How's the quality?"

"Worse than your porn," Erik said, smiling.

We sat there in silence for a second. We were the only customers. Empty bistros in Normandy flashed though my eyes. "Have you seen *Sex, Lies, and Videotape*?" I asked.

Erik stopped eating my fries. "I never saw that one. But if you're referring to what I think you are—" He wagged his finger at me in a Clinton–Lewinsky way. "Not my style."

I didn't care if he was talking cheating, amateur porn, or any perversion or fetish I might have triggered. I was busy amortizing his shyness, his exclusivity on me. On us. I believed what I wanted to believe.

Erik picked up a toothpick and my book. "So, how you've been?" he asked, skimming the back cover.

Alone, I thought. "Busy," I said.

"How's Chicago?" Always browsing.

"Lake Forest? A joggerland." I stuck to short responses, few words, my rally against his business-as-usual catch-up, as if the whole summer that we didn't speak had never happened. *Ask me why I'm here, motherfucker.*

But Erik kept on chitchatting, " . . . bio versus pharmaceuticals versus generics . . . ," his toothpick fencing.

"You know something?" I cut in. "I'm here to see you."

"Wanna get takeout and go home?" he asked with a cocky smile.

Fuck takeout and fuck you. "Let's get rubbers first," I countered, pathetically trying to handle—undo the undoable, really—my perfectly dismissed confession. I wanted to whack his fucking face, so I walked up to the register and paid.

That night I couldn't get any shut-eye on Erik's futon because of the high-tech indoor city lights, so we slept and fucked sideways in the four-foot-high storage bedroom above his stove. At some point, a used rubber fell into a pot below.

"Why do you spell Erik with a *K*?" I asked, looking at the rubber floating on two-day-old marinara sauce.

"I feel more Scandinavian," he said.

"Why's that?"

"Fewer hang-ups. I throw away the sauce, rinse the pot, and keep eating."

I fell asleep with my arm under his neck.

AT FIVE TO NOON THE next day I was at Sant Ambroeus on Madison Avenue. There were no stools at the bar. The two guys standing there, one in aviator sunglasses, were drinking espressos while reading Italian newspapers. Farther inside the restaurant, women were already having lunch, most of them on their cell phones.

Andrea walked in, sparkling like her pearls. She was in her late thirties, about five-ten, with long straight blond hair and an American clean and busy-looking face, wearing a cypress-green coat and matching scarf. "Best espresso in the city," she said with a firm handshake through butter-soft leather gloves.

"Excellent," I said. "Thank you for making the time."

"Of course. We call it Lunch and Learn." Andrea nodded to the maître d', who approached her and whispered something in her ear. She nodded with a confident grin, and we were led to a corner table. A double espresso was placed in front of her as we sat down.

"Thank you, Todd." She took her gloves off, studying me. "So, how are things in Chicago?" she asked and immediately busied herself with a PalmPilot, or some such device I'd never seen before, which slid open and unfolded three times into two screens and a keyboard. Suddenly her fingers froze. She looked up. "Wait. Let's get to know each other. Who are your sponsor, mentor, and buddy?"

I knew two of the three, though I wasn't a hundred percent sure who was what, or what the titles meant exactly. I was ready to share some names when Todd leaned over me: "Would you like something to drink?"

"Just water."

"Try the espresso," Andrea demanded. "We won't have time for coffee after lunch."

"Espresso."

"Good." She looked pleased. "So what's going on in Chicago? And why are you here?"

I took a sip of water carefully; her Batman accessory was taking up half the table. "It's a fun project," I said. "We are building their 2010, 2020 anti-infectives strategy, which is exactly the type of work I always wanted, you may recall from my interview. I—"

"Stop," Andrea interrupted. "Let me tell you what's going on in Chicago." She downed her espresso. "They need speed and innovation. As simple as that. They need speed to deal with the blessing turned curse of having too many drug candidates in the preclinical stage. Of having too many choices. And they need innovation to move beyond the pharma sector's expectations. Can we *do* that? Can we fix their opportunity cost of predictability? Can we speed up their disgracefully slow growth?"

One of her screens flashed and I thought of Erik's apartment.

Todd looked at me. "Would you like to hear the specials?"

"Just tell him the signatures," Andrea ordered.

I SPENT THE REST OF the fall traveling between Lake Forest and Manhattan. Fourteen-hour workdays were followed by weekends, seven of them, with Erik. After one of those Friday-evening flights, I ran into schoolmates from EBS. There was an assumption in our greeting, an implicit expectancy, as if Terminal C at LaGuardia were an alumni lounge. Jokes about "the coalition of the willing" mixed with talk of Starbucks's European expansion and the new governor of California. Then more jokes about Alkis and his latest girlfriend, and, although we parted with unrealistic promises, for the first time I felt somewhat integrated into my new world, made up of work and Erik.

At the curb outside the terminal, waiting for a cab, I considered the idea of just going along with Erik as is. No confirmations. Everything unexpressed. Maybe our status quo was not a bad thing, after all. A balance not to be discussed, nor disturbed.

Maybe all I needed was a glossary to trust and translate. When Erik said "I so wanna suck your dick," I could interpret affection, even love. *I still have a chance*, I thought as I slid into the backseat of the cab and right into old hopes and habits.

My weekends' main activity was following Erik around Tenth Avenue in west Chelsea, his district, one of the last downtown neighborhoods where you could still forget you were in Manhattan. Nightclubs and galleries had started to move in, but the landscape still had a Pittsburgh feel about it, a sense of industrial abandonment. Erik pointed at rezoned fields full of trucks, and lots that were up for bidding. We strolled by rail yards that seemed to go nowhere. Everything around us looked stout; nothing was conventionally pretty. Rectangular structures occupied more than a block, streets tunneling through them. There were no shops, nothing, just random pedestrians for whom I couldn't see a destination on the street. Or some kids just sitting there, staring at us, under the High Line—the abandoned freight railroad that blocked the sun from Erik's apartment. Soon the landscape became repetitive. We would turn the corner to more barren streets, some of them as quiet as those in Lake Forest.

We walked to Billymark's on Ninth Avenue for two-dollar happy hour, and from there up the street to the Pakistani kitchen for dinner with Melissa, Erik's "favorite cabdriver," the only cabdriver he knew.

Once at the restaurant, Erik picked up the neighborhood's paper and checked the column by the journalist, who had written that Erik's "use of a rent-subsidized apartment"— Erik being the manager of the district's community board— "was a conflict of interest."

"Well, it's up to the board now," Erik said and shrugged,

clearly indifferent to our faces, which were turned radioactive green by the fluorescent lights reflecting off the restaurant's pistachio walls. I needed sunglasses—our table, chairs, and pakora sauce were all in pastel yet shining colors. An old guy in what looked like a corner shop within the restaurant yelled in Punjabi through his internal window. When I read his sign out loud, "We fix all cell phones," Erik shook his head as though I had crossed some line of political correctness by noticing a cell phone shop within a Pakistani restaurant.

I let it go and made eye contact with Melissa. She was a Barbara Bush look-alike: hair, wrinkles, surprised-looking face . . .

"It's for the tips, Stathis," Melissa said, catching me gawking at the large cotton camellia brooch on her L.L.Bean flannel shirt. She turned to Erik: "What you gonna do if they evict you?"

"They'll be doing me a favor," Erik said. "I live in my work, I walk too much. I'll move to the Bronx, with you!"

"Then we'll be neighbors!" Melissa laughed. "I can take you into town on my morning shifts."

"You know I can't afford you."

"You gonna bike or run to work?" She kept laughing.

"Lady, you saw me jogging once and you almost ran me over."

"Parks are for runners. Streets are for cars."

"Not in my district. We'll make it a walker's hood." Erik's Southie was acting up.

Melissa looked at me. Her eyes were wide open. "He was jogging in fucking Harlem!"

"I was legit." Erik smiled.

She forked some chicken. "He was running naked in a snowstorm," she said with her mouth full. "No one around. I thought I would be the last person to see him alive. I honked, I yelled . . ." She waved her fork at Erik. "He kept running. I had to chase his freezing ass down the street."

"Sorry, I don't run in a team." Erik laughed.

"What's wrong with that?" I said.

"I don't need one more class in my life. I'm not like you," Erik said, satisfied.

I wasn't following, but I could tell he smelled blood.

"Let's see," he said, and looked at the ceiling. "Stanford class of '98? EBS '03? Command '03? Bay Area Sailing Team I-don't-know-when . . . What's next? Friends of the High Line, class of 2004?"

Was I accused of being a zealous immigrant? Today's version of the never-ending American story? A successful Melissa? Fine. I was an educated immigrant. He knew that, he acknowledged that, so why couldn't education be our bond? Our stick between Melissa and corporate? If we had anything in common, we were both into reconciling reality with ideas. We spiced things up—like the smell from the kitchen, which was getting stronger by the minute. The Pakistani music louder; the same song had been playing for half an hour, pounding my head after my absurdly long week, flight, and lack of sleep in Erik's sarcophagus of a bedroom. "Isn't that how you grow up in this country?" I countered, feeling the swollen glands in my neck.

"I didn't choose this country."

"You came back," I said.

"To do my share."

"Of what? Declassification?"

"Yes." Erik laughed. "Whatever it takes."

"And you picked the right hood?" I pressed.

He pushed his plate toward Melissa, who was already eating his chicken bites, and motioned to the waiter for more beers. "I picked the only hood where we can preserve without penalizing the classless," Erik said.

"So preservation is to blame now?" I smiled.

His manner changed. "*I'm* the journalist, amigo. I didn't say that. I said urban preservation criminalizes poverty. That's how we preserve in this country. We push the poor out of the city."

"Three more beers! Now!" Melissa yelled, eating with her hands.

I looked at her dirty nails and mustache. Cabs were parked and double-parked on both sides of Ninth Avenue. What if Alkis or Paul walked in at that moment?

"That's the way to do it," Erik said to Melissa, and I wondered if—correction, *when*—Erik would pick up a New York accent.

FOUR

TWO WEEKS BEFORE CHRISTMAS, ERIK told me he was going to Hawaii for the holidays to cover an eco-event and kayak with his brother. He didn't ask me anything about my holiday plans, which were non-existent.

"Your name is at the airport in Athens," my sister told me that same week.

If I traveled back to Greece, the army could force me to enlist for a minimum of eighteen months. I'd lose both my job and my American green card. So, once again, my sister and I talked about our never-materializing plan: that I would buy the whole family a trip somewhere in Europe. My father's work, my sister's kids, my mother's health and fear of flying: the trip was always postponed for one reason or another. By 2003 I hadn't seen my family for three years, a period long enough that I could pick up on the pity on colleagues' faces when I had to respond to their query on how long had it been since I'd visited Greece.

"You're choosing comfort and privilege over family," Paul told me at a conference in downtown Chicago when

I dodged his question about when my next trip to Trikeri would happen.

I was not proud, but I didn't doubt that my choices were right, necessary. "Even globalization has its limits," I retaliated. "You know better, Paul. You just came back from"—pretending to be—"surfing in the South Seas."

He took a sip of his pink cocktail. "You know why I like you?"

"'Cause I used to let you copy my homework?"

"Because you're a white-collar prostitute with a small-village story to sell," Paul said.

Whatever.

And yet, driving back to Lake Forest by myself—the rest of the Commanders on their way to Washington or San Francisco—I was restless. Paul wasn't from a shitty island. He didn't know what it meant to grow up among a population of two hundred, or what rural life is really like. Not all of us were born to be my father or Jeevan, who spent their lives fishing and fixing boats for tourists like Paul and his friends. Whoever had the luck or the balls to ditch that might actually get to open a savings account, or drink wine that leaves less of a hangover than retsina. I worked for it. I studied, I put in the hours. I deserved it both ways: my family *and* Command. Fuck you Paul, *and* Christmas. And that Friday-night jam.

In my room at the Deer Path Inn, I ordered a steak and called Reception to ask how to get a DVD.

"We have a small collection at the front desk," the Russian receptionist said. "I can bring it to your room so you can choose."

"Thank you, but I'll come down in a few," I said, and hung up.

I took off my shoes and lay on top of my bedspread. I lit a cigarette and dialed my sister from Mrs. Frederick's phone. Now that I'd been gone for a decade, our weekly calls were more or less standard. We would talk about our parents, my nephew and niece, and the new family dog, and then she would thank me for the money I wired on the fifteenth of each month.

I had just made a paper boat out of the Guest Comment Card when my sister told me that a marine patrol had retired our father's fishing boat.

"An ad hoc inspection," she added, distracted.

"Oh," I said. "Maybe it is for the best . . ." I stopped mid-sentence. There was bittersweetness in the sound of my voice.

Then she surprised me: "Are you happy?"

We never got personal, acknowledged our time apart, or talked about our hopes and yearnings.

"Yes," I managed, turning my paper boat into an ashtray.

"That's good," she said. There was something aged in her voice.

"It is."

"Markos started taking English in high school. He wants to study in New York, like you."

"Well, I went to school in California," I said, instantly realizing the idiocy of my argument. This wasn't going well. "We have a few years for that one, right?"

"Six," my sister said.

"That's a long time."

"It seems that way."

Was she referring to me? Was this my taxing call, my bill for walking? I took a drag and recalled the night I had found out about my scholarship to study abroad. I ended up at the top of Pelio, the lights from Volos across the bay giving in to the dawn. One of the few moments in my life that I thought I had perfect clarity. I would leave home—too island-isolated, too windy to speak or hear emotions—and find myself. Learn and gain, even destroy—the way the Greeks have been rising and falling for three thousand years now. But here I was, thousands of miles away, lured by the Eriks of my new world—equally muted islands—by their WASPy heritage, by their dividends. Sure, I was an Associate, I was one of them, but I'd traded my island's silence for that of New England. It was ironic, really; I finally had the balls to talk emotions, but there was no one around who'd listen.

"*Hello?*"

"I'm here," I said into the receiver. "How about we get Markos a computer for Christmas? So he can practice."

She took her time. "When do they celebrate Christmas in Brindasi? The same days we do?" she asked.

"It's Brin*di*si," I said. Since I left Greece, I had never corrected my sister. Our call was becoming unbearable. I fought an impulse to hang up. "Of course they do," I added.

"Are you drinking enough orange juice?" she asked me.

I left my room for the reception desk in my suit and socks. The Russian woman was alone behind the desk, reading a paperback of *Under the Tuscan Sun*. A DVD folder, open in front of her, had *Pearl Harbor* and *Monsters, Inc.* in its first page.

"A few are out." She put her book aside. "But most of them should be there."

"I'm sure I'll find something," I said. "I just wanna veg, really."

She smiled. "I know. That's my favorite thing to do after work too. Usually with a movie I've already seen."

I flipped the page. There was *Lord of the Rings* something, *Chocolat*, an empty holder, and *Erin Brockovich*.

"Are you going to New York for the holidays?" she asked in a harmless Midwestern way.

"Er, not sure." I concentrated on the folder in front of me. An image of my unfurnished apartment in San Francisco— thus, my holiday plans—flashed through my mind.

"Oh, you *must*! It's the best time to visit New York. John and I were there last Christmas. We went to three Broadway shows. Have you seen any plays this season?"

"Yes. I mean, no. I mean, only Off-Broadway," I lied.

"We love that city. The restaurants, the museums . . . We went to Tavern on the Green, where John proposed. It was so romantic. The next day we had brunch at Pastis, in the Meatpacking District. It's so much fun. Have you ever been?"

Work lunches aside, Erik's three-dollar beer and spicy

chicken had been my only wine-and-dines in Manhattan. In fact, west Chelsea was the only neighborhood I knew. I followed its district manager around like a puppet when my base was in the six digits and New York was waking up from its 9/11 and dot-com mournings—people drinking and dining in the four corners of each Manhattan intersection.

"Yes, it's fun," I agreed. "Couldn't get a table, though." I flipped one more page, to *Forrest Gump*, *Braveheart*, and *Titanic*. Could these movies be more fucking predictable?

"Have you been to the Guggenheim?" she asked with a scouting look on her face.

Still in my suit, the radiator's heat hitting me, I was nauseated. My only entertainment options, straight from a Dallas/Fort Worth inbound flight, lay in front of me. And this Russian-Midwestern receptionist kept rubbing it in.

"I have a friend there," I said, loosening my tie.

Her Midwestern smile turned Russian. "A special friend," she said—she didn't ask.

Special alright. I thought of the public hearings that Erik ran and I attended, standing at the back of the room, sometimes straight from the airport after seventy-hour weeks when I didn't know if or when I'd see him again. I wished she'd shut the fuck up.

"I'll take this one." I took out a disc and closed her stupid folder.

"Oh!" She was surprised. "I love that movie." `

I rushed back to Mrs. Frederick, threw *Forrest Gump* behind the door and my jacket on the couch, and downed an Ambien with a minibar vodka. It was dawn when I woke up, starving. I found my dinner on the coffee table and had it for breakfast, with my tie still on.

That Saturday I talked Erik into a Los Angeles stopover, where I'd invited myself to spend the holidays with Alkis and his girlfriend.

"We'll be at the Chateau," Alkis told me from London.

I was puzzled. "Chateau?"

"The Chateau Marmont," Alkis explained. "Call them soon, they book up fast."

"What damage are we talking here?"

"You've been on expenses for four months now, you wanker. What on earth are you crying about?"

I hung up and dialed the number he gave me.

"Good morning, Chateau Mar*mont?*" someone answered, practically singing to me. I couldn't tell if it was a man, a woman, or a child.

"Uh, reservations," I said.

"For the restaurant or the hotel?"

"The hotel."

"Hold on, please."

"This is Derek's suite at Chateau Marmont's reservation line. Please leave me a message and I will get back to you."

I just held the receiver. Derek's voice made me uncomfortable; his busy indifference said I wasn't good enough or something. I hung up.

THE RUSSIAN GAVE ME A lift to O'Hare, but not before a "long overdue" tour of Lake Forest that in an unwary moment I had accepted. We started from the Inn's own wedding suite, where she pointed out to me a white hart or stag, the Inn's crest. Something that I was "probably familiar with from Alexander the Great." We drove by Lake Forest College, a fitness center, and Mr. T's or Michael Jordan's residence— she wasn't a hundred percent sure whose.

My cell phone flashed Andrea's number.

When I picked up, there was some static. "I'm on my way to Lake Forest," Andrea said. "Are you at the Deer Something Inn?"

I tried to explain my situation, but she spoke over me. "Stathis, meet me at the Admirals Club at O'Hare in thirty minutes. It's across Gate 8. Terminal 3. I have another call I have to take. I'll see you soon," she said, and hung up.

FROM A LOOK AROUND THE Admirals Club, you could tell it was Christmas. Club members and ground staff (one in a red-nosed-reindeer sweater) were in corporate cheer. Andrea waved to me from one of the sofas overlooking the terminal, at the back of the lounge. She wore a wool coat, its red echoed by her lipstick.

"Stathis!" She smiled her bleached teeth to me. "I'm sorry I didn't have a chance to brief you from New York, but everything happened so suddenly," she said, and threw an Airborne tablet into her Perrier, making a double-bubble drink.

"I was on the phone with our client throughout my flight, so I'm glad I got hold of you."

Our client? I tried not to look confused as I sat next to her. Too much perfume. "That's okay. Of course," I said, warily.

"I'm heading to an off-the-record meeting with your friends in Lake Forest," she said. "We want to get their metabolics therapeutic area too, but they are already in talks with McKinsey, so we have to act fast."

I tried to warn her about the bubbles mushrooming above her glass, getting ready to spill all over her laptop, but she was on a roll: "You guys cannot handle both anti-infectives and metabolics by yourselves; we need to beef up the account. I'm getting a team together from Washington."

"That's good news," I said.

"It is, isn't it?" she said, flattered, almost flirty.

Andrea wants my validation?

She took a sip from her Airborne-Perrier, which dripped orange from her red lipstick. Then she reached into her reptile-leather briefcase and handed me a folder.

"What is this?" I asked.

"This is what I'm going with for the pitch," she said busily, checking her phone.

I looked at the folder's title and almost laughed. "Er," I said, and made myself cough. "This is Command's recommendations to their number-one competitor, from few months ago." *What's going on here?* I thought. "We're not supposed to even look at this." Let alone use it.

"It's only directional." Andrea played with her phone nervously. "Stathis, you're in the service business now. This is leveraging our knowledge bank. It's called *best practices*. It helps our clients." She started playing with her pearls, 'cause she was fucking lying. This was against Command policy. You can't have teams working for competitors see each other's work. She *knew* that. She finally looked at me. "I just e-mailed you a copy of this deck. Get online, delete the graphs that I have already marked, and change names, of course." She rolled her eyes. "Just go through the whole thing and treat it with some imagination. I want to leave something behind with them, today. Now, I gotta call Washington. What time is your flight to LA?"

This was fucked up. I wanted to talk to Alkis. "I'm boarding in twenty . . ." I tried.

"No worries. We'll get you upgraded on the next flight out." She smiled harmlessly, but I had frozen.

"Stathis, this is common practice. We've been using best practices to position our clients for success since long before you joined us. Honestly, if you can't support me on this I'll have to keep that under consideration for the rest of our work in Lake Forest. Where are you staying in LA?"

I leaned back on the sofa to take the situation in. "I think the Chateau Marmont," I mumbled slowly. "But they are full," I added quietly. What the fuck was I saying? What the fuck did my hotel have to do with any of this? Crazy bitch.

"Andrea, I'm not sure I'm comfortable with this copy-and-paste thing between competitors—"

"Okay, I'll call Washington and explain that you're not capable of on-the-fly teamwork. I'll ask for remote support from there." She picked up her phone again, but paused and looked at me. "What is it going to be?"

Anyone who has ever worked in the service industry knows that when you join a firm, you want to do everything by the book. But you often find yourself debating how this book translates to the real world, to the client's wish list, or to your VP's demands. You don't want to be difficult. Sometimes you don't even want to deal, so you escape to comforting thoughts. I would see Erik soon. Everything would be all right.

"I don't want this to have my name on it," I murmured, and opened my carry-on to get my laptop.

"Who said it ever would?" Andrea asked and gave me a glance like I was a toddler riding my first bike. "Great!" she added. "I knew you wouldn't want to start at Command as anything less than a straight team player. Don't forget to highlight speed and innovation. I want it in every slide possible. I'll get you to the Chateau. Let me call Washington and then Andre."

"Who's Andre?" I asked.

"The Chateau's owner."

FOR THE TWO NIGHTS THAT Erik stayed in LA, I checked out of the Chateau Marmont and into the Standard, down the street.

"Will you cut off the labels in your shirts too?" Alkis laughed when he found out about my "downgrade."

I said I would, barely listening to him, counting down to Erik's arrival.

"Genius to moron," my indisputable mentor said, pitifully, and I was back.

"Actually," I said, "how about I stick 'Armani' on your rubbers so your girlfriend might finally get to have an orgasm."

To Alkis's surprise, I didn't pick Erik up from LAX. I didn't even offer, trying to somehow square things with Erik in my mind. Then, of course, he didn't mention needing a ride, feeding into our rivalry.

At the Standard, I opened my room's door to a flashing camera.

"Feta *Cheese!*"

Erik carried a bag the size of my work briefcase. He was bloody good-looking. "My fancy, horny Greek!" he yelled, surveying the room. "It's good to see you, brother." He gave the room another once-over and then said: "*And* your minibar! Let's get you drunk and throw you in the pool."

"Let's totally fuck," I said, and belts and buckles hit the floor.

"Hey, I gotta be out of here by six," Erik said. "Okay if I borrow your rental?"

It took me a second to breathe, but by then we were making out, so I got away with it.

"You bet." I played too cool to ask why. What the fuck *for*?

"You okay?" Erik asked when I couldn't come—my mind was spinning, speculating about Erik's business in LA. "You used to bust a nut on demand. What happened? Did you just fuck the doorman?" he laughed.

"Yikes," I whispered.

He squeezed my balls, which made me super hard. I blushed, bit his neck, and came soon after.

"GET YOUR DUBYA, YOUR WALLET and come to Matsuhisa for dinner with us," Alkis ordered me as soon as I answered my cell phone, a little past seven that evening.

"Negative," I said. "Erik and I are meeting a Greek guy who dropped out of Harvard to go fight in Afghanistan . . . You there?"

"What're you talking about?" Alkis asked, clearly amused.

"Not exactly sure yet. An old friend of Erik's, a London Greek, Constantine something, happens to be passing through LA. He is on his way to Iraq via, um, Mexico? He became—" I snorted—"a *mujahid* in the '80s. He is a war correspondent now."

There was another pause.

"Actually, I'm looking forward to this," I said, trying to cover up my anxiety before meeting my opposite: this guy who gave up London for the Middle East, my hero's hero, plus a Greek. A triple hat.

"Are you guys doing drugs?"

"No!" I choked while lighting a cigarette.

"Hold on a minute," Alkis said. "Is this the guy from that shipping family who they thought was dead? The one that Paul's ex-girlfriend dated for like a week, ten years ago?"

This was getting complicated.

"No clue," I said, letting my smoke out slowly. "But I guess we'll find out."

AN HOUR LATER I WAS driving Alkis's rental on Sunset, hitting holiday traffic. No one was moving except a guy behind me riding a Ducati, changing lanes. As his BMW jacket zig-zagged into my mirror, Alkis's question about Constantine began to make sense. I thought maybe I had overlapped—I must have—with some of Constantine's brothers or cousins right after Trikeri. At thirteen I got a scholarship for the premier high school in Athens. It was a Greek institution, where 80 percent of the students were sons of politicians or benefactors and came to school in BMWs. The rest of us, from around the country, came on grants. We didn't mingle.

I had been stuck in traffic for a good hour and a half when Erik rang.

"*Embros*," I said.

"Where are you?" Erik ignored my Greek.

"In Echo Park, I think. Trying to find your no-sign bar on Sunset."

"It's a former cop hangout."

"And that will help me spot it how?"

"Just a drink-ordering tip."

"You're worried. You shouldn't be," I said, and Erik hung up.

When I finally found the garage-looking building, the only sign said COCKTAILS, in neon. I walked in and saw Erik seated next to a skinny guy at the end of the bar.

I was hearty, Greek: "*Kalispera! Eimai o Stathis.*"

"My name is Zemar," said Constantine, looking in my direction but not straight in the eye.

I sat on Erik's right and ordered a beer. On his left, this Zemar or Constantine or whoever, bearded, tired, with veins and wrinkles everywhere, with nothing Byronesque about him, held his bottle with both hands. I could smell his body odor from my seat.

Erik was in the middle of a story about the last time they had seen each other, in Egypt, but Zemar was drifting away. He didn't blink, even when he was asked to answer a question or pushed to deliver the punch line.

Suddenly, Zemar woke up: "How is your brother?" he asked Erik.

"Kevin is great," Erik replied. "He moved to New York about a year ago. He's dating this fashion girl. My mother wants grandchildren, so the pressure's on."

Zemar forced a smile. A couple of teeth were missing.

"He would have stopped over had he known you'd be in LA," Erik said.

"Is he still working with your father at the hospitals?" Zemar asked.

"Well, yes and no. They started a biotech fund together. And now a bunch of Kevin's mates from Wharton have jumped in. It's actually taking off," Erik said with a who-would-have-thought shrug. He quickly transitioned into a story about when Zemar dropped out of Harvard fifteen or twenty years ago and disappeared into the Hindu Kush mountains to fight against Red Army leftovers and Arabs. He asked Zemar about the tribes' religious conflict with Islam, about paganism and mountain legends. Honestly.

Still, Zemar took him seriously. He answered slowly, patiently, even smiled here and there, showing more wrinkles as he defended Islam from Erik's "Hindu mountain spirituality." But Erik kept going.

"I do not like horned phantoms!" Zemar told Erik at one point, and I almost spilled my beer. Were they on drugs? We were post-9/11, in the middle of an illegit invasion, and Erik, a journalist, was chatting with a war correspondent about fucking ghosts and Sanskrit epics that I bet he'd Googled. Or had they made sure they rushed through the good stuff before I arrived? Was this a conspiracy?

"Where I live these days, they have a white stag for a crest," I said. "A Russian told me that Alexander the Great, a *Greek*, captured it. Maybe he dragged it all the way out to Afghanistan and became a ghost," I said with a grin.

Neither of them laughed or said anything. Zemar's grip on his bottle got tighter, his yellow fingers brighter. Erik looked at me—for the first time that evening—like I had committed sacrilege. He turned back to Zemar: "When is your wedding?" he asked.

"We are still working on the date. Jennifer is converting."

"Becoming Greek Orthodox?" I said. No doubt in my sound.

"Muslim."

I was drinking fast, and I didn't give a rat's ass if he had changed his name, his religion, or his fucking sex, for that matter. But a high school pride, an elemental instinct, had been ticked off, and I wanted to be acknowledged as one Greek to another. "Where do the tribes stand post-9/11?" I asked.

"I am not going to discuss any US involvement," Zemar said with an air of statesmanship, setting boundaries.

"I'm sure it's hard for you," I pushed. "I mean, staying objective. From a warrior to a correspondent . . ."

"*Why?*" Erik jumped in. "Isn't that what you *consultants* are going for? Advise *and* stake? Alkis and his equity-based fees you make fun of?"

Was Erik in love with him? Or was Zemar just Erik's wet dream of a career path? A guy who'd been given all the opportunities in the world but chose extreme hardship and poverty, who reduced Erik's hanging out with Melissa to a fucking hors d'oeuvre. "If you see the two as comparable," I said to Erik, looking at Zemar.

Zemar let go of his beer and stared back at me. His bottle was full. "Shouldn't we?" he said. "We don't live in a lab. There's an opportunity cost in everything we do. Didn't they teach you that at EBS?"

"Isn't your family in shipping?" I asked.

Erik's lips parted. An I-don't-believe-you're-going-there expression was on his face.

Zemar locked on me. "How big's your dick, mate?"

"He'll fill you in on the opp cost there. But I can tell you it's Greek," I said. "And since we're not in a lab, maybe you'll get a better bang for your buck if you invest in sustainability. Like labor issues. Or, God forbid, if you pay taxes on your family's vessels instead of flying first-class to Peshawar."

"Shut up, Stathis!" Erik said.

"No worries, I'm done," I said, and stood up like a madman. I tossed a ten onto the bar and started for the door.

"Where are you going?" Erik asked.

I turned. "To the Chateau Marmont," I said, surprisingly together. "To get drunk and get blow room-serviced for Christmas. Which, by the way, I can afford, after working my ass off in Lake fucking Forest."

I got out onto the street in a rage. Racing down Sunset, changing lanes like a motherfucker, I wanted to make a U-turn, go back, and beat the shit out of that beer-petting freak, *and* Erik. But I saw a NO U-TURN sign—a sign, I thought—and sped onward. I checked in at the Chateau without checking out of the Standard.

Maybe because of my flustered face, or for some reason, Josh at the front desk upgraded me to a cottage at the far end of the property. "An elevated house with a private balcony overlooking LA," Josh said.

I opened the cottage door—no luggage, no porter—and saw an old wooden floor. The cottage smelled like my grandmother's house in Pelio. I downed both minibar vodkas and called for more. But I was restless, I couldn't wait, I couldn't sit still. My Erik-anxiety and my grandma's smell were creeping up on me.

I walked out and into the garden, all the way to a dead end with a hidden table behind the pool. Two girls were there, looking as if they had just stepped out of a Pimm's commercial.

Was I at the party in Bungalow 3 the night before, the one wearing a red scarf asked. She had a certain birthright in her voice, a curiosity toward me mixed with boredom.

"I'm from Greece," I said, for no reason.

Was I there working? her friend asked me while petting a golden retriever.

Was she asking if I worked in LA? Or at the hotel? Suddenly all I wanted was to go back and hide in my room.

"I lost a friend," I said, and turned around.

In the cottage I drank from the room-serviced bottle till I passed out with my cell in my hand.

Erik's number buzzing on my palm woke me up. I jumped. "Erik," I answered before it got to ring twice.

"The game's on," Erik said.

"Where are you?" I heard my own voice, sounding sleepy but thrilled.

"Outside the Chateau Marmont, on Sunset. I think."

"Walk to your right. You'll see a door with no sign on it. Before the parking lot. I'll meet you there."

I left the cottage barefoot and rushed down from the balcony, three steps at a time. Pacing through the garden toward Sunset, I cursed the cross-shaped pond that I had to navigate around. I opened the garden door and found Erik standing on the pavement with his bag.

"Wanna play?" He grabbed my hair and kissed me. I felt his tongue in my mouth. "Hey—" he slowly pushed me back—"Zemar's off to Mexico tomorrow and needs a place to crash. Do you think we might have a sofa for him?"

"We're good," I said, and tried to look into his eyes, but Erik shoved his tongue back into my mouth.

I knew he wouldn't be there if it wasn't for Zemar being desperate, and yet little was better than nothing.

"Mint," Erik said, pulling out.

SMOKING NAKED IN BED, I punched Erik's shoulder. He snatched my hand and I knew, right then, that things were about to change.

"Why don't you just say it," Erik said, and looked at me.

"I totally fucking love you."

He took a drag from my cigarette, first time, and palmed the right side of my face with, what I saw, care in his eyes. "I better swallow you then," he said.

ERIK'S SNORING NEXT TO ME woke me up. I stared at him, trying to spot REM in his eyes, his involuntary smiles or angst, his dreams, but I couldn't. Then I looked at my watch, which said six a.m. I got up but couldn't find my boxers. I picked up Erik's from the floor and threw them on, then walked into the living room to a smell stronger than it had been the evening before. There was incense burning, and wood. Zemar was sleeping on the sofa next to his traveling bag, which had been half emptied all over the floor. It seemed like everything Zemar had was in pairs. There were two cell phones, two beaten-up passports—one British and one that I couldn't make out, not Greek—two linen scarves, English pounds, bandages all over, two syringes, a standard Ronson lighter, and a duty-free pack of Marlboros. Two books lay on the coffee table: *The Plague of Fantasies* was next to Michelin's map of Mexico.

I took a pack of cigarettes, along with his lighter, and walked out to the balcony. I sat on the top step and lit up, dazed by the city lights still clear below, a sparkling chaos that beckoned me to sort it all out. I spotted Sunset and then gazed east, trying to discover both Echo Park and the reason I lost it. I remembered yelling at Zemar and, through him, at Erik and myself, battling posh communism and perhaps my walking away from home. *Two birds with one stone*, I thought, and smiled. I dragged on my cigarette on the balcony's concrete floor and drew a matrix, just the way I nailed case studies at work: *X*-ing privilege against collectivism and *Y*-ing life goals against upbringings. Erik and I were at odds in this two-by-two, but a year on, finally, it looked like our prisoner's dilemma might be giving in. I said *I love you*, he swallowed my come. Was I decoding? Was I translating? "None of your fucking business," I murmured to myself, laughing, and manned up to walk down the steps and smell the roses in the garden.

"*Kalimera file!*" someone yelled. Good morning, my friend.

I turned and saw Zemar's silhouette, his linen scarf worn as a turban, lit by the Gucci billboard behind the fence.

"*Kalimera file*," I echoed, thumbing his lighter, perfectly curved, begging to be touched, and I felt myself bending my life even further. If Zemar was the prototype, I had to cut deeper between my work and my inarticulate, interpreting life with Erik.

FIVE

THE NEXT EIGHTEEN MONTHS I lived in hotels. I spent half a year at the Soho Grand in New York, four months at the Lancaster in Paris, another four at the Forrestal in Princeton, two at the Berkeley in London, and one at XV Beacon in Boston. They were all small, theatrically decorated properties that catered to long-term guests by offering insanely addictive service. Suitcases were magically unpacked and repacked. My favorite books appeared on my nightstand, and new underwear in my drawers. If I had a good day, cocktails were complimentary. If I got sick, a doctor was sent to my room, and my handwritten notes were couriered to the client. Shopping, gift wrapping, VAT-refund processing, and personal reminders in Moleskine pads cushioned me. Everything was available yet only when I needed it.

Sure, I worked crazy hours and with difficult teams, but, much like the expensed luxury I lived in, everything about my work was someone else's long-term commitment. I built portfolio management models that helped clients decide on billion-dollar investments, I developed product-launch and acquisition strategies for years to come; but they were all other people's challenges. I was protected by project-specific deadlines; clients, cities, and Command teams came and left. I made short, forceful friends—and enemies—that I rarely came across again. And soon this detachment at work spilled over to the rest of my life. Attached Commanders honored personal commitments Friday to Sunday, crossing the continent or the Atlantic twice a week, but singles, or semi-singles like me, decompressed on weekends right there in the hotel.

"How is hotel living?" I played back Paul's question over my room's speakerphone in Princeton. "It's just like work, really. Promiscuous," I said with a nervous laugh. "We're talking no responsibilities. When, if, I want to spend a weekend at my home in San Fran, *great*. Otherwise, all options are open."

I could hear Paul smoking.

"If you think about it, it's not a bad deal at all," I went on. "I'm homeless, but in first class."

"I think you're bullshitting me, Greek boy," Paul said.

"Come again?"

"You sound lonely."

"How's London?" I changed the subject. "How are *you*?"

"Everything is fine, everything is good. It's just a bit strange being single."

"If anyone can do it . . ."

"Screw that," Paul said.

"Well, being single may be good for you. You said you wanted to rediscover yourself, remember?"

"I suppose," Paul murmured. "Please don't do that," he said firmly to someone in the background, then to me: "*Malaka*, what are you doing this weekend? Come hang out here with us, in London."

"Us?"

"Alkis and I are throwing an EBS dinner this Saturday night."

"IF YOU WORK IN MANAGEMENT consulting, you can keep reinventing yourself," I half joked at Paul's party. "Being on a project means that you are in town for a few months, with an expense account and twenty-four-hour service. The options on how you present yourself are unlimited. What's not to like?"

"Careful, now. Real options and hedging cost. There's no free lunch." Paul handed me his new business card: wealth, asset, private equity, and custody management. "All in lower-case Calibri," he said, pointing at his card.

"You mean there's no free lunch for your *clients*," I said.

"What's that supposed to mean?" Paul asked.

"Means your ass is a different story," I replied.

"I don't make the rules, Stathis. I just play."

I thought of his father, who did make the rules, who'd probably gotten Paul his new job after he'd spent a year drinking in the Pacific. And why shouldn't I get a free lunch, or some no-strings-attached ass, for a change? All that when, slowly but steadily, people were cutting me out, right, left, and center.

By 2004 I had become so virtual, so conditioned to my self-exile, that old friends and acquaintances gave up on my schedule, my availability (or lack of it), my "flakiness," and finally "you!," as I read at the end of a collapsed e-mail conversation with ex-colleagues from the Bay Area. "Stathis who?" someone from the group had replied-all. "You're supposed to meet him in Café de la Presse and he's in Amsterdam."

That summer, insomnia settled in. I became an after-hours Birkenstocked fixture at the front desks of my hotels. When a useless Ambien gave me the munchies, I shared the midnight burger right there with the reception staff; often it wasn't even charged. Discussions and etiquettes started to slack, and the night crews would quickly position themselves as the have-nots in our relationship, with all the boldness—the cockiness, really—of having little or nothing to lose: "You work too much," these kids would tell me.

"You should buy a Daytona."

"Upgrade to a bungalow."

"Work faster."

"Quit your job."

"Go to Jericoacoara."

"Have a three-way in your cottage."

When I left for work a couple of hours later, the same shift would see me out: "Good morning, Mr. Rakis," they would say firmly, businesslike. Like a Cinderella-esque switch had evaporated our nighttime equal standing.

Other guests, sometimes colleagues, would pause an extra second at my lack of grooming, and even when I was freshly shaved—a habit that became less sacred—I lacked the chivalry that the typical Commander projected. Among my kind, there was usually sophistication and neatness around our appearances, and I showed neither. Partners with the "smart" accounts, their entourage, and a good number of "hi-pots"—high-potential Commanders—went for the angular Savile Row cut. Lower in the food chain was a compulsion for a Ralph Lauren kind of properness that bordered on a manicured, Christmassy, my-mother-bought-me-this-shirt look. I had joined an army of eunuchs with a handful of Euroglitz Brown graduates in four inches-high-collar shirts.

Andrea, in her high heels and pearls, would now and then comment on my "amusing" or "random" tie knot, my mismatching belt and shoes, and once, after a client presentation, my "weathered" Filofax. Wireless gadgets were "a Command privilege, a shield," she explained, "subsidized by our professional development expense accounts." I would get internal e-mails about a new Apple series, a special offer on Montblanc accessories, or an Etro suit sale, but I had neither an iPod nor a French-cuff shirt. My three suits were solid brown, gray, and black. Not having a navy-blue was more than anti-Command; it was almost anti-American. My anachronisms, my perceived masochism: "How come you jog without an iPod?" an early-twenties Business Analyst asked me. "Why do you take notes by pen? Why don't you just IntraPoint in real time, like the rest of us?"

None of that really bothered me. Neither did my privileged solitude, which slowly slid from fun to lechery. Sleeping around became a hobby. In hotels, I laid receptionists, maître d's, competitors, flight attendants, and, once, a business-school professor. "Wanna get a drink?" turned into "Wanna get naked?" turned into "Wanna fuck silly?" All in the name of managing insomnia and—in all seriousness—in order to run into a better Erik, while I was busy lying to the real Erik, pretending I had meetings near him, hoping I'd jump on a plane and spend a weekend with him somewhere, anywhere in the Western Hemisphere.

"Bro! That's crazy. I have to be in Montreal for work the week of the fourth too," I said over the phone, excited but careful, trying to keep despair out of my voice.

"Is that right?" Erik mumbled, typing something.

"I'll get the Molsons if you buy eggs on Sunday," I said. "It's a good deal, Erik."

"Don't you need to prepare? Pick your fonts?" Erik cat-and-moused me while we talked out my second obviously made-up business trip that summer.

"They're Canadians."

"Mm-hmm." Was he acknowledging my political incorrectness? Reading an e-mail? Watching *War-on-Terror* in the background?

"WE PROMOTE STAFF EXPOSURE," ANDREA said during my semiannual professional development meeting with her.

"I don't want to be exposed . . ." I joked, but her expression didn't change.

"You see, Stathis, any quick specialization to a specific industry, like biopharma, will deny you the advantages of what I call 'corporate window-shopping,' which is one of management consulting's main attractions. Very few people get to play in different sectors like we do." She adjusted her earring, and a Krupp-sized diamond ring glittered. No window-shopping there.

I nodded.

"Now, I want you to *live* for speed and innovation. That's what our clients want and need."

"Speed and innovation," I echoed reassuringly.

She was dating a Fortune 100 CEO, and as her jewelry increased in size, so did my aversion to her. Obviously she wasn't there for the salary, and with most partners courting her for her man's business, she had turned into the perfect bitch. The last thing I wanted was to be the bitch's bitch. Plus, after she had cornered me at O'Hare, there was no trust lost between us.

"Speed . . . and . . . innovation," she repeated slowly, as if I doubted her.

I nodded again. What the fuck? I get it. Move on.

Within weeks, contrary to Andrea's advice, I joined Command's biopharma practice, a move that kept me bouncing between the East Coast and Europe. Soon enough, I realized that pharma managers didn't trust Hamptonites or groomed, testosterone-deprived intellectuals to build their strategies. What Command VPs were missing—out of privilege or success—was that clients were equally self-absorbed in their plainness. Strangely, my Command abnormalities gave me my first breakthrough: I was not 3G-accessorized, I was not intimidating. Jersey clients saw their own dullness in me. We identified, we joked, they "could be consultants too!" I became their first point of contact. See, my insomnia went beyond the mundane; it protected me from jumping to hypotheses and conclusions. I was a voyeur in client meetings. People talked too much. You shut up, and you got it. I let clients play out their thoughts and then intervened on their terms. I became "the weird Greek guy" who made Senior Associate in sixteen months because I was lonely, Erik-obsessed, and depressed.

"MATE, WE *HAVE* TO GET out of consulting," Alkis said, a couple of hours into our red-eye to Paris.

I laughed. "We've been promoted," I said. "We're about to lead a big biotech project in France."

Alkis shook his head. "Jesus, Stathis. You still think consulting's a career."

"I never said that," I protested.

"Command trains us to grow *nominally*! The partners will never let us get paid in equity from clients. Nominal growth!"

He waved his hand at a slight angle. "That's all you get. Failure. Nominal growth is *failure*."

"We offer independent thinking," I said. "Objectivity. We can't get paid in equity. We *shouldn't* get paid in equity."

Alkis made a face. "What?"

"Equity is a conflict of interest. It's obvious," I said, and looked around. We were the only two people awake in first class.

"Whatever, mate," Alkis said, and clicked on his Outlook. "This is too good a week to argue. I love my ex-client."

"Did you extend your last project?" I asked, more lost than curious.

"*God*, no! The client there wasn't getting it, so we fired him." Alkis laughed.

How does one fire a client? Was this some consulting joke I had missed? Or did Alkis get someone literally fired during his last project, in London?

"Fired?" I said.

"Okay, want to hear something really sexy?"

"What?"

"I penciled down the head of BD at News Corp to talk about social networking opportunities."

"You got a meeting at Murdoch's?" I said, still bugged by the "firing" comment.

"Stathis, I don't have meetings. I have *discussions*," Alkis said seriously. "Fun, fun, fun," he whispered, tapping his laptop with his thumbs.

But in early 2005 *everything* was "fun" and "sexy." At Command, our EBS "tribe" had brainwashed itself into "fun." Projects were "value-adding," "strategic." "Ride the wave!" people said. Downside risks were seen as independent, impossible to be aligned in a row. Discounting them or treating them like any other absurdity—say, the fear of flying, or terrorism—was "leadership," "good decision analysis." Our world was an upside-heavy dependency diagram, a 1950s superhero with an expanding torso yet very skinny legs.

Alkis's iPod, laptop, and coffee—all black—lay spread on his tray table. *The Aviator* was playing on his video screen. I looked at his gizmos and wondered how Alkis had those instincts, which we were never taught at Command. I glimpsed DiCaprio in a state of paralysis on the screen, and thought of how Erik would react to Alkis's new meta-consulting world. For some reason my mind went to al-Qaeda, and I imagined us being shot down right at that moment. Not an absolute loss, I thought, seeing Alkis smiling at his Outlook screen. But a sudden turbulence made me change my mind.

"I'll go check if Gawel has any questions for tomorrow," I said.

"He's back in business," Alkis murmured, glued to his screen.

I found Gawel, the Analyst who would be helping us in Paris, sleeping under the *Harvard Business Review*, *Wallpaper*, and a blanket. *Fast Company* was on the floor by his Princeton duffel bag. Once again, I thought of Erik, and how would he describe this scrawny Tintin look-alike twenty-nothing-year-old Pole tucked in under his subscriptions in business class.

Sinking back into my seat, I was ready to close my eyes when I caught Alkis watching a video—on his laptop this time—that showed a preacher in front of a massive, bright screen in a packed theater. The guy talked eagerly with his hands as people cheered. I changed my angle to get a better view, risking more of Alkis's "markets can demystify and democratize anything," only to see Steve Jobs talking to Apple executives in a company auditorium. I looked at Alkis beaming, oblivious to my peeking, back to Jobs, back to Alkis, and I began connecting the dots between Command's narcissistic credo of "haute thinking" and Alkis's "ubiquitous commoditization" and equity obsession. For Alkis, for all the Alkises, strategy, retail, entertainment, personalized medicine, seduction, *anything*, could be deciphered into a recipe-driven craft. There were no business art forms left. With the "right story," generations of skill sets could become irrelevant. We were back to a 1960s conglomerate thinking, when anything could be led by any one of us.

WE CHECKED IN AT THE Lancaster on rue de Berri, off the Champs-Élysées.

"We are a *hôtel particulier*," our porter said, squeezing with us into the hotel's tiny red elevator.

I didn't know what that meant. "Hotel what?" I asked.

The porter pressed the button for the top floor. "We believe that privacy is the new luxury," he said, seriously. Seriously.

"Are you coming to L'Avenue tonight?" Alkis asked me. "I told Gawel to book a table."

"Room service," I said, trying to sort out the connection between privacy and dwarf spaces.

"Suit yourself," Alkis said, and checked his watch. "Listen, I need to power-nap for forty-five, then hit the fitness room. How about we get together around two to go through tomorrow's schedule?"

"Power-nap?" I was jet-lagged; I saw ridiculousness everywhere.

"Yes, you put your muscles but not your brain to sleep," Alkis said casually. "Which reminds me, we need a proper gym. Gawel should Google that."

"Why don't we just ask at the front desk?" I said.

He gave me his you-are-delaying-deliverables face. "Stathis, you still think that *google* means *Google*? It's a verb! It means he needs to take *care* of it."

DURING MY FIRST WEEK IN Paris I was at the client's headquarters till eleven each night, trying to figure out what exactly we were supposed to do there. "A portfolio management exercise for their pipeline. Pretty straightforward," stated Andrea's one-line e-mail from New York. By Friday, Alkis and I were at odds on pretty much everything: from which of the client's drug candidates we would assess, to the evaluation process we would use, to our communication style, all the way to our shirts and ties.

We spent our first weekend between Command's satellite office in Paris and the business room of the Lancaster. Alkis was all about: "I'm from Bayswater . . . there are right and wrong answers, Stathis . . . at the end of the day, markets are linked, so we can buy, bypass, or pass on *anything*," while he accused me of being "too process, too West Coast, too decision-*fucking*-analysis."

"I HEAR THAT YOU AND Alkis had a smooth takeoff," Andrea said as the two of us strolled down rue François 1er toward avenue Montaigne. It was a freezing January night.

I rubbed my hands together and put them in my coat pockets. "So far, so good," I said.

"Let's go for a quick drink at L'Avenue," Andrea said, peering through the windows at Céline. "It's important we spend some quality time together before the project takes off." She scrolled through her BlackBerry with her gloves on. "I have an hour. I want this to be our time." She looked at me. "*Your* time. How are you feeling?"

"I'm excited," I said, unexcitedly.

Once at the restaurant, we sat at a table for two by the door. The whole place was made of red velvet. I heard some Greek from farther inside, but I could not spot the table.

"The client loves you," Andrea said, taking her purple gloves off one finger at a time.

"Nice gloves." I returned the compliment in her currency.

"Lambskin," she said, satisfied. "Should we get some appetizers too?" She made a naughty face.

"I'm Greek. I'm always hungry."

She put the menu down. "Okay, let's not confuse things. We'll get to your Greekness in a second." She corrected her posture. "Stathis . . ." She tilted her head sideways. "You will be in Paris for a while. Of course, I will be dropping in to provide you with thought leadership, but you will have to make some tactical decisions here by yourself. Is there anything I, we, can do to help? Let's get personal!" She let out a nervous laugh.

Who was *we*? Command? The partners? Alkis? Someone she was fucking on the client's side? And what did she want from me this time? I couldn't wait for this project to really take off, and then end, so I could get back to the States to be with Erik—whatever that meant. "I've done it before," I said.

"Of course you have. Still, being away is never easy. Okay, let *me* start." Her voice turned girly. "These days, because of my fiancé, I live between New York and Washington."

"You live in Philadelphia?" I said.

"Let's order," she said, thrusting her scarf off.

The light hanging above our table hit the pattern of gold skulls on her scarf, piercing my eyes. What's wrong with me? Work's the only certain thing in my life. "It was a joke," I tried.

"It was a great joke," she said flatly, then ordered a couple of appetizers, reading as much as possible from the menu, working on her French accent: " . . . *raviolis frais au saumon. Et champagne, s'il vous plaît.*"

"Dirty vodka, straight up," I told the obviously American waiter. "So," I paused before my recovery line. "You were saying your boyfriend lives in Washington?"

"My boyfriend lives in several places. His job takes him all over the world."

"I know who you're dating," I said. The whole company did.

"Oh . . ." She tried to mask her brag as surprise. "You do? How come?"

"My Productivity Assistant told me. I mean, the guy runs a Fortune 100 company."

"Oh, that . . ." She waved her hand dismissively.

Yes, *that*. That's why you made Partner, remember? When I brought up Porter's Five Forces, you said you hadn't seen the movie yet; and now you want to provide *me* with "thought leadership"? The only thing you're providing me with is the cure for my hangover, with your first-class narcissism. "I got confused when you said *boyfriend*," I said with the tiniest of smiles. "He is sixty-five, seventy? Man-friend, maybe?"

"Whom are *you* dating, Stathis? I didn't have a chance to ask my PA."

"No one," I murmured.

"And why is that? Handsome, smart Greek guy like you?"

I was debating between *It's none of your fucking business* and *I couldn't find good dick in New York.* But plan C took over. "I've had commitment anxiety since 9/11," I said as touchingly as I could.

Andrea looked puzzled. "I'm sorry, did you lose someone?"

"No. But I'm still dealing with the aftermath."

"Stathis, it's 2005. Maybe . . ." It took her a second to work out that I was BSing, but it was 9/11, so I had PC immunity—she couldn't nail me on this one. She audited me for a moment, possibly weighing a full-blown assault—but then again, it's hard to read through Botox. "Work!" she announced, walking away from the turbulence. "We discussed lots of therapeutic areas today during the client meeting. Antiangiogenics, metabolics, etc., and most of them may well end up being within the scope of the prioritization exercise that we'll do for them, but I believe there's real value in some more peripheral areas."

"Like?" I asked.

"Like . . . like the lifestyle space that was brought up." She looked away, as if thinking this through for the first time.

"You were the one who brought it up," I said.

"I did, and for good reason. It's an area where even marginal investments from the client could attract significant benefits for them—"

"I think it's interesting to put a light on Lifestyle," I interrupted her. "I don't see why it can't be included in our pre-evaluation phase."

"I believe it should receive more attention than just that," she said, playing with her pearls. "I want a Command squad team to screen *everything* out there that could be an alliance or a potential joint venture for the client. From cosmeceuticals all the way to nourishment, weight, and hormone lifestyle opportunities. It's bio-*life* sciences, Stathis."

This didn't make any sense. "Lifestyle is an interesting space, Andrea, but . . ." I shrugged my shoulder. "You were in the conference room. They talked unsatisfied areas, diseases begging for breakthroughs."

"Aging is a disease too."

I couldn't tell where was she heading with this crap.

"Andrea, they were talking RNA, DNA transistors. Pill nanomachines. Don't you think they are putting *real* innovation at risk if they move away from their core science?"

"*It's all out there!*" she shouted. "They should just go and *buy* innovation!" Some Russians next to us turned. I had never seen her lose it like that before.

An intense silence followed while she recovered. Composed again, she went on reciting the strategy trend of the moment: a fad in which big corporations would pay lip service to breakthrough work but actually outsource it, and instead push their internal focus to side areas, like innovative go-to-market, management, and operational processes.

"I thought you believed in hard-core innovation," I said carefully. "I didn't realize that you had become a Bhidé fan all of a sudden."

"Stathis, you think you're so clever, it's almost cute. *Almost.* What you don't understand is that I don't give a damn about the HBS loser you're trying to intimidate me with. And you know why? Because I have Greeks like you to write HBS case studies for me."

"Why did you join Command?" I asked her.

"Why did you move to the States?"

I didn't respond. To fuck Erik?

"Allow me," Andrea said, leaning forward from across the table. "You moved to the States to trade up. Whatever that was for you. Your work, your relationship, your one-bedroom. That's why people move to the States. To trade *up.* Our country was founded on Wall Street principles."

"How does one trade up a cosmetics baron?" I asked.

"With a buyout emperor," Andrea replied without thinking, and *fuck!* Now her whole bio-lifestyle spiel made perfect sense. Suddenly there was no doubt as to why she was pushing for beauty creams. It was pretty basic, really: even a simple announcement by the client that they were shifting their focus to Lifestyle, and their valuation would get a hefty correction. Her fat man-friend could buy the client at a discount.

"Suppose we talk them into Lifestyle," I said. "Hasn't your man-friend gone shopping for biotechs these days?" Her bracelets clattered. "Allow me, now," I went on. "Coincidence, I'm sure, but . . ." I made a what-do-I-know face. "Just thinking out loud—couldn't someone speculate some convenience here too? Say, an acquisition? Look at biotech versus cosmetics multiples, and—"

"I don't understand what you're saying. I don't agree with you," Andrea said, shaking, which made me register that we were not talking management consulting anymore. We were talking insider trading. I had to think fast and smart—and where the hell was Alkis when I really needed him?

"Andrea, you *cannot* not understand what I'm saying *and* not agree with me. Pick one."

SIX

THE MOMENT WE WRAP THIS project I'm done with Command," Alkis told me on the Lancaster patio. He had just gotten back from an interview with a bank in London. It was our second month in Paris, and Andrea's potential plot had brought us closer. He poured half of my scotch into an empty glass. "This business with Andrea is just nuts. The bitch has no idea what she is doing," he said, and motioned for a drag of my cigarette.

I passed him my smokes. I could tell that his interview had not gone well.

"Why would I want to make a million off her insider job, risking *my* name, when I can make twenty by building it up legitimately?" Alkis said.

He and I had finally reached some balance. We divided up the work. He'd be creating the client's alternate R&D portfolio strategies, and I'd evaluate them. Of course, there was some overlap when it came to deciding metrics of success, or when we picked distinctly different R&D strategies worth evaluating; and we shared poor Gawel, our Business Analyst, who swung between reporting to an evil and a less-evil project manager.

"Let me guess," Erik told me over the phone as I entered my room after thirteen hours of nonstop work that Sunday. "You think you are the less-evil manager."

"I'll give you that one, 'cause I'm exhausted," I said, checking my watch. It was half-past midnight.

"You know that you can be intellectually obnoxious, right?" Erik went on, but I didn't pick up on any lecturing in his voice. He came across as protective, if anything.

I threw my laptop on the sofa and hopped onto the bed, crashing into the breakfast-request card on my pillow that doubled as my wake-up call at seven each morning. "Try intellectually dead right now," I said.

"That's funny." Erik snorted a laugh. "I leave Port Authority when you leave your client, but in a different time zone."

"Stop bragging."

"That's why you make what you make. I didn't go for that," Erik said without hesitation.

I thought of his father's hospitals and his mother's book deals. Erik was judging me from behind trust-fund doors. I wanted to rally all the juice left in me and fight back, end things right there, but a deeper fear stopped me. Whether his approach to life was a result of luxury or principles, I was still drawn to his fuck-you independence, to his carelessness, which I could never experience except through him. I was the Senior Associate who fell for the communist, and I brought home the bacon. Now we could do anything we wished. Surf between self-interest and self-respect, live the quantum life

I studied: impossible for anyone to know both our positions and our momentum. We could get some curry with Melissa before she took us to the airport, fly off to help tag threatened sharks in the Bahamas. We could check TomDispatch's US imperialist theories on our BlackBerrys during French Open breaks. But how do you confess to that? How do you commit to spontaneity when its definition is its undefined randomness? How do you write an algorithm for chaos? "Anyone who considers arithmetical methods of producing random digits is, of course, in a state of sin," von Neumann said. Isn't staging a lifestyle making a joke out of it? Out of us? Wouldn't I be exposed to Erik as a poser? Wouldn't I lose him? So I had to apply myself harder to the one thing I had: work. I had to stay on top of things, become more and more what Erik officially condemned while hoping that deep down he understood our unspoken symbiosis, and that he found me smart and interesting and potentially lovable.

"Which is such a stupid New York thing," Erik said, bringing me back. I had no idea what he was talking about.

"I see," I said.

"Listen," Erik said. "How you choose to work is your business. But the way you're working right now can bloody kill you."

"If I didn't know better, I'd say you sound caring," I tried.

"I want you to be good at what you do," Erik said. "How's your sleep?"

"I have a feeling that tonight's going to be just fine."

"I miss you, man," he said.

"I think tonight's gonna be excellent."

"Clown."

We laughed. I grabbed a pillow to shove behind my head, and Erik said: "It would be fun to do a road trip in France. We could even go for a run in the forest, in Montmelian."

My exhaustion vanished. I didn't need a pillow; I was already up. "Really?" I said.

"Would love that, amigo. But I have to be in Tahoe end of this month. There is a summit I have to cover for *The Nation*."

A brief silence followed.

"Wanna . . . come along?" Erik said timidly, and I felt a second rush.

"That's a tricky one," I said cautiously, detaining myself. "I was planning a Friday-to-Monday trip to New York in a few weeks. I guess I could steal an extra day and meet you in San Francisco. I still live there, remember?"

"It's a date."

Six hours later I was up by myself—no latte, no knocking at my door.

Walking on the Champs-Élysées' forty-foot-wide side-walks, the stores still closed, everything clean and in place, my whole life felt simple, really. The client, Andrea, my sister, the Greek army. Riding in an empty train, I imagined my weekend with Erik in San Francisco. I pictured us driving up the coast on Route 1, or in Tahoe, or wherever—in the city, in traffic, it didn't matter. Then I started making a list.

I had to find an Erik-restaurant. Buy some furniture before he arrived. I would have to move fast, but I would be in California—I could just walk into Crate and Barrel. "Simple and quick," I said out loud, and a cartoon balloon popped above my head: it struck me that speed and innovation, Andrea's own medicine, might be just the weapon I was looking for to fight off her scheme. I wondered if there could be a link, a common denominator between being fast and being novel—and what if that link was exactly what I felt in the train: simplicity? I arrived at the client in serious brainstorm mode. I began to look for simplicity everywhere.

"HOW ABOUT WE EXPLAIN MODERN portfolio theory in the next slide?" Gawel asked me hours later. We were the last two bodies left at the client site.

I kept PowerPointing, but Gawel went on: "Andrea said that Markowitz's efficient frontier is the best way to show the bang for the buck for Lifestyle."

"Are you sure she didn't say Malkovich instead?" I asked. "Fuck Markowitz and fuck Andrea."

Gawel didn't say anything.

I stood up. "Gawel, it's okay, it's fine. Of course we'll use portfolio theory. But look at you." I grabbed his iPod from the top of his gym bag. "*One* button!" I leaned over his desk and clicked on his homepage. Google came up. "*One* entry," I said.

Gawel didn't know where to look.

"Relax," I said, and stopped his chair from swinging. "We will still use good ole Markowitz to figure out which of their drug candidates they should put in clinical trials, but we need to camouflage our prioritization."

He was fixated on his Google screen.

"Listen. We need to mask your portfolio prioritization model. How can I explain this . . . Clients don't have time to understand how we do what we do, the same way people don't have time to read manuals before they use their phones. Nobody *cares* about understanding how things work anymore. They just want them to work. We need to build an iPod-like portfolio management model. A Google-like interface around what we do."

"I'm not sure I'm following you," Gawel said. "I'm not sure Andrea will understand. I'm not sure Alkis will understand, either."

"Leave Andrea to me. Don't worry about Alkis, goddammit. Alkis comes every time Steve Jobs launches a product."

It was after-hours and I was on the verge of a breakthrough.

THE FOLLOWING THREE WEEKS WERE my most productive in Paris. I knew I couldn't challenge Andrea to her face, but once the simplicity virus got into me, I saw a chance to distract the client—maybe I could sabotage her plan. Everything had to look simpler. In the client reports I prepared, I killed Command jargon everywhere I could—from footnotes all the way to hard-core analyses. I replaced the word *probability* with *uncertainty* or *chance*. I simplified my work and told the client to do the same. I was a decent brander: "Innovate through Simplicity" was my message. The French liked it, or at least they were curious about it. Alkis loved it. "You're selling them simplicity, whatever *that* means, instead of Andrea's Lifestyle junk?" he laughed. "Kudos for screwing over the bitch and her boyfriend. I knew the moment I met her she'd be a filthy cunt."

With Alkis watching my back, I marched on. But Andrea was skeptical.

"We are far from a simplistic company!" she e-mailed me, cc'ing Alkis.

I contemplated replying-all and spelling out the difference between *simple* and *simplistic*, but did not. I did not have to; the more the client liked me, the more Andrea had to turn a blind eye to my ways.

She kept crossing e-mail swords with me, of course: "Whatever process you agree on with the client, I still want to see an attractive Lifestyle strategy in the alternatives that we will evaluate."

I did. I evaluated Lifestyle like any other strategy we developed, because now I could afford to. The client had already adopted me. I was their portfolio management "conservat*eur*," and therefore Andrea's Lifestyle travesty would not receive any special treatment. No favors. Yet I was still on thin ice with Command. I had to justify my simplicity, my process of abbreviation.

"I'm not cutting off Command intelligence," I explained in an e-mail to Washington. "I'm embedding it."

"Tricking managers into consulting crap is innovation in its own right!" I joked with Alkis while I was packing for San Francisco.

He threw his head back, faking an out-of-control reaction to my nerdy hilarity. A bank had just offered him a job, and now he was raiding my minibar.

"Mate, the real innovation is that you saved our asses from Andrea's whip," Alkis said, then turned sharply serious: "For now. I'm out of here, but I want you to stay away from her. Got that?"

Once again, he was fathering me.

"Are you joining the capital markets for ethical reasons?" I tried to shift our chat. But Alkis was right. I thought I could outsmart Andrea, and that illusion allowed her and Command to have a hold over me.

IT WAS A MUGGY NIGHT when I walked into my apartment in San Francisco. Paul, lying on my sofa, was reading *Wired* magazine. I ran over the dates in my mind. It had been a good five months since I'd stood inside what I officially called my home.

"Are you indispensable now?" Paul asked, tossing his magazine on top of my Starving Students moving box, which he used as a coffee table. He stood up. He looked thinner than he had the last time I saw him, a year before in London, when he had quit his bank job to go around the world again, and once again, yes, to "reinvent" himself.

We hugged awkwardly.

"Well, who isn't these days," I said. "How are you?"

"Not bad, actually," Paul said. "Not bad."

"I'm sorry about your mother, Paul."

I had heard she'd passed on.

"Yes." He shrugged. "Thank you. I got your e-mail."

"When did you come to San Francisco?"

"Right after the funeral. About a month ago."

Through a hole in the moving box I got a glimpse of my hummus-stained Finance book and remembered the cold weekend in France when I had first met Erik. I began counting the years since, but stopped. It didn't matter; I was about to spend the weekend with him.

"How was Asia?" I asked eagerly, covering for my silly face.

"Fun. You must go."

"How long did you backpack for?"

"Four months," Paul answered.

"Did you see anyone?"

"I spent a week with my ex in Hong Kong." He forced a laugh. "She's married now."

"I didn't know that," I said.

"Yeah. It was a bit intense." He looked at me briefly. "I mean, it was interesting. She is into the whole baby thing. It's on my blog."

I was about to check on him, how he felt, the works . . . but I saw my semi-inflated airbed and realized that there was no door to my bedroom, though clearly there used to be one. I wasn't sure where to start, but Paul was on a roll: "I'm having dinner with an investor in the Mission. You should join."

"Investor?" I asked, my eyes still glued to the space where the door should have been.

"Accosting has been getting some serious traffic, so we'll fund a media company behind it. An umbrella for more verticals."

"Accosting?"

"AccostingCelebrities.com."

I gave Paul a funny look. He had been to university. His father was a prime minister, for Christ's sake. "Seriously?" I said.

"Yes, traffic's been crazy," Paul continued, oblivious to my surprise. "We are like: 'Yes! Come work for us. Sure, invest in us . . .'"

"No, I mean, right. I mean . . . Seriously? *That's* the name of your blog?"

"It's a media website. You get the updates."

I had never really figured Paul out. He had a couple of million in the bank and a thirst for social peeping—a creepy obsession that went all the way back to EBS and kept him from doing something with his life. Was this website part of his fight against his supernova parents? Or had he finally given up on competing with them? His chosen path forward to make fun of his heritage.

"Are you accosting your father?" I giggled.

"Funny, Stathis . . . We just signed a lease for a small space in Nolita. I have to be in New York next week." His cell phone rang. "Speak of the devil. It's my ex. Her husband is helping me with Accosting. I got to take this. Hello?"

I looked at my watch, popped the one Ambien I had not used during the flight, and walked into my open bedroom. I closed the window and sat on my airbed, feeling it deflate for two seconds before my ass touched the wooden floor.

I grabbed some of my mail, which was spread out next to Paul's paper-thin laptop, bleeping that it was out of battery. An EBS Hong Kong wedding invitation in some green "fabu-lously ever after" recycled paper—why was I even invited?—envelopes from PG&E and Gap, and two handwritten cards, one from my nephew showing a fishing boat and wishing me happy birthday, the other with Klaus Maria Brandauer, or Klaus Kinski, or a clown of some sort, in a colonial outfit walking on a rice field. "*File, Kales Giortes.* A year ago you took me in. Zemar." I stared at the pink stamp from the Union of Myanmar, mailed ten months back, but my eyes slowly got distracted by the prehibernation countdown on Paul's laptop. An Ambien animistic empathy urged me to plug it in, relieve its cries for help, as my mind flew back to the steps of the cot-tage at Chateau Marmont, where I'd stood with Zemar. "You don't know how to be in this world," Zemar had told me, smiling sheepishly, stoned and smacked up, as we looked out on the city lights of LA. "You've been dealt a good hand. You were born smart and handsome. I used to do your job. I've seen many Andreas and Eriks. It's all about working the hand you've been dealt, Stathis. You are not playing your cards right. You want to become Erik, who wants to be me, who wanted to be Erik's brother, who's obsessed with Erik. You don't know your full potential. You'll outdo them. And then you'll quit. We all do," the junkie said, and rested his hand on my shoulder.

A MISSED CALL ON MY cell phone woke me up the next morning. I listened to Erik's message—canceling his trip because he was "coming down with something." I called back instantly, but it went straight to his voice mail. "Feel better" was all I left.

"Paul," I shouted.

No one answered.

I needed coffee dangerously. I got up and walked into the kitchen to make some, but all I found was an empty box of instant next to Starbucks molded cups and notes from EBS-ers who had passed by. I couldn't even make out the handwriting in most of them. Then I just stood there and felt the pain.

"Fuck this!" I crunched up cups and notes—nasty coffee everywhere—throwing all kinds of shit in the sink. "And fuck me," I whispered.

Unshowered, still wearing the same clothes from the flight, I walked down the street to Café de la Presse. I got a latte (weak, a milky joke) and tried Erik once more but, again, I only reached his voice mail. Why wasn't he picking up? He wasn't fucking dying. I hung up in a mix of outrage and guilt: he was sick, I tried to convince myself.

I asked for an extra shot in my latte and called my super about the bedroom door. He didn't know anything about "any door," but he wanted to discuss with me "the serious complaints from the neighbors." I said I'd have to call him back and dialed an ex-colleague from Redwood City, but, after several rings, that too went to voice mail. Through the café's windows I noticed Crate and Barrel across the street. It was a moody San Francisco morning. I strode in with my triple-shot latte.

"And how are *you* today?" Jane greeted me at the door, under a poster of a sailboat that reminded me of my nephew's card.

"I want a coffee table," I told Jane without smiling back. For all practical purposes, I was a guest in my own home.

I spent the rest of the day putting together five pieces of wood. In the evening I went out by myself to get drunk and laid, and almost succeeded.

I was busy fucking on the half-inflated airbed when Paul walked into my no-bedroom-door one-bedroom.

"What the fuck!"

"Shit. I told you there was a chance of this happening." I threw my boxers on and hopped into the living room. "I would have closed the door if I *had* one, Paul."

"I'm sorry," Paul said, and let out a nervous laugh. "We had a small accident. But don't worry, the door's getting fixed."

"Accident?" I said, breathing heavily.

"My chess guru was doing an attention exercise and it turned into overdose. We broke down the door. We had to."

I stared at Paul, flustered. Neither of us spoke. I was so tired of him and his bullshit.

"Stathis, it's getting fixed!"

"A chess guru was here," I said, flatly. "Is he okay?"

"He's fine, he left you a note. He's paying for the door."

"What's an attention exercise? Actually, I don't give a fuck. How about some privacy?"

He gave my boxers a glance. I was still hard.

"*Now!*" I yelled. "Privacy ain't a luxury, you know."

Paul looked at me like I was speaking Greek.

"You're testing my patience, Paul. You, your stupid work, stupid Erik. *Everything!*"

Paul smiled just a notch, as if he was getting a kick out of disobeying orders.

"Then go down on me, bitch," I said, straight-faced.

"*What the fuck?*" the naked guy shouted from my bedroom.

Paul stared at my crotch without moving. He didn't blink.

"That's what I thought," I said. "You're a freak, Paul. A rich stalker with websites. You should be locked up. You're a sociopath, *exactly* like your father. You know *exactly* how to be in this world."

Paul laughed. "Erik taught you all that?"

"Fuck Erik. You both've been dealt a good hand and you're fucking it up. I'm gonna play my hand right."

"Yeah," Paul said, nodding toward the naked guy in the bedroom, who was sniffing from a tiny bottle. "I can see that."

On my way to Paris I didn't stop by New York, even though, after four voice mails, Erik bothered to invite me for "a quick stopover to hang out." He was "bummed for not making it out West, passing up some good change too." But healthwise, he said, he was better.

It was a long flight. Long enough for me to consider scenarios. What if Erik had asked me to stop over in New York only *after* I mentioned Zemar's card from Myanmar? What if his work in Tahoe had already been canned? My unfulfillment soared at thirty-five thousand feet. I was exhausted, and desperate for a clean sheet of paper.

SEVEN

BACK IN PARIS, MY HIATUS from Erik was protected by eighty-hour weeks. Work was my medicine. I obsessed. I fought Andrea on Lifestyle relentlessly, all day long via e-mail on my BlackBerry, all the way back to the Lancaster. "Fuck the West Coast nice guy," I signed my notes to Alkis.

Fuck them all: Andrea, Command, WASPs, Erik. I decided to be Greek and proud. It was 2005; we had nailed the Olympics and Eurocup. Finally, Greekness, that unprocessed masculinity, was selling. I would be the "peasant" consultant. I played up my Greek accent and took cabs instead of using our car service. I talked to the client spontaneously, using ungrammatical words like *optionality* instead of Command's *real options* mumbo jumbo.

"Strategic engineering," I cut off Andrea, in a packed conference room, as she rambled on about Command's "decision analysis–backed hybrid alternatives" in a pathetic attempt to return the discussion to her Lifestyle agenda.

"How manly," the client-lead gasped, touching her gold necklace.

"We take risks, 'cause that's what men do," I said, and eyebrows rose in response.

"I'll teach you backgammon, show you how to deal with strategy and risk," I talked back to Andrea when she threatened me with sensitivity training. With her Lifestyle pretty much bypassed by the client, I was growing some balls.

I BEGAN TO HAVE FUN with phallic capitalism. I spotted a polished, feminine side in the white-collar man and pounded it; wasn't that expected of me? To be Greek? I dealt with privilege like a man, as though luxury was an accident, a by-the-way. I lived in hotels—"to be by the clients"—and slept around, sometimes with people I'd present to a few hours later. "It's a guy thing," I told Alkis, who, primed for his banking job in London, partied along with me.

We went on working and drinking until, a couple of months after San Francisco, Andrea requested a debriefing meeting in New York.

Checking in at the Soho Grand, half awake, with two Ambien finally kicking in to end an all-nighter that had rolled into a transatlantic flight, I texted Erik: "I'm in town."

We spent the weekend in my hotel. We didn't talk about San Francisco. We didn't argue about globalization, west Chelsea, consulting, Andrea, Zemar, Melissa, not even what used to be my "ridiculous accommodations." My fear of asking for anything more, coupled with the battery-safe mode that the French and Andrea kept me in, led to an Erik-you-win state. Which, oddly enough, and for the first time, made simply hanging out with him pleasing. I would spend a string of weekends in New York that winter.

"COME TO THINK OF IT, Paris to New York isn't much longer than New York to San Francisco," I told Alkis over the phone while waiting to board at de Gaulle.

"Funny, that."

"Here we go again . . ."

"No, wait," Alkis said. "I got a case study for you. You make VP, but Concorde's been long retired. It's tricky to jet-stalk these days, isn't it?"

"My next project is in New York," I said, raising my voice. "Working on it. You know that."

"What if it's not? What if it is? You've no *shite* what I'm talking about."

Shite, indeed. He was talking about Erik like he was my vice, when I thought that the worst was behind us. We'd even diversified our whereabouts—carefully, of course—to include hangouts near my hotels in Soho. "We have tequilas at Café Noir and burgers at Kenn's Broome," I mumbled into my cell phone. "Two bucks more than Empire Diner."

"*What?*" Alkis laughed. "Are you losing it, mate?"

"Sorry," I said. "I don't sleep well. They're calling my flight."

AFTER PARIS I PUSHED FOR a project in New Jersey so I could spend my weekends in New York. With Erik.

"Less expensive than those Friday-to-Monday trips to San Francisco. And much more productive," I sold to Andrea. "But I need a hotel downtown," I added, hoping to seal my non—west Chelsea bars with Erik. "I have to be close to the Holland Tunnel to get to Princeton on time."

"That's understandable" was all Andrea said.

By early 2006 I even gave up on trying to notch down my accommodations for Erik. He didn't get the difference between the Mercer, the Soho Grand, and the W. They were all "Marcjacobsland" to him.

Sunday mornings, with Erik still sleeping next to me, I would room-service a latte and catch up on the week's e-mails. Around 10 a.m. Erik would curse something and crawl out of bed to go pee.

"Can't do it with a hard-on," I yelled to him on the Sunday I heard him pissing onto the cement floor and the porcelain seat, and finally into the toilet bowl.

"I ain't Greek," Erik said, muffled, sleepwalking back to bed.

I fought off the temptation to call him on the cleaning staff, his turf. A couple of hours away from the first EBS–Erik brunch, I was tense.

Tucked in, Erik turned onto his stomach and put his hand between my abs and my laptop. "Tell your client to push the boat out again," he said under the pillows. "'Cause budget is a dying species, right?"

I clicked on "Empty Recycle Bin," and that crunchy tossing sound came up. There.

He got me on the ribs and I punched his left arm, hard.

"Motherfucking *fucker*!" he yelled.

"That's the cleaning crew calling you."

Two separate showers later, we dressed and walked in
silence down the street to Bubby's. New York's winter breeze
pierced us. I was still jumpy. The brunch ahead was already
smothering me. I felt trapped between my two worlds: too
communist for Alkis, too Republican for Erik.

Björk was screaming and Alkis smiling as we entered the
restaurant, packed with tall investment bankers and their
Asian girlfriends. I winked at Alkis, which was all I could
do with a dozen or so people in the ten feet between us. Next
to me, an iPod-ed seven-year-old stood on a bench in a sea
of *New York Times* sections, sticking crocodile-dog icons on
the restaurant's window. I saw Paul, down the bar, paying
for a couple of pink drinks in pyramid-shaped glasses while
answering his BlackBerry. He was in "gym-sofa clothes," per
the instructions in Alkis's girlfriend's "NY brunch for the
unacceptables who skipped the engagement party" Evite.

Then we were pushed. I grabbed the sticker-graffiti kid just
in time, as he fell over the edge of the bench. "Here, buddy," I
said, handing him his Keith Haring play–touch screen from
the floor.

"Hey, mate!" Alkis said, wrapping his arm around my
neck.

"Alkis! Congrats! I was looking forward to this," I said.

I was about to make sure Alkis and Erik reconnected on firm ground, but two hands belted around me from behind.

"*Malaka*, amore," Cristina whispered in my ear. She smelled like peaches. "You are too handsome," she flirted with Erik, while she was still holding on to me. She reached over and gave him a quick kiss on the lips.

"This is Cristina, my fiancée," Alkis said, faking an apologetic face.

Then Cristina turned and kissed me. She looked curvier, definitely healthier than she had the last time I'd seen her with Alkis. She gave me a big Italian smile.

"Hi," Erik said to Cristina.

"They told me our table's next," Cristina said. "Oh, God! Who *is* this guy?" She touched Paul's arm as he squeezed toward us, BlackBerry first.

"Paul," I said. We hadn't seen each other since San Francisco.

"Stathis." Paul kept typing.

"Hey," Erik said. "Good to see you, Paul."

"Hi."

"Oh, Paul is busy," Cristina said, teasingly. "He just launched a new blog for Wall Street."

"It's a *media* venture," Paul corrected her without looking up.

"A media venture," Cristina echoed. "He's been looking at corporate lofts since Thursday."

"Anything good?" Erik asked Paul.

"Not a thing," Paul replied. He finally looked up.

"Takes some walking."

"I just want it done and over with," Paul said, but the beeping sound from his machine distracted him. "Okay, this is priceless. It's the third time they've rescheduled this week." He smiled. "I'm sorry. My New York Realtor is utterly insane."

"What are you doing with Wall Street?" I asked Paul.

"We are launching AccostingPE. It's a private equity outlet."

"He's turning Accosting into the next Condé Nast," Cristina said. "Oh my God, did I choose the wrong guy?" She laughed.

That was impossible.

"Cristina is psychic," Alkis said with a laugh. "I mean, we're all in the business of the future," he added, this time seriously. "What's the next premium, the next big thing? Health? Security? Sex?" He tried to reach Cristina's neck, but she slowly pushed his hand away.

"Are you guys here for work or fun?" Erik asked Cristina. He looked genuinely interested.

"Both," Alkis stepped in. "Cristina is here for work and I had a meeting in California. So we were like, let's just take a couple of days off and hang out in New York."

"What does Cristina do?" Erik asked.

"She's with PPR."

"What's that?"

"Gucci."

I saw Erik's *but-of-course* look.

"You remember Erik from the forest?" I asked, trying to make Paul stop typing.

"Yes," said Paul. He gave Erik a glance. "You're that journalist from Oxford, right?"

"Well, not exactly. Not anymore," Erik said. "Now I work for the city."

"Oh, my ex-girlfriend's law firm was on Chancery Lane. I'm the only person I know who actually likes the city. We used to lunch on—"

"I work *for* the city. Of New York," Erik said.

Paul narrowed his eyes. "Are you from New Jersey?" he asked Erik.

What on earth . . . Erik would never acknowledge an insult to Jersey, and Paul somehow knew that, so I was both curious and terrified to see where Erik would go with this. But Alkis jumped in:

"Hey, Paul!" he shouted. "Why can't you lose weight as fast as you lose your hair?"

Erik turned to Alkis slowly, signaling that he was not through with Paul. "How long we got you in town for?" Erik asked Alkis.

"I was hoping to leave tomorrow," Alkis replied. "But I'm not sure if Paul's done with the third degree."

"What are you cooking *this* time?" I asked Paul.

"Come on, now," Paul said shyly, like he was asking for forgiveness about San Francisco. "We are covering the turn-around of a public telecom in Europe, and Alkis is advising them on private equity compensation for their management team."

I knew about Alkis's project. I could see how this topic could go south, fast.

"Are you guys doing private equity in the *public* sector?" Erik asked Alkis.

"Well . . . I guess you could say that," Alkis admitted. "But we are open-minded about it."

"And how exactly do you do that?" Erik asked, his laugh lines shaping. Here we go.

Alkis paused, which was enough for Paul to butt in: "They are multi-stakeholder minded while bottom-line focused," he said seriously. No one spoke, so Paul went on with his shit. "It's in the art of giving advice, really. Stathis can explain this better. He's a consultant."

"What about continuity and sustainability?" Erik asked. "Is that part of your art?"

There was another uncomfortable silence until Cristina reached Erik's arm. "I'm so thirsty. Darling, you are taller and stronger. Will you get me a Bloody Mary? Virgin, darling. Please."

"I'm not sure I can reach too far with this arm." Erik gave me a dirty look and began to shuffle toward the bar.

I was Paul-gripped.

"*What?*" Paul finally yelled at me.

"The art of giving advice, Paul? *Seriously?*"

"Want my Erik review now or should I e-mail it to you?" Paul said.

I was ready to "fuck you" him again, along with his website, his father, and his country—I mean, I'd never work there, or would I?—but Alkis laughed. "You twats!" he sneered. "What the hell are you crying about? You both bull for a living."

"We can't all be in private equity, Alkis," I said, annoyed by being equated with Paul. "Some of us have to think about R&D. You never know, you might need innovation after you cash-cow everything with other people's money."

"*Yeah*, Alkis," Paul shammed.

"Watch it, I still have pictures of you on a leash," Alkis threatened him.

"Be my guest!" Paul chuckled. "It's not like my father's getting reelected anyway. Post them!"

But Alkis wasn't listening. He was busy lifting the Haring-graffiti kid.

"Oh, thank you," the kid's mother said as she searched for her son's iPod between the Week in Review and Sunday Styles. "It's a white Shuffle," she told Alkis, worried.

I noticed the boy's Athens 2004 Olympic T-shirt and thought of my niece, more or less the same age. How many times had I actually seen her? Three? Four? Then, from the corner of my eye, I caught Erik squeezing his way back through the waiting room, tomato juice spilling over the polo of mine he was wearing, and I was happy for the distraction, one of those everyday things—a bad haircut, an unprocessed hotel receipt—that help me forget where I really am in my life.

"My hero!" Cristina welcomed Erik back. "Now, Alkis tells me that you grew up with Constantine."

Erik gave me a quick look. "Well . . . I know him," he conceded. An Erik first. "Why? Are you a friend of his?"

"I knew him at Harvard," Cristina said. "I haven't seen him for years and years. How is he? I can't believe he's getting married!"

"He is. I don't see him often myself. In fact, he was closer to my brother. He shows up out of nowhere every few years."

"That's *so* Constantine," Paul said, making both Erik and me turn. I hadn't seen this coming. Things were getting odder by the moment.

"His name is Zemar now," Erik said, louder than necessary, and—surprise—one more silence followed as it dawned on me that everyone seemed to know Constantine or Zemar as this ghost, who randomly materialized in Greece, my EBS world, and Erik's, too. A phantom that blurred segments of my life that I was trying to compartmentalize. I knew there was more here than I could work out.

"Right," Cristina at last giggled. "Of course. Makes sense. I knew he had converted—"

"Oh, he was always a wildcat," Paul interrupted. "But fun. Though somehow he always scared me. There was a darker side. After all, he did date you, Cristina!"

"Crist*ina*!" Alkis pretended fury, and Paul laughed.

"Briefly," Cristina said, and pointed at Paul. "Your ex dated him too. Gosh! Who didn't? All my girlfriends were crazy about him. I mean, in those days. I haven't seen him since that ski-safari at Val d'Isère. When was that?" She looked up. "Seven, eight years ago? He was high for the whole week. Still, I liked Constantine. I *like* Constantine."

"Think of him as a brand," Paul said, which sent Alkis into a fit, and half a Bellini over my ass.

I tried to dry my pants with my hands while scanning the dining room, pretending to be oblivious to the whole Zemar circus, but these guys wouldn't stop.

"Honestly, he needed to settle down," Cristina said, her face brightening. "I was watching Reuters, streaming from Iraq, the other day and I thought of him. I even asked my HP for resolution."

"Your Hewlett-Packard?"

"My higher power!"

The maître d' asked us to follow her.

I was drained when I finally sat down and ordered a beer. As soon as it arrived, I had the longest sip and checked out. When Alkis started on his Schwarzenegger meeting—accents, cigars, Learjet seating—I got up for a smoke. "I love Americans!" someone from our table shouted as I left.

WALKING BACK TO THE HOTEL, Erik and I did not speak. In the room I flipped through TV channels indefinitely, unable to concentrate. Everything blurred into one show, as if extreme makeovers happened after hurricanes in Florida, and polar bears were endangered in Iraq.

Erik changed into running clothes and stood still in the middle of the room. I pretended to pay him no mind, trying to postpone the EBS–Zemar tsunami coming my way, until I couldn't anymore.

"What?" I broke the silence, still looking at the screen.

"This ain't gonna happen."

He wasn't talking about Zemar or EBS. He was talking us, already speeding down a one-way street. So I doubled, had to, hoping to salvage whatever I could. "It never was, Erik."

"I was about to say . . . again."

"You didn't," I said, still looking at the screen.

"So you're ready for an all out. Good. You and me both." He walked out wearing my sneakers and slammed the door.

I turned off the TV and looked at the remote control shaking in my hand. I got up, grabbed a scotch from the minibar, and dimmed the lights to Alkis-power-nap level. I downed the whiskey and lay back on the couch, listening to my watch ticking, feeling the ugly side of uncertainty building up in me. At work I sold clients "the beauty of potentiality." "Its superiority to actuality," the "value in *not* knowing" about the launch of a product, potential infidelities, or the success of a dinner party. Suddenly my "accept everything as a string of probabilities" line was a farce, a travesty.

I was still on the sofa when Erik returned. His nose was running. He undressed and jumped into the shower. I stared at my underwear in the middle of Erik's puddle of soggy clothes on the bathroom floor until steam filled the room and I could no longer see them. The running water stopped and the shower door swung open. Erik came out in a hotel robe, took a V8 from the minibar and *National Geographic* from the side table, and spread out on top of the bed covers.

"Good run?"

"Yes. Did you *power*-nap?" He raised his eyebrows. I could see his balls.

I didn't reply, still trying hopelessly to avoid the inevitable.

"What?" he said. "Are you gonna chicken out now?"

"No," I said. "Let's fight. Isn't that what you came here for? And cross your legs, will you?"

"I don't do that."

"Then wear some underwear, 'cause I'm tired of being shown your hangers."

"You should try and show yours every now and then. You still got them, right?"

He made a cylinder with the *National Geographic* and started to tap his thigh.

"Dude, if you're going to keep tapping your bible like that, swear to God, I'm gonna puke."

"Nah, I'm just a joker, man. Isn't that what you're into?"

"Yes, we're all clowns. And you're too fucking quick for us, Erik."

"You're not bad yourself. Negotiation-analysis guy! Come on, pick a frame. Isn't that how you guys talk when you fight? No, wait! I got a couple for you. How about Alkis and his futurism? Or Cristina's ski-safari? Yes, you are all clowns. You belong onstage. Really."

"And how's that different from . . . Oh, me? Oh . . . er . . . I . . . see . . . went to school in, uh, Connecticut." I went for his Southie accent. "Hmm . . . well . . . it was in New Haven, you know."

"I ain't your fucking Gawel, Stathis! You haven't figured that out yet?"

"Answer the question," I said. "You went to Yale. How's that shitty little stage any different? 'Cause it's hysterical, really."

"There *is* a difference. There're ways to spend your time and money. You sell privileged ignorance or indifference. I'm done with your EBS bullshit. You're on your own."

My heart was pounding. "You need to make money to be able to spend any," I said.

Erik stared at me, stunned, for a good three seconds. "I don't have sixty bucks for fuckups like you," he said, stood up, and grabbed his backpack, searching for something inside. "Fuck," he muttered.

"Neither do I. That's why I see them when I see them. And I eat with Melissa and listen to her. It's called *life*. And if I wanna have an impact, I have to listen and talk. I don't ban. I don't become *binary*, Erik, with-us-or-*against*-us."

"You excuse them, and that makes you a *pathetic* little dick." He started packing.

"Man, you're not *listening* to me! Are they clumsy? Fucked up? Sure. But who isn't? Look around you. Sustainability? There was never *any sustainability*!" I pointed at his magazine. "Open your fucking bible. It's full of life cycles. This notion of perpetuity is made up! Fahey went to fucking business school. Mike Davis used analysts to write his books. What the *fuck*?"

Erik laughed. "You cunt! Weren't you the one asking Zemar for sustainability? Know what? You think you can consult me, but you're just being dumb. Or you'll say anything out of desperation."

I was standing next to him without breathing. "Either way, fucked up," I said.

He let his backpack drop. "I don't want to see them again."

"How old are you?"

His eyes narrowed. "I want to punch you so hard right now."

I pushed him onto the bed and pressed hard against his torso. "Look at me, man."

"Fuck you," he whispered.

"Look how good I am. Just *look* at me."

He cupped my face, hurting me. "Move to New York," he said.

Locked in his stare, I felt his breath. I was living by the day.

EIGHT

DEEP, DEEP DOWN, SOMEHOW, SOMETHING didn't go exactly as planned, and that's why most of you are here." That was our dean's opening line in his EBS welcome speech. Four years later, nothing could better have captured my move to New York.

"What does it matter where you live?" Alkis said over the phone from London. "You are a consultant. You live where you work." Plus, I had nothing to figure out about New York, he argued.

"I got New York credit!" I joked, but he had a point. Empire Diner, US Open seats from Command, Melissa, ambitious misfits. I could see my move as a simple technicality.

In February 2006 I called my super in San Francisco and told him that I wouldn't be renewing my lease. He could keep my airbed and coffee table. In return, he agreed to ship my EBS books across the country.

The night I moved in, the bartender at Billymark's fixed three tequila shots. "Here's to our neighborhood newbie!"

"Easiest move ever!" I cheered my sublet of a small studio— it had a decent patio, though—down the street from the bar.

"You call this moving?" Erik laughed. "Stathis, you never moved! Everything's furnished, delivered, how do you call it, er, outsourced!" He kept laughing. "Three times a day, seven days a week."

"Who cooks for one?" I said with a shrug.

"You're making a Chateau Marmont cottage in west Chelsea," Erik said, and downed his shot.

"Yeah, okay," I said, and threw mine back.

Erik nodded to the bartender. "Keep them coming."

My first official fall in New York was split between workdays in Princeton and weekends in my studio, on West Twenty-Ninth Street. In New Jersey, I led a Command team in building an oncology strategy for a major pharmaceutical company that was fighting off a biotech. I was assigned Gawel and Justin—an Alkis mini-me, a fresh-from-Tuck, work-and-party-hard associate. Things ran smoothly.

Erik—his place a couple of blocks from mine—was on my patio with or without me. He fought off squirrels and brought over leftover plants from Hudson River Park by Twelfth Avenue. He had people over, and let friends of friends crash in my absence. He drank my wine and moved my *Economist* stash next to the toilet because "they wanted Clinton to walk," he explained.

"I thought they kinda retracted that," I lazily protested.

"The damage was done, wasn't it?" Erik responded quickly. "And they didn't exactly oppose the invasion in Iraq either."

He made Greek salads—good ones, too—in my strictly-one-person kitchen, and talked about how he'd make "real salads" when the tomatoes he planted came into season, "if those damn squirrels don't get 'em first." He began to befriend my neighbors and the kids on the basketball court across from the post office at the end of my block. He went to "organic bullshit" markets and found furniture on the streets on Wednesday nights, our neighborhood's recycling day, and carried them up the two flights of stairs.

"Have you heard of bedbugs?" I asked once. But when it came to domesticity, I was always brushed off.

"Didn't you use to take in dogs from around your village?"

I began to register details, the silly trivia people talk about when they describe relationships: the exact spot on Erik's face where he always started shaving. The way he took off and put on his work shirts—already buttoned up. His gym-like rhythm while working on the patio: brisk before a halt, then all fired up again as he moved a plant or a bag of soil. His caring, protective voice when he talked on the phone to his older brother, Kevin—a strange dance that I couldn't explain except by the fact that Erik was the book-smarter of the two. In a way, Kevin gave me hope. I would never become Jeevan, the saint, or Zemar, the daredevil, but I could be Kevin, accepted and loved just the way he was, the fund manager absolved.

"Plants are more important than art or work," Erik said that spring, and another time I would have fired back, "What about people?" But the patio was bonding us, we were getting along, and I was in New York, finally making a home.

SOMEHOW THINGS BEGAN TO MAKE sense. Between managing Andrea and having Erik and that silly patio, between reading, cooking, and drinking, I thought I was on my way to adulthood. I was relaxed, and it turned out to be one of the most peaceful, productive, and loving times of my life.

We read on a futon that Erik had dragged onto the patio next to the tomatoes, beneath quarreling squirrels, neighbors having sex, and sirens screaming down Ninth Avenue.

"I kinda like the police sound track," I said during a nonfiction Sunday.

"Narcissist!"

I chuckled. "Where did *that* come from?"

"You'll get it," Erik said, and kept reading.

"I grew up listening to waves. Sirens are exciting."

"They're exciting 'cause you'll never be chased by them."

"'Cause you have?"

Erik turned and gave me a *wanna-bet* smile.

"Oh, yeah?" I said. "Got a record too?"

"Damn right!" Erik said, and touched the scar on his upper arm.

"I thought you said that was a car accident."

"During a chase."

"*Really?* Did you hit a supermarket in Roxbury?"

"Punk!" Erik laughed. I laughed back.

"I know you wanna tell me," I said.

He put his book down. "Okay. So we're leaving a Red Sox game and the brakes die on us, and we red-light a major one."

"I believe you," I said unconvincingly.

"Now cops are chasing us, but we can't stop. So my cousin fences the car right up next to the wire of this parking lot. Windows smashed, paramedics, cops don't buy our story . . ."

"Did they take you to your dad's hospital?" I asked seriously.

"Fuckass!" Erik jumped on me, but I was expecting him, so I sprang off the futon. "Stop dancing," he yelled and threw my copy of *Real Options* after me, which I kicked in midair.

"Bequia! One on one!" I said, and started tapping our soccer ball with my knees.

"You were lucky," Erik mumbled.

"Keep telling yourself that."

"Stop talking. You'll drop the ball two floors down to Guadeloupe again," Erik said.

"You didn't pass it to me right. Look! Look how you're supposed to hit the ball. Above the knee, Erik. On the thigh. Jump and swing. Jump and swing. Control, don't trap."

"You play soccer like you dance *zeibekiko*."

I laughed but kept freestyling. "You play *football* like a dancing slave. Said Zemar taught you?"

Erik threw his Mike Davis at me and I kicked the ball at his face. Making a fist in time, he bounced it off the patio.

I ground my teeth. "It's a *sublet*, you dick!" I said as seriously as I could. "Gotta be decent, discreet."

"Dance *now*."

I burst onto the futon and onto him, clamping his neck with my knees. He tried to break loose and grabbed my crotch. "You wood?" Erik laughed.

"Is your verb-skipping a Southie thing?" I squeezed his neck harder. "Or is texting fucking with your brain?"

"*C'est quoi ce bordel?*" my neighbor shouted.

"Greek slut!" Erik said.

"Bloomberg whore!"

Weather permitting, we slept outdoors. I barely thought of Greece.

WEEKDAYS IN PRINCETON, WE WERE making progress, getting closer to solid findings, but somehow I wasn't translating goodwill to more work. I wasn't really selling.

"Business development is the only way to partnership," Andrea murmured during my professional development meeting as she flipped through my "Basket of Skill Sets" folder.

She was still sore about Paris, and she knew that I suspected her motives and moves. She still had the upper hand, but now she was a touch scared of me too.

"I lifted 'Business Development' to 'Primary Focus,'" I offered.

She dropped my folder onto her desk and turned to her new espresso machine, which was sitting-pretty on a tea trolley I had seen in conference rooms. She pressed the machine's big round red button and went back to my "2006 Goals" subfolder and my "Focus Card," which she put between my "Upward & Downward Evaluation Matrix" and my "Command Years Scorecard."

"Yes, I see that," Andrea said, nodding. "It used to be under 'Substantial.' Are you sure you don't want an espresso?" she asked, and once again leaned over the machine, which was warily silent.

"I'm good, thanks," I replied, worrying that her new toy was broken, and what impact that might have on my professional development.

But then she turned, holding a glass filled with espresso. She leaned back against her desk, not quite smiling, one hand flat on my folders, the other holding her cup, and enjoyed a sip.

"Stathis," she said, looking quickly up to the ceiling. "Your basket is strong. You're in the tenth percentile on both leadership and quant. You get good client feedback, and Command is not an up-or-out firm, but . . . What I want to see next—what *your* challenge should be next is to introduce clients to more of our offerings. And the ticket here is . . ." she prompted me with her free hand: "Something sexy?" She tilted her head. "*Innovation!* What else?" She raised a shoulder and took another sip.

Seriously—after her failed insider-trading trick in Paris, Georgina Clooney was back at her innovation tune. She was so shameless that I had to look away to avoid laughing.

I left her office wondering how Andrea's innovabullshit and seven folders of my professional development, of *my* bullshit, could make middle managers buy more slides and Excel spreadsheets.

A week before Thanksgiving I dispatched Justin to research literature on how to "introduce management frameworks to corporate America." "And I want sexy stories," I ordered. I'd never used the word *sexy* at work with a straight face before.

Two days before the holidays, Justin walked into our Princeton war room with his Victorinox carry-on in tow. When all nine pockets were empty, we were buried under a mountain of books, articles, and Post-it notes on business frameworks exploiting metaphors from history and war ("Alexander the Great's art of strategy"), instincts and emotions, paradoxes and controversy ("Teams don't work," "Throw your annual budget plans in the garbage"), family life, ecosystems (animals as well as cataclysmic events), thermodynamics, mythology (including fucking Greek gods, or was it Greek gods fucking?), cognitive behavior, semiotics, and the Zen impact on the bottom line. Honestly.

I spent the rest of the morning feeling like I was stuck at the business section of Borders at Logan, thinking about the man-hours wasted on those metaphors. But it was the mid '00s; there was time and budget for anything.

Later that day, I was on the treadmill at the client's gym, smiling, thinking of Erik's reaction to the "labors of Hercules in the corporate boardroom." Still, I knew I had to push things to the point of ridicule to have a chance at being heard, and hopefully sell—and for the life of me, I couldn't get Oprah off my treadmill's screen. I pressed the Channel button twice, but she was still there, looking astounded, when an Aztec warrior–heart-monitoring-gloved hand pointed at the side of my treadmill's frame.

"You need to plug in here first," a familiar voice said.

I reduced my speed and saw Justin, beaming next to me in hard-core athletech gear. A bottle of smartwater and a video gadget were hooked to his gladiatorial Home Depot–like belt. His T-shirt said: "Hwa, Won, Yu."

"I didn't know you worked out," Justin said, all cocky after his intervention.

"Surprise," I said. "I didn't know you were off to Baghdad."

"Funny, boss. Are you just running, or working on volume too?"

"Running, mainly. And how many times have I told you that I am not your boss. We don't have bosses at Command. I'm your senior, and it's for this project only."

"Trying to look young now, are we?"

From the corner of my eye I caught Gawel, in a plain T-shirt and shorts, looking our way from the other side of the gym. Without a suit, he looked high school.

"What's . . . 'Hwa, Won, Yu'?" I struggled.

"They are hapkido's main principles," Justin explained. "Nonresistance, circular movement, and water."

"I'm surprised they didn't jump out of your suitcase this morning," I said, but Justin was fixing a button on his fist-weapon glove-watch.

"I gotta keep moving, boss. If I drop below my heart range, my monitor will beep."

"We can't have that, now," I mumbled, and went back to my Hercules thoughts and my skepticism about placing myself in this stupid business-metaphor fad. What I needed was a potent nondrug paradigm that I could just plug into Jersey pharmacos. *But how can I turn an indie script into a summer box-office hit*, I thought, when I noticed Master Justin, two machines down, stretch-stepping while browsing a big-screen catastrophe on his gadget. Could I be missing some sort of sensation here? At the end of the day, who was my audience, and what did they really need in order to have a good day at work? These were managers who would pick the *New York Post* over the *New York Times*. A corporate-world craving everyday, Brooklyn thrills. I had to make my projects newsworthy. Keep them simple, but give them a populist twist: a surprise, a juxtaposition. I started sensationalizing our oncology project, Murdoching its challenges and deliverables.

The next day I walked into our war room feeling smart. "Let's have some fun!"

"Mornin'," Gawel and Justin mumbled.

"We'll work like restaurant chefs," I said with a smile.

Gawel turned. Justin kept typing.

"Stop e-mailing," I said.

"What's going on?" Justin asked. "You need a latte?"

"Stop talking," I told Justin. "Now, I said that we'll work like restaurant chefs. So let's find out what's seasonal to put in the specials." I paused, with a grin on my face.

"Could you—"

"Okay, here is the one-liner: We pick a current affair and we build a framework around it. Then, and *only* then, we fill it up with the client's numbers."

The guys nodded to each other, puzzled.

"Just bear with me. For example, our client is getting murdered by this aggressively low-priced biotech, the underdog, right? We are supposed to present final recommendations end of February, which, if you Google, is Oscar season. So we can approximate their market to a duopoly and use game theory to build a couple of defense strategies, including a dominant one that we could call *A Beautiful Mind.*"

"No shit."

"I'm not *done* yet. We'll use the bar scene from the movie to show how it's possible to improve the client's odds by helping them find their Nash equilibrium and settle on it. How they cannot protect their market share if they go into a pricing war, as the underdog *knows* that *they* know that with such a move they'll lose money." I stopped to breathe.

Gawel stared at me responsively, giving me a scary high. There was science behind my nudging—game theory worked, they could outfox the bio—nevertheless, I was making something out of nothing. I was adding to Justin's suitcase and getting away with it, crafting more "entertainment" for managers; me, who'd studied quantum physics, for God's sake. Was I turning into a tabloid? Into the dark matter and energy I learned about in school?

Maybe a little nudging was okay, for *this* project. Sell, get promoted again, and rethink things.

"Seriously, it was nominated for eight Oscars," I half joked with the client-lead a couple of weeks later. "I bet our biotech friends have seen the movie too."

He was amused, but intrigued enough to buy that they were "Nash-locked" with the other side.

"Unless, of course, we change the rules of the game altogether," I continued. "Strategy two: 'Deterrence.' A much riskier strategy, and a really bad movie."

A door had just opened, and Andrea had somehow been left outside. I am almost free, I thought.

IT WAS 2006 AND EVERYBODY was smiling. "Uncertainty is your friend," I preached at the backgammon tournament I set up on the client's outing. "It's a better strategic game than chess. See, if we lack uncertainty, then all rents will end up being equal, as strategies *can* and *will* be replicated."

I became Jersey-provocative. Whether they believed me or not, they smiled.

I started to excite pharma executives, and that spring my "Innovate through Simplicity" taunt had a small following. I was the Commander whom Andrea would "kidnap" for thirty-six hours to send to an innovation panel in San Diego. And I was game. Flying in and out of towns, I rationalized my abuse of Ambien. I even groomed—some. I dropped by Kiehl's in Barneys and accepted Andrea's Outlook invite— "tentatively"—for a fitting at Dunhill. I got promoted, tripled the money I wired to Greece, and started to call my sister more often, as though something was about to happen.

But what could I do? Quit Command and get a real job? Move back home? I was the youngest Senior Engagement Manager. I was practically Andrea-free. I could work things to my equilibrium, the way I did with clients. Greece hadn't called me back yet. My sister never said: "We want *you*, not your money." Not openly, not to me. And Erik? Well, I was a manager now; I would sleep better soon. I would work out my physical and mental depletion and help him fix up the patio. I could even bribe the Greeks and visit Pelio with him. Teach him how to fish and dive for clams in the Aegean. Things would get better because I was in the driver's seat.

"Pick a nice location for your big day," I told Alkis over the phone after he reminded me of his mortgage and wedding plans with Cristina. "'Cause I'm so ready for a real vacation."

"Whom with?" Alkis laughed. "Your sister? Or Erik, *again*?"

Bastard.

"How many times have you proposed but changed your mind?" I said viciously. "I bet you've racked up some loyalty points at Cartier by now."

"That's right, I changed *my* mind. Something I seriously doubt you're able to do yourself. It's funny . . ."

"Funny what?"

"You outsmarted everyone in our Negotiation class and now you're scared to ask Erik to move in with you."

Pick your fights. Deflate. "I don't even have enough room for my three shirts," I said, and tried to laugh.

"Well, that's all you got, mate. Fucking empty shirts."

I knew that Alkis cared, but he was complicating things. He was off the point, he was wrong. Things were balancing out, yet they were still fragile. There were no pockets for Erik, everything was on a continuum: from my job, to my friends, to the books I read and the sports I played. He referred to my approach to life as "New York retail. Everything exchangeable, no questions asked." He saw no commitment on my part, "no staking whatsoever. Like your life's a Command project," Erik said, but all I read was affection, his approval of what I did through playful attacks, the way my father had picked on my algorithmic approach to fishing. All fun and games, till a patio night that spring when I saw an end in Erik's words: "No irrevocable commitment of resources, no decisions. No balls," he spat.

"Come again?"

"Isn't that what you teach your clients? Optionality? Hedging? Guess what, you live it," Erik said.

It was his gut, not his words, that made me go: "I haven't hedged you."

"You never bought the option, I ain't your put," he said, sucking an old paper cut on his thumb. "I ain't adding to your risk-free ride. Your commitment's to what you don't have."

Erik paused to suck his fucking thumb while telling me that he's not mine. And his casualness, this paper-cut insignificance, tore down our pathetically planned patio in my mind.

As the weather got better, Erik started making a point of avoiding dinners and concerts. "I can't afford your eating alfresco," he'd smirk.

If I got a freebie or tried to pay, he'd dismiss me.

"Dude, I won't be part of your agency cost!" he said, throwing my jargon in my face when I offered him Command seats for the Yankees.

I thought of clients listening to me, Gawel admiring me if not adoring me, and I fought back: "You get too much pleasure from telling us that you don't have a TV," I countered when Erik shed a discussion on *Lost* during a dinner he joined at the last minute.

When the check arrived, I bundled resentment in camaraderie and passed him a fifty under the table. He grabbed my hand, pressing hard on my wrist till my fist opened. "Pick it up now," he said, satisfied.

By summer our fights were constant.

"You realize that you've developed wardrobe syndrome," Erik told me at 192 Books when I asked for a separate receipt for *Guns, Germs, and Steel* to expense on my Command account.

"Lost you," I lied.

"You did, didn't you?" Erik mocked. "Let me explain. You can link anything to your work, to your clients. Expense it. Everything's wardrobe, used once for a performance. Your *relocation* was part of your professional development. You're still hotel living."

I tossed away the receipt, but Erik kept staring at me with pity.

"And for what?" he said. "For smart-ass work stories and silly dinners."

It was the first time I was completely sober and wanted to physically hurt him.

"Have you seen *Vanity Fair* at home?" I asked as casually as I could. "I can't find it."

He gave me a shrug.

"The issue with Soros and your father. Thought I left it on the patio, but I can't find it. Did you take it?"

Erik shook his head in disbelief. "Mother . . ."

"You know which one, right? The one with the photo of your dad among his clients? Those 'five remarkable women' or something?"

"Ask your higher power to find it for you," Erik said, and walked out.

"Hey, wait a minute!" I yelled after him on Tenth Avenue. "You walking out on me? Come back! 'Cause when it comes to your family, your definitions are *so* strict. *Hey!* 'Cause I can be a Jeevan too, an eco-warrior, a great communist!" I shouted. "Or are you guys hedging? You run for office while your brother takes over your dad's clinics?"

Erik stopped. He turned around and walked up to me, his finger pushing hard on my chest. "*Listen* to me, Feta! If you wanna fight, have the balls to talk about *me*! What I *do*, instead of who I *am*. Got it? You ain't in fucking *Europe* anymore."

Right there on Tenth Avenue, smelling coffee in his breath, splashes of his spit on my face, I knew we were close to an end. Maybe he'd never seen me as an equal. I didn't. We'd met fleeing our homes but heading in opposite directions, crossing each other in an accident that I might have dragged out for too long. Seferis's poem came to mind: Helen and Paris never made it to Troy. The war was fought for nothing, for an empty shirt that ended up there instead. A decade after I'd left Greece, both Alkis and Erik were right. I was wardrobe. I was a fucking empty shirt.

NINE

UK COMMANDERS HAVE A MORE accurate use of language. It goes back to their schooling," Andrea said, projecting different typefaces on the wall of her office. "Good communication allows them more client impact. They advance faster."

Good for them.

"There is something crisp and clean about London's style. See there?" She circled an *H*, using her laser pointer.

What the hell was she talking about? Was she selling me a type of font or assigning me to a project in England?

"Are you a Verdana or a Calibri person?" she asked, pointing back and forth between impact and mission.

I didn't know which one was which. I truly couldn't see any difference.

"Er," I wavered.

Andrea looked at me in shock.

"Calibri," I gambled. Calibri was the font on Paul's old business card. For some reason he was proud of it.

"Really?" She played with her butterfly-shaped necklace. Now that she was engaged to her CEO, pearls had been replaced by gems. "I don't mean that their actual streets are clean. I mean that there's something crisp about the way people live in London."

Freak.

"I meant Verdana," I said. "Ah, *crisp*! I get it!" I tried to end her font-masturbation. I had to finish the PowerPoint deck for the next day's client presentation. It was a big meeting. A five-billion R&D investment was at stake. Andrea knew that and she was wasting my time, our time, by flexing her muscle, showing me who's boss, playing up the importance of bullshit. Or, worse, she was slowly setting up one of her work traps again. "I'm off to Princeton. You'll get the client deck tomorrow, first thing," I said, and walked out.

"Seven a.m. sharp!" Andrea shouted after me.

I left New York Verdana-committed—I mean, what the fuck—but something sad was bugging me that I couldn't pinpoint, something bigger than Andrea and her petty power games, or even her insider plots. As I sped down Fifth Avenue, the Ramones yelling, "I don't wanna live my life again," it hit me that I was afraid to leave Command. I didn't want another job. I didn't want to reboot into another three years of the same parody, desperate for downtime but always yearning for a project or two. I was too American to quit, too Greek to pretend I liked the constant all-nighters, the working on the weekends and holidays.

By 2006, I didn't know many people who were happy to be consultants. The few of us from my class who were still here, the plateaued ones who hadn't followed Alkis to an investment bank or a hedge fund, were carried by the inertia of depression. Drinking, cheating, obsessively exercising, crying, chewing Paxil, and snorting cocaine, we simply acted out while we waited (hoped, at some level) for all of this to end involuntarily, or to "come to terms with the brand-management job at a client campus in south NJ," Alkis reminded me in his latest e-mail. He signed, "Come-to-Lehman, Alkis," and I deleted him from my BlackBerry, Mailbox & Handheld, while checking in at the Forrestal in Princeton.

IT WAS APPROACHING TWO IN the morning when I signed for the third round of room-service martinis while still working on our real-options approach to optimizing the client's licensing choices on pre–clinical trials compounds.

"How about we change the legend in the last chart?" I shouted to Gawel from across the suite as I charaded to nightshift Anthony for cigarettes.

"What are we going for instead?" Gawel yelled back at me.

"Call the distribution's tenth percentile 'Surprise' and the fifth percentile 'Bombshell,' and if we must go further we'll '9/11' it or something," I said. I eyed Anthony for a cigarette that we weren't allowed by Command policy, anywhere, anytime. With the partners at DEFCON 2 on smokers, I was discreet.

He winked and passed me his pack.

I put a twenty in his pocket. We'd done this before.

Gawel stopped typing. "Stathis, how tactful, I mean, how politically correct do you think this is?"

"It's not," I replied, joining him at our war table. "So there's a chance they'll like it."

Gawel mumbled something about Andrea to himself. The woman had recently made Command headlines when she quoted Samantha, her favorite character from *Sex and the City*, into a client pitch. Her upcoming wedding with the cosmetics baron was the only reason Washington had let the "incident" slide.

"Yeah, she'll die of shame," I mumbled back.

"Stathis, I know you're one of them," Gawel said, his eyes fixed on his screen.

Little prick . . . What on earth . . . "I'm one of lots of things."

"I've seen you smoking outside the Soho Grand," Gawel said awkwardly. "You can smoke, I don't care. My father's Polish."

What did "My father's Polish" mean? That he was not? As opposed to his mother? It was 2 a.m.; I was on my third martini and desperate for distraction. "So that makes you what? Polish? Half Polish? A quarter? American?"

"I'm Polish American."

"Well, I'm half Greek and half Greek, so I need to smoke."

Gawel let out a shy smile. "I won't tell. You are safe with me."

I offered him Anthony's pack and he took one. I threw him my lighter. When Gawel finally lit up—second try—I saw his hand shaking. I was typing a note to Andrea, explaining our progress on the presentation, when her e-mail hit my screen. "What the hell is she doing up at this hour?" I mumbled. We had agreed on a 7 a.m. deck transfer. She didn't understand what "a cumulative distribution and a standard deviation" meant in my last draft. I sniffed to cover my laughter and restrained myself from reading her e-mail out loud. She finished her note by adding, "I found two typos. Something that really, really, exasperates me," and she hoped that "that was a one-off thing."

I clicked Delete and caught Gawel downing his martini.

"What was that?" I said.

"I told you, I'm Polish."

"American."

"Er, what time do we present tomorrow?"

He knew. I looked at my watch. "We present in six hours, if that's what you're asking."

"Stathis, I, you know . . . I have like . . ." Gawel was stuttering. "I have a half-hour drive to my hotel on the other side of Princeton. Plus, I need to be back here for printing by seven tomorrow. You think . . . would it be okay if I crashed on your sofa?"

I thought we might get to this, but still I felt a cold sweat. I looked at his messed-up hair, his cleft-chinned face colored in by an early-twenties abashment, while I was lonely, horny, and sad. His fingers swayed on his keyboard, and I thought of my no-war state with Erik since our fight on Tenth Avenue outside the bookstore two weeks back. Whatever our no-fighting, spend-the-minimum-time-together relationship meant for our future, it was still better than nothing. I had slept only with Erik in New York. *Get your own fucking room*, I thought. "Only if you snore," I said.

An instant grin. "Why?" Gawel asked.

I finished my drink. "'Cause I'll snore in my bedroom. And trust me, you'll need to cancel it out."

He went back to his computer, beaming. I smelled the vodka on his breath from across the table. I was helpless.

A sloppy e-mail to Andrea later, I placed a blanket by Gawel, who was pretending to nap. He bent to reach it and grabbed my hand without looking at me. We just stayed there.

"I know," I said.

His grip got tighter, and quickly, superstitiously, I told myself that I loved Erik, privately, the way I used to cross myself before diving into the open Aegean, embarrassed to think that someone might see me. Gawel trembled when I kissed him. He hurried off his socks and unbuttoned me.

I felt his tongue clumping the head of my dick and I heard his T-shirt shrieking as I tore it.

"*God*, swallow my dick!"

I came fast down his throat just as his come hit my shirt, two feet away. Then he leaned back on the sofa and rested there, without spitting or rinsing.

"We all deserve some pause after coming." I sat next to him. My dick and balls aside, I was fully dressed.

"Okay . . ."

"Something someone told me once."

Gawel laughed. "Even Alkis?"

"Even Andrea." I pulled Gawel sideways, spooning him in his T-shirt leftovers.

"Stathis . . ."

"It's gonna be okay," I said. "We'll be okay."

THREE HOURS LATER I WOKE up without an alarm. I had fallen asleep holding him. No Ambien, first time in a month. Gawel was facing me, still asleep. I left without showering, in the shirt I had slept in, spotted with come. I lingered at the door for a second, thinking of writing a note, but where would I start? "Good morning. Have a good time printing the client decks!" I left the hotel for the client at six, feeling grateful that I had a presentation to do and Andrea to deal with—another first.

Gawel walked into the conference room as I was trying to calm Andrea down; she didn't find the deck's colors bright enough.

"It's Command's standard template," I explained. "Morning!" I shouted toward Gawel, who was holding a bunch of printouts under his arm. Andrea, in orchestration mode, didn't acknowledge him.

"Morning," Gawel replied without looking my way, counting the printed decks.

I was about to press for a look, but he slipped out to fetch extra highlighters. I almost stormed after him.

"*Focus?*" Andrea yelled.

I was taken aback. "I'm listening."

"I mean the *projector*, Stathis!" She jolted a metal box and one of her flamingo-painted nails irked and bent against the lens. "*Damn it!*" she cried.

PRESENTING, I SURPRISED MYSELF. DISTRACTED by Gawel—the little punk was taking notes, avoiding my stare throughout the presentation—I was lighter, lean, Command-crisp, while Andrea cut in every three minutes to say, "Which is one of the reasons we are here today."

"ISN'T IT GREAT WHEN WE all play nice?" Andrea said at the end of our postpresentation debrief.

Gawel nodded.

"Right." I collected my papers.

"I'll see you tonight at the benefit," Andrea said, ready to stalk two clients from our meeting whom she spotted as they were about to enter the next conference room. All of a sudden, as if she had changed her mind, she stepped toward me: "Presenting in a dirty shirt is unacceptable."

"I got Parkinson's."

"Come with me," she ordered Gawel, her stare firmly on me.

I traced him with my eyes. At the corner, he looked back and gave me a timid smile.

I drove back to New York in joy and fear. Gawel's last look was playing again and again like breaking news in my mind, giving me a thrill, a hard-on, and a silly face I had last worn before EBS. Then fright would float in and I'd try to calm myself by thinking things out in a rational way. Gawel, Erik, Command, me—all I needed was some order, some quality decision making, just like I did at work. How about the utilitarian approach, "the greatest happiness for the greatest number," I said out loud, thinking of multi-variable decision frameworks, while my brakes against the tunnel traffic screamed how multivariably, multi-back-and-forth, utterly multi*fucked* I was. The more I thought about it, the more panic snaked into me. I knew I had crossed a line, and with a subordinate to boot. Unethical, stupid, and dangerous.

In the tunnel, I switched on the headlights and thought of our office ordinate. This trick made us all look more or less together, commanding, attractive even, coating what happened with Gawel so that it looked almost involuntary. He was the apprentice and I was the mentor, and, after four years of battling with Erik for interrelational supremacy, this clarity was in its own right a romance. That and the fact that a young man listened to me, looked me in the eye, and idealized me—*me*, of all people—turned a blow job into the first light coming from Tribeca while I was exiting a four-year tunnel of emotional depletion.

In Manhattan, on my way to the office, I stopped by my place to shower and change my shirt. Throwing my keys on the coffee table, I noticed Erik's brother's invitation for that evening: "Kevin's new pad is finally ready!"

What if Erik finds out about Gawel, I thought. "Science fiction," I said out loud, and jumped into the shower to scrub it off.

I stood there motionless, looking at the blue tiles on the shower floor—water pounding my head and chest—thinking of what on earth I'd talk about with Gawel at the benefit, his ginger hair and blue eyes, and I started to jerk off, ruffled by the fact that I'd have to sneak out in time to make it to Kevin's; Zemar's latest cryptic postcard; back to Gawel taking my dick, doggy-style this time; Erik's soft snoring, which I'd grown to like; Alkis and Cristina's e-mailed sonogram; two clients, one hopefully new; Jeevan's peaceful stare, fishing at sunset before jumping off the boat to cool off; and fucking Erik by the wash of the sea, until I came.

THE LIGHTS DIMMED AS A picture of the High Line was projected onto the fifteen-foot screen of the Wall Street ballroom.

"I have powers of subpoena, and if you don't quiet down I'll cite you," Eliot Spitzer said from the podium. The eight hundred attendees of the Friends of the High Line 2006 Benefit laughed. "For me, it is part of what makes Manhattan, Manhattan," said the video narrator, identified as "actor, NYC resident," and people applauded.

Andrea leaned forward at the Command-sponsored table. "He's at the central table in front," she whispered to no one in particular, and the ends of her hair dipped into her risotto. A couple of junior associates stretched to catch a look of the movie star.

"Gawel didn't make it?" I asked Andrea, relaxed.

She kept looking at the screen, enchanted. Rotating pictures of west Chelsea mixed with quotes from activists, actors, and politicians identified as "High Line supporters."

"You're almost on what I call a flying carpet. It's a completely different vantage point."

"It's up in the clouds."

"A demiparadise."

"It really works for everybody. Because this is, in fact, going to be one of the coolest places to live in all of Manhattan."

"I didn't invite analysts," Andrea bothered to answer me at the end of the slide show.

Then footage from a public hearing I had attended during one of my New York weekends, back in 2003, played. It showed an artist sobbing, explaining to Erik's community board that the High Line was the first thing she looked at when she woke up in the morning. In the video's background I made out Erik, with a microphone, facilitating the hearing.

Then I spotted Paul, sitting pretty at the table to my left. When we locked stares he motioned to the screen—where Erik was still visible—and threw a piece of bread my way, which I caught before it hit Andrea.

"I hope you *do* realize that we are here for a *number of reasons*," she said with a *what-the-hell-do-you-think-you're-doing* face.

"There's sauce in your hair," I said.

The lights came up and the New York attorney general presented awards to a fashion designer, an actor, and the City Council speaker, all of whom were honored for "their early and continued support of the High Line project."

"I did *exactly* what Josh and Robert asked me to do," opened one of the honorees.

I stood up to go out for a cigarette.

"Don't leave yet!" Andrea grabbed my wrist. "I want to take a picture of all of us in front of the High Line."

"Sorry?"

"Oh, they do that every year. Everybody has their picture taken in front of a life-size High Line poster."

"I'll close my eyes," I said, and wiggled my wrist free.

Outside, Paul was smoking, holding a gift bag with a beach towel in it. I motioned for his lighter as I noticed the flags on the Museum of American Finance across the street: "The Money. The Power. The History."

"I need one of those," I said, pointing to the towel, but Paul turned and looked at the flags.

"I thought all you wanted was a beach shack back home."

"That, too. The *gift* bag." I pointed again. "My towels are all white, stolen, and stained by Erik."

"So, you don't come." He passed me the bag. "Take it. Let's get out of here."

"A partner-bitch is inside."

"Fuck her."

"Someone has to," I murmured. "For everyone's sake."

Paul was on his cell phone throughout our cab ride to my place. "I enjoyed working with you, I learned from you, but you were born to apologize! It's 2006 and privacy is getting redefined . . . No, no, *no*! We are not stalking them, we are *accosting* them . . ."

Once home, I got two beers from the fridge, turned the music on, and walked out onto the patio. It was a clear June night, and I could still hear Paul inside: " . . . thank you for your administrative . . ." mixed with Jamiroquai's " . . . this corner of the earth is like me in many ways.. . ." when the sound of Gawel's incoming text went off.

"How's the benefit?"

I had a moment of low-oxygen dizziness, mixed with an about-to-get-busted rush. I sat down, loosened my tie, and thought of Gawel, wondering how it would feel to be twenty-three again. I remembered the years right after Stanford, working in Redwood City. I went to the supermarket and cooked. I had routines, for Christ's sake. I wasn't exactly Gawel, but I was less jaded back then. If I had an affair or got promoted, I was childishly proud. I believed in myself. And what if I'd met Erik then, prior to all the EBS and Command decay, when I had a real job and real friends? Would I still have fallen for him? Followed him to New York? Or, better, would I be equally obsessed with him if I had real problems, like making rent or getting a job? Maybe not. But there I was, not twenty-three any more, not middle-aged either, in a smart suit and loosened tie, on my patio, gazing at the Big Dipper and the North Star, replaying my juvenile habit of making sure I knew where Polaris—my grandfather's compass during the war—was in the sky above.

Fucking Erik was my war. A craze, a luxury excused by the circus that otherwise surrounded me. We had time to "stand up for our favorite type of font," address "the nonsmoker's identity at work," or text each other the ridiculously obvious while, *because*, our Alkises could "fire clients." We had legitimized our silliness, we *were* silly, so why not make a war for Erik, Grandpa? I was still within my social standard deviation.

"On the Andrea side," I began texting my work-nonwork response, when Paul walked onto the patio.

"I'm heading to Soho House. Do you care to join me?" Paul asked as I heard Erik jogging up the stairs to my apartment.

"No can do," I replied. "It's Erik's brother's party tonight. An uptown thing."

My apartment door squeaked open and Erik dashed to the patio, where he came to a halt. He glanced at me, then at Paul, then back at me.

"Erik!" Paul waved. "It's been a while."

It took a second.

"Right," Erik said, and ducked back in. I heard his beer cap hitting the dirty dishes in the sink.

"Good day?" I asked Erik when he surfaced again.

"So far."

They bumped shoulders as Paul stepped inside, his phone ringing madly.

"What's this jackass doing here?" Erik asked while marching to his tomatoes.

"We ran into each other at Andrea's High Line thing."

"Of course you did," Erik said over his shoulder. "What the hell was he there for? Stalking the romantics, or helping them out?"

"Watch it," I said. "You're supposed to be High Line impartial, remember?"

He turned and looked at me with narrowed eyes.

"I'm just saying," I added quickly. "We don't want the district manager to be cited in blogs with funny HL quotes, now, do we?"

Erik shook his head. "HL? Seriously?"

I smiled, confused, like I'd missed his point.

"Does the towel on the coffee table say *High Line*?" Erik went on.

"It does!" Paul hopped back before I had a chance to speak. "It's from a princess turned fashion designer," he said, rowdily. "You wait. Five years from now you can make a killing with your towel on eBay. Just don't mark it."

I almost fell from my chair. "What the *fuck*, Paul?" I said, and tried to laugh it off.

"Hey, I just used the bathroom and wanted to dry my hands—"

"That's cool." Erik gestured to me. "I can wait to make a killing, but you don't have to, Paul. Why don't you build a kiosk on Seventh and Eleventh that sells maps with actors' addresses in the Village?"

"Actually, we're doing that online," Paul said smugly. "You and I, Erik, define privacy differently. Stathis is from the Balkans, he understands."

"No, he *doesn't*."

I felt busted. Like my balancing act, my having it both ways, was coming to an end.

"Transparency is not a crime," Paul said. "We chronicle trivia, details, in real time."

"Since when does acknowledging that you're doing something shitty actually legitimize it?"

"Since people are fed up with hypocrites," Paul answered calmly, and I put my cell in my pants pocket. "I have to run. I'm meeting friends from London," he continued, checking his Timex. He turned to me: "I'll leave your name at Soho House."

THE BUZZ FROM KEVIN'S PENTHOUSE got louder and louder as we cruised up, making the elevator operator less and less audible until he was practically muted. Still, Erik laughed at the guy's joke about the Mets.

The door opened onto a hallway that led to a crowded living room. Most of the women were in flowery dresses, the Madison Avenue–goes-Nolita type. Guys wore work suits or Patagonia shirts, and Lance Armstrong wristbands. They were all tan, and they mixed like they knew one another. Catering staff in bow ties served the decades-younger guests, which was bizarre in New York—uncomfortable, almost. I lost Erik to his Exeter schoolmates—"Hi . . . yes . . . been a while . . . good to see you too"—and looked for a vodka rocks.

"I'll take care of you," a waitress, who'd have long been retired had she lived in Europe, said to me.

With my drink firmly in hand, I crossed the living room and stepped out to the balcony, with its Spider-Man view. My eyes hopped from skyscraper to skyscraper before they laddered down to Park Avenue, which was covered with streams of red and yellow car lights. "Me and My Monkey" came on. I lit a cig and smelled Andrea's perfume.

"Stathis!"

I saw Helen, Erik's brother's girlfriend (sort of), showing off her brown hair and white teeth to me. She was in a black dress that turned into jewelry around her neck, leaving her tan shoulders naked. Northeastern, beautiful, early forties, she looked older and more together than the rest of the women there.

"Hi, Helen," I said.

"So good to see you." She kissed me slowly on the cheek. "How are you? How do you like New York?"

"I'm good. And the city looks pretty steep and steely from here. Kevin's view is unstoppable."

"It sold him on the penthouse. Adore!" She waved her hair as she bummed a cigarette. "So, how is the love these days?" she asked teasingly.

I lit her. "Tested?" I said.

She took her time exhaling. "Then you'll learn something."

"I usually don't."

"I like this," she said, feeling the cotton on my shirt, but I wasn't sure if she was talking about the fabric.

"Thank you." I smiled at how comfortably I accepted her compliment. "And coming from a fashion executive . . ."

Helen gave me a plotting stare. "I don't learn either."

"How do *you* feel in your ignorance?"

"Wonderful!" Helen laughed. "I just focus on sex. You should try it," she said.

I felt my phone against my ass and remembered Gawel's text, which I hadn't returned yet.

"And I stay busy," Helen continued, playing with her glass of champagne. "We are moving our offices to the Meatpacking District. You'll come to the party."

"Is that an invite?"

"Oh, Stathis, stop flirting. You know I can't compete with a communist in bed."

"Ha! Erik's not a communist. He's an independent, he

says." I rolled my eyes. "And how's sex with the family's fund manager?" I tossed back, and looked away at the Citigroup building.

I sensed Helen leaning toward me. "I wouldn't know," she whispered.

I had to think about this, so I turned strategically, covering my surprise with casualness, when halfway around I saw Erik through the window, talking to a news anchor inside.

"Unlike his brother, Erik loves contradictions," Helen said, picking up on my sighting.

"Tell me about it," I murmured, glued on Erik.

"But they are both surprising," she said, before kissing me and stepping back into the living room.

"Hey! I need more," I shouted after her, wanting more of her allusions. A couple on my right turned. I rattled my ice cubes their way till they looked elsewhere.

An hour later, things had slowed down. Erik, seated on a buffet table, held court among the ten or so guests left at the other end of the living room. He was talking with his hands about technology and globalization. I caught bits and pieces: " . . . didn't reduce the gap between haves and have-nots . . . the incestuous connectivity . . . a perverse interface . . . believe it or not, they gave business class a high out of disruption . . ."

I stopped listening and squatted by the fireplace. Most of the furniture had been removed, which made Kevin's living room look ridiculously large for New York. One of the framed photos above my head, on the mantel, showed their family with the Clintons in Chappaqua. Hillary looked at Erik's father—her signature you-got-me laugh on her face—while Kevin, on his knees, petted a Lab with Chelsea. Then I turned to my left and saw Kevin in the flesh, seated by himself, taking his right shoe and sock off, and I thought of the coincidence of two people taking their socks off in front of me within twenty-four hours.

"Marathon training is killing me." Kevin massaged his foot.

Even though he was seated, you could tell that he was six-three, six-four. I saw Erik in him. "What time do you run?" I asked.

"Before work. I'm in the park by seven," Kevin said.

"And what time do you go to bed?"

"I try for elevenish." He stretched his toes. "But these days I am not that good at it. We're in the middle of an Avastin me-too due diligence, and it's running us around the clock."

Two bow-tied women asked Erik to move so they could clean the table.

"Stop showing off your foot size," a guy from Erik's circle yelled to Kevin from across the living room. "It doesn't work!"

"Hey, try training on triple-E 13," Kevin shouted back at him.

"I bet they're broken in by now." Kevin's friend walked over. He looked at me: "He's been in the same stinky sneakers since Wharton."

"He's been in the same pleated pants since Wharton," a woman joined in. "And they have to go."

"I need the pleats, Kimberley. Need the space. Otherwise I feel constricted," Kevin said, and winked.

I grabbed the lion's head on the fireplace and pulled myself up. "It's been a long day," I told Kevin. "I gotta head home."

Kevin stood up, half-barefoot. "Captain Stathis! It was good to see you. Hey—" he squeezed my triceps. "There's some biotech stuff I want to bounce by you. We should get together."

"Anytime," I said. "And thanks for tonight. Fun."

Erik was still binge-talking. He looked my way and made a military salute.

I raised my eyebrows and walked out.

In the cab, Erik's good-bye kicked off a lecture in my head from Alkis about "plateau-equals-failure" frustration. I was ready to call it a night, but the booze in me questioned my plan. "What happens when I'm not there is irrelevant to me." Another Alkis-aphorism that I found challenging in New York. Wanting something to go my way, I decided to ditch Paul and Soho House.

Half an hour and an Ambien later, I was backwashing a beer on the patio when I heard Erik skipping up the stairs. The door creaked and banged, and I saw him—he didn't say a word walking in—pick up some paper from the coffee table. He yawned, and with his free hand he reached the top of the patio door, stretching out his shirt, making visible the thin line of hair that reached down from his belly button. Unlike me, he was still as lean as he had been when we met in France.

"You didn't go out with Paul," Erik said, checking both sides of Zemar's postcard.

"I didn't know you were coming."

He let go of the door. "Interesting," he said, and Frisbee'd the card to the sofa. "Why? Were you expecting someone else?"

"Would that've been a problem?"

His body language changed as he walked by me to his plants.

I felt the Alkis-plateau again. Slouching in my chair, I knocked over my beer bottle and sent it rolling to his pots. Erik picked it up. Then he turned and looked at me. "Are you high?" he asked.

"Will you answer me?" I insisted.

"Yes, it would have been a problem," he replied, impatiently. "You're my bud, right?" He bent over his plants again.

"I'm your *bud*? What's that? 'Cause I'm done trying to interpret what you mean," I said. "Fuck that," I whispered.

"Then go to bed," Erik said, feeling the leaves, sticking his hands in the soil.

"Why? You horny?"

"I lost my wood when I saw you with Paul. Plus I don't wanna get anything on your High Line towel."

I stood up, holding on to the back of my chair. "Right, of course. The High Line, our dead moose."

Erik stopped nursing. "You're a fucking mess. What did you take? Ambien?"

"You can't change the subject on me twice."

"Fine." He stepped toward me, and our faces leveled. "Tell Paul and Andrea that the wait at St. Vincent's is an hour long, while their cash goes to a rusty railroad, which—"

"*Paul's* cash?"

"*Which* is the roof to the homeless whom you guys will push to Jersey after you're done with your renovation."

"Is that your worry?" I laughed. "'Cause homeless'll come back. They always do."

"No, *you're* my worry. You talk safety on the streets, then you run amok with your pills at the Standard. You use the fear of developers so Barry and Diane can sell more shoes and ad space."

"Maybe you can talk some sense into them at your parents' parties," I said softly, which made the sound of the incoming text on my cell more acute.

"Wanna check that? It might be your new pen pal, Zemar."

"You love me?" I said.

He stared in disbelief, not moving.

"I fucking love you," I said. "Do you love me?" I reached for his shoulder, but he struck my hand down, soil flying from his hands, sobering me up.

"Look at you. Smart and *pathetic*. Actually, no, you're dangerous. You take something bad and you turn it into a joke. You *masturbate* through simplicity."

I felt like I was at the end of a rush. "Then it won't stick, will it?" I said. "But here's what does: masturbators like your brother bragging about their dick size."

"Swear to God, leave Kevin out of this."

"Oh yeah? Tell me, how is his size any different from your dad's money he inherited? Or did he work for his dick?"

His fists formed.

"What?" I shouted. "You don't *look* at me? 'Cause I talk money? What the fuck you gonna do when you have to split half a billion with your brother? *Huh?*"

"You Greek piece of *shit!*"

I felt the cement burning my back, the soil from his hands scrubbing my neck, the metallic taste of blood as his watch sliced my lip, happy Ambien flashes of me swimming with my sister in the Aegean, sleeping with Erik in Normandy. He locked my neck with his elbow. I got his stomach from the side and saw his fist coming down on my face, suddenly stopping midair.

"*Come on, you dick!*" I yelled.

"You're not worth my punch." He spit hard on my face. His liquid fogged up everything.

PART II

After Erik

TEN

July 2006

THERE'S A HEAT WARNING OUT," the driver says as we cruise along the Jersey Turnpike back to Manhattan.

"Got any limo-bar peanuts?" Justin asks him.

The driver studies Justin in the rearview mirror. There's no bar in the car.

Justin glances at his watch. "It's after nine. I need a burger, boss," he tells me. "I need some alcohol immunity before I get to those girls downtown. Wanna come along?"

I get that Friday-night air in his voice, but it's Wednesday, which reminds me of his calling card—martial arts, partying, and seventeen-year-old girls—and the fact that we have nothing in common.

I reach for my cell phone and speed-dial the office. I get Andrea's voice mail and I start summarizing the presentation we just wrapped up. It was my first big pitch without a VP in tow, so I work in a couple of self-deprecating expressions, Washington's favorite way of signaling confidence and comfort when describing a kick-ass meeting: " . . . if I could still think straight at the time . . ." I hear myself babbling, " . . . which, of course, was the most unintelligent thing I could have said . . ." By the time I hang up, I'm disoriented. It may be the haze or just my exhaustion—I've already put in forty, fifty hours this week. I rest my head back and fall in and out of sleep.

"Boss, the girls are fun," Justin insists. "Tatiana is *nuts*. You should totally come."

I have a slight fever and I need a drink, badly. I worry about the note I got yesterday that I have to vacate my sublet by the end of the month, and about the fact that I have been officially and irrevocably beaten out of a four-year on-again-off-again relationship, when I was always on. I haven't slept ten hours since Sunday, trapped in an Ambien drowsiness that I have come to like; it dulls the pain some. I don't want to talk to anyone, and I definitely don't want to hear how good I still have it.

"Not a hundred percent," I tell Justin, but the idea of being alone scares me too. Numbing myself and watching others is how I deal with rejection.

Justin faces me. "You owned the room today, Stathis. You were technical but philosophical. I think they really liked us."

"They were easy on us," I mumble.

"Nah, you nailed that Black-Scholes question. Andrea would've frozen. How do I get to be a manager like you two years out of business school, man?"

It's been three years, and his sucking up is pre-drinks, so he's trespassing. I look at his tight suit. "Wear a fucking suit," I say.

"It's McQueen," he shoots back, fingering his sleeve.

"I know how much you make," I say, looking out my window.

"Barneys Warehouse! Know what, I paid for it like fifteen seconds before the blackout."

"And?" I don't get it.

"The registers went *down*, boss."

I can see him, all proud, paying for his *Esquire* kill seconds before New York time-traveled back a hundred years. I'd tell him to try Dunhill next, but I'm getting desperate for downtime. So I bring up martial arts—he does Brazilian jujitsu for two hours a day—banking on ninety seconds of zoning out while he talks.

THE OUTDOOR STAIRWAY LEADING INTO the basement sake bar on Ninth Street is jammed. I smell caramel and dog shit from the garbage of the coffee shop next door.

"Our friends are inside," Justin shouts at the doorman, but he doesn't care.

I'm sweating like a pig. My shirt sticks to me in this muddy, gross New York weather that braces scrawny East Village kids while suffocating the rest of us. I pull my tie off and stuff it in my pants pocket.

Inside, we move through a dark bar area. At the end a Japanese curtain is lifted, revealing an even darker vault-like space, the whole thing no larger than a New York one-bedroom, filled with claustrophobic booths, graffiti, and people with silver rings in the wrong places. We stand out in our suits, but no one looks at us.

Justin sheds his glove-tight jacket in one move. The collar of his shirt is the only thing not glued to him as he snakes to the last table, where two girls are sitting. "This is Kate and Tatiana," Justin says, beaming. "This is Stathis, my project manager."

"Good to meet you," I say.

Kate smiles and looks at me for a good three seconds. She says nothing.

"Take your jacket off, Stathis?" Tatiana says, and brings a piece of white fish to her mouth. She can't be more than nineteen. I try to figure her out before answering her command-question. A hundred pounds, olive skin, there's an appetite in her green eyes I've only seen on horny peasants in my village in Greece. She swallows and waits for my reaction as soy sauce drips from her hands, while her stare says: This is my table, motherfucker.

I mumble something even I can't hear and sit down opposite her. She's in a man's black suit and a T-shirt that says "Baghdad" under a Disneyland logo. She takes her jacket off. I can't believe she's doing this with sauce still on her fingers, but she does, bored, as if it's a routine. I can see everyone's nipples around the table. She has ridiculously perfect breasts.

For the next fifteen minutes Tatiana devours three hundred

dollars' worth of sake and bizarre meta-sushi plates while she flirts with Justin, talks to Kate, and stares at me.

"You know I'm quietly judging you," she says after our third eye lock.

"Beg your pardon?"

"Seen *Magnolia*?" Kate steps in. "It's a quote from the movie."

I take my jacket off too, to show ease—something I only do in client meetings. "What do you do in New York?" I ask Kate. She's beautiful in an American way, freckled.

"Where I come from, this is an impolite question," Tatiana says.

"Tatiana grew up in Aix-en-Provence and Laurel Canyon," Justin volunteers.

I nod, though I haven't been to either. I'm not sure why he's sharing this. What's he trying to explain? Her aggressiveness, her looks, or her taste in movies? There's definitely something moving in her soup.

"Yes, on holidays!" Kate laughs.

"I was at boarding school in England," Tatiana explains. "And Kate's a stylist." She adds this casually, as though my "impolite" question is suddenly forgiven. "Kate is all about the electronic-bohemian look. She's a genius."

"I just don't want to work for people who lunch," Kate says, and kisses Tatiana quickly on the lips. "I don't want to play on people's insecurities. Honestly, I want to make luxury a small fraction of anyone's wardrobe."

"Isn't that what it is already?" I ask.

"God, no!" Tatiana yells with a rhetoric-giggle. "It's so unbalanced! You shouldn't have to buy *only* indulgence. You can use uniqueness, suspense. Why don't we see current affairs in fashion? I want to be inspired by the Middle East crisis. Reality. Crime. Seriously!"

I'm confused, and it's not just my exhaustion. "Isn't the purpose of luxury to escape reality?" I object, but Tatiana shakes her head.

"No, no, *no!*" she insists. "That's exactly what we're talking about. We need to redefine it. We're talking luxury that everybody, and I mean *everybody*, can use for self-esteem. It's about reality, not escape."

I have no clue what we are talking about. My mind drifts to my mother's gold cross and wedding band, the only jewelry she ever wore. I remember her probing a gutted sea bass to find her ring after she lost it while sorting my father's catch, and me spotting it in his nets, saving the day.

Some nigiri lands in front of me and I'm back to Tatiana. The girls are already off on a "new New York" discussion. How "all these glass condos will bring back Gotham." They talk about how the "best views look *into*, not out of, the units," about bird shit on the glass that will make peeping in on people "like watching old damaged footage."

" . . . spiderweb-looking window cracks . . ."

" . . . most interesting suicides . . ."

I feel spent. I understand enough to know that they'll keep cruising through topics for the rest of the night.

"How is our godmother?" Tatiana suddenly asks Kate.

"Oh my God! You won't believe this," Kate says. "She's hosting this new reality show in Spain. It's insane, honestly. They take old, mentally retarded people and make them sing and dance to sleazy songs. Totally out of control. Live, with hundreds of sixteen-year-olds screaming."

Tatiana's eyes widen. "Love it!"

"I thought you were into artsy movies," Justin says. "Like *Magnolia*."

Tatiana reaches for his hand. "Justin, babe . . ." she says. There's polite contempt in her voice. "The only difference is from post-, okay, apocalyptic, to post-postmodernism. Remember the frog scene in the movie? The plague scene? What's the difference from the reality show? In Spain, the singers are plagued people, when the real plague is all those kids encouraging them and making them stars. That's where the real art is, the performance. Really."

Justin looks at me quickly. He takes down his sake like water. Suddenly I feel protective of him, which I've never felt before.

"Do they shoot in asylums or do they escort them into studios?" I ask.

Tatiana's eyes lock on me. I can see she's about to lose it. "You know, Stathis? The writers that you read have not written a single word in *decades* to criticize TV commercials showing chimpanzees in dresses drinking tea. It's 2006 now, and we talk about it. And that's shocking to you. Makes your nipples stiff."

My first thought is, *I don't know what to argue first.* My second thought is, *I don't have to. All I want is to sit back and be distracted.*

IN A TRIBECA BUILDING WE walk down the hallway that leads to the loft Tatiana shares with a photographer. To our right are life-size cutouts of Saddam Hussein and Martha Stewart, smiling and posing in front of a wall with dozens of Gucci and Nokia logos. I hear Mick Jagger singing "You see I bounce back quicker than most" from inside the loft, and I'm both relieved and scared that it won't be just the four of us.

"Is your roommate here?" Justin asks Tatiana.

"No," she says, confused, and opens the door.

The music and the AC burst through as one shock wave. I walk in and fall into a post-sake take-it-all-in state. A canopy bed at the center of the loft sits on an island of beach sand. It's surrounded by freestanding floor-to-ceiling photographs of a toddler smoking, slum houses, and a portrait of Edgar Bronfman Jr. flanked by two other CEOs. A gigantic puzzle of *The Scream* is half-finished and glued to a wall like mold. Its remaining pieces, thousands of them, are scattered between clothes, Polaroids, glue traps, pizza boxes, and jewelry. There's a real or fake Mao leaning against the bedroom wall that's been vandalized with mascara and earrings. Strangely, I don't see any sand scattered out of place.

I sit on a sofa surrounded by kilims, arabesque art, and large ashtrays—I recognize a couple from hotels I've lived in. Across from me, hanging on the wall, is a leather costume, a woman's one-piece bathing-suit-shaped outfit that looks like a motorcycle. It actually has steering handles with rearview mirrors built onto it. Justin touches one of its mirrors, which is tilted to face upward, and then puts his finger on his tongue. He picks up a rolled twenty-dollar bill from the floor and goes into an all-out hounding around the coffee table.

"Is this your mother's?" Kate fiddles with the motorcycle-looking dress.

"Thierry gave it to her when she went to Cannes," Tatiana says. "She hated it, so she gave it to me."

"Adore!" Kate says, stunned. "When are we going to LA to raid her wardrobe again?"

"Stop obsessing about my mom! I'm the beautiful one," Tatiana says, and walks to the fridge. "There's no sake, so we're having tequila," she shouts over her shoulder. "Stathis, this is a mobile sofa. Push the pillow all the way back so the cushion wraps around you."

I try it. The three of them switch into production mode automatically. Tatiana prepares shots, Justin sorts out the three walled iPods, and Kate goes through the large wooden box on the coffee table. She empties US Open tickets, jeweled sex toys—or just jewelry—shutoff notices from ConEd, and pictures of Tatiana with the Dalai Lama, Monica Lewinsky, and her look-alike mother, until she finds the two tiny plastic bags she was searching for. She waves one of the coke bags to me with a *Eureka!* smile on her face. I nod and look away. Through the bedroom door I see what must be an Oscar statuette on the floor, peeking out beneath dirty laundry. Then a screen starts to unfold slowly from the ceiling, with a live version of *Heartbeat City* playing on it. Tatiana gives Justin a massive coffee-table book with Brezhnev kissing Erich Honecker on the mouth on its cover. Justin starts to cut cocaine on the propaganda kiss and talks about Bungalow 8.

HALF-NAKED ON THE FLOOR, JUSTIN ropes his shirt around Tatiana's long hair. She snorts two lines and then tries to do a tequila shot off his abs. Justin laughs, and tequila rushes, pauses, and rushes again from his stomach onto the sapphire rug.

"Are you having fun?" Tatiana asks me, resting her head on my lap, her feet on Justin's chest.

"Did you do the graffiti on the Warhol?" I reply.

"Stathis, you don't really own art unless you make it your own. Same way you don't really own your sofa until you spill something on it," she says, and she begins to unbutton my shirt while Justin rubs her feet, kisses and makes out with them.

Kate leans over and helps Justin out of his pants. Then she whispers something in Tatiana's ear and the two of them get up and go to the bedroom.

I look at some framed lace panties on the wall, trying not to think about how many work rules I've broken so far. I have to review the bastard.

Justin, in his boxers, paces around the loft. "Got Viagra or Levitra on you, boss?"

I stay silent, a license we both know I burned some two hours ago. But Justin's antsy. "I've done seven big ones. How the fuck am I gonna fuck her now?"

"Sorry, I didn't ask for any on our way out."

"That's dick!" Justin says. "Cialis?" he asks with a childlike hope.

I spot a Dartmouth logo on his boxers.

I'M LYING HALF-NAKED ON THE canopy bed with sand all over my sweaty feet. Tatiana, next to me, tries on my tie as a bra. "I wear only men's clothes," she explains.

"Things in common."

She cuts lines on a bed tray while the speakers sing "must have me confused / with some other guy," mixed with lusty giggles from another iPod. Across the loft, in the bedroom, I see Justin, naked, pushing a shiny dildo into Kate; I realize it's the Oscar. They moan-laugh. Tatiana takes off my tie and puts two bumps on her tits. I do both of them and suck the leftovers. The coke, bitter, slides down my throat. Tatiana wants me to take off my pants, try on her Disneyland/Baghdad T-shirt.

"Why?" I ask.

"I want it stretched," she says, and snorts a line.

"I don't sleep with girls."

"I'm . . . I'm twenty."

"I like guys," I say.

"I don't believe you. You're depressed." Then, "My room-mate moved out. Move in with me."

I don't laugh or say no, which is utterly insane. I studied physics and have an MBA, a fucking job. I wire money to my parents on the fifteenth of each month. I ran into decadence before but managed it. So why do I feel like I just landed where I'm supposed to be: with the totally flawed? "I don't want to be alone," I hear myself saying.

"What is his name?" Tatiana asks, and I hear compassion through cocaine.

ELEVEN

WITH OBVIOUS AND DELIBERATE LABOR, the cabdriver doles out one-dollar bills to change my twenty. I'm late. "Keep fifteen," I say, and he briskly hands me a five that appears out of nowhere.

I jump out into a cool New York evening and onto the square pavement off Sixth and Bleecker. About fifty people are dining at a flock of outdoor tables, fenced in by another twenty who are waiting to be seated. I catch Italian, Spanish, and broken English.

Tatiana, in an oversize white shirt, probably mine, sits in the eye of the storm. She touches the lower arm of a dark-haired guy who's with her. Her long brown hair hides her smile, but I see those large green eyes spotting me. She lets go of his arm.

"My VP has issues," I say when I reach them. "I'm sorry." I lean over Tatiana and she lets me kiss her on the lips, but she's all business.

"This is my roommate, Stathis," she says. "Ray is my train-er. He just came back from Iraq. He was in combat there."

"Excellent" escapes my mouth, and I immediately wonder what exactly *excellent* means here.

"Hello!" Ray stands up and shakes my hand, which is unheard of below Fourteenth Street. An inch shorter than me, lean but solid, he has a rude boy's face and two days' beard.

"Welcome back," I say, sitting down across from him, Tatiana on my left. Her eyes are fixed on him, but so are mine.

"I've been back for three months now, but thank you." He grants me a surprisingly innocent smile.

Desperate for post-Command vodka, I scan the pavement for a waiter. When one comes by, Tatiana calls out eight or nine plates, all in Mediterranean languages and single words: " . . . osso bucco, *controfiletto*, *croquetas*, *gamberoni*, two vodka martinis, and a bottle of Cortese." Ray orders whiskey. I don't say a word—don't have to. I just sit back and watch Tatiana's cell phone vibrate nonstop, practically crawling around the table.

"I didn't know you worked out," I tell Tatiana after our waiter leaves. "Which gym do you guys go to?"

"No . . ." She shakes her head. "Ray trains in a private space on Perry Street."

I look at Ray's biceps under his white T-shirt and try to remember the last time I worked out. Probably before I moved in with Tatiana, a good month ago. I tried doing push-ups at her loft once, but the smell of her bathroom— of puke, permanently—got to me. I'm not entirely sure whether Yolima, our housecleaner, actually exists, or whether the sheets on my canopy bed have ever been changed.

"How long have you two been training?" I ask.

They check with each other. "We had some cancellations," Ray says at last.

"We've worked out once. Anything else, Stathis?" Tatiana says, and loosens my tie with one jerk.

She peeks at her watch, which I notice is my watch, the same watch that Erik once borrowed. "It's stressful. I'm afraid I'll lose it," he told me when he returned it to me the following day. Now I wish he'd kept the stupid Rolex. Maybe I would see him wearing it if we ran into each other, in that happenstance way that people play out in their minds when they go through breakups with no closure. My problem: I don't seem to be able to stomach things and move on. Three months on, all my calls to Erik unanswered, and I still don't hit the gym or choose my own food in restaurants. I don't make decisions, so Tatiana, my new "higher power and concierge"—yes, fuck you, Erik—makes them for me.

I spend my nights in restaurants and clubs now, or at Tatiana's loft listening to coked-up nonsense from her boyfriend—of the week—her schoolmates, crashers, Black-Berry'ed drug dealers, cousins, and "coworkers." I don't even know what exactly she does for a living. Is she an actress? Model? Stylist? Nothing? "Tati's a collector of all trades," Kate, a permanent standby, joked once, but not really. "She has an appetite for food, clothes, *people*. She has an appetite for adopting, like she did with *you*." Kate laughed at me, or with me, the latest member of Tatiana's surrogate family. "No, seriously," Kate insisted. "What interests me is how Tatiana sorts through New York. She's an artist. A *life* artist."

Yellow and green dishes arrive, sparkling in olive oil. Tatiana speed-fires through three plates of shrimp and fettuccine while she rants about movies, Nokia gadgets, and beer. Works for me; I'm happy zoning out.

"You know that, right?" Tatiana suddenly asks me, as if checking to see whether I'm paying attention.

"Er, yes, love beer," I mumble.

"I'm talking about Stella *McCartney*, Stathis." She turns to Ray: "There's nothing Stathis doesn't get. It's just that he's a bit preoccupied right now. He's heartbroken. But he'll be better later tonight."

Why? "Later?" I ask, but Tatiana ignores me.

"Ray, how long did you say you were overseas?" she asks.

"I was on active duty for two years."

She goes tenderly for his hand, but at the last second she picks up her vibrating cell phone instead. "My lover!" she yells, answering. "When did you get in? . . . Oh baby, are you jet-lagged? . . . How was the set?" She laughs. "I'm at Da Silvano . . . with Stathis . . . roommate . . . of course . . . *When I think about you I touch myself* . . . Miss you *more*! . . . Okay, I'll see you in a bit."

"Who was that?" I ask with a full mouth.

"My mother," Tatiana says, casually. "She just got into town. I think she's depressed. We have to go see her." She reaches for Ray's hand, and then mine. "*Please* . . ."

I try to read Ray's reaction to the mother-love chitchat, but he just keeps sipping his whiskey.

"Is she staying with us?" I ask.

"No. She's at Soho House," Tatiana says, and gets up. "I'm sorry, I'll be right back." She bolts inside the restaurant.

For the next ten minutes, she'll be throwing up two hundred dollars' worth of pasta, which means that I have to play with the army. I look at his thick, bushy hair—probably compensating for years of crew cuts—his on-and-off abashed smile, and I wonder why he enlisted. I wonder whether he's a Republican, and which square state he's from, but I don't care enough to ask—I'll probably see Montana about one and a half times in my life. Plus, his ease reminds me of stupid Erik.

"Is she any good?" I open.

His childlike smile disappears. "She's very flexible," Ray replies.

Jarhead here gives as good as he gets—I'll show you flex, buddy. "Why'd you join the army?" I demand.

"I wanted to be in the Marine Corps Reserve."

"What did you do in Iraq?"

"I was a combat rifleman instructor. For the infantry."

"I don't know what that means," I lie.

Ray looks right at me. Why do I want to pick a fight? Ain't I exhausted enough?

"Land soldiers," he says. "You fight on foot. Face-to-face."

"You must've seen some intense stuff over there."

"You have no idea."

I tilt my head, unsatisfied.

"What?" Ray asks.

"Try me," I say.

"There's savagery that you don't get in your movies."

My movies? I saw *Occupation: Dreamland* when I lived at the Mercer. I have seen your fucking *life*, redneck. "Do you support the invasion?" I ask, and suck down what's left of my martini.

"To some extent."

"And which part's that?" I spit back.

"We removed a butcher and his gang."

"Even if we butcher our way through to get to them?"

"You'd think there are better ways," Ray says with a shrug. "But you can't do things by halves."

"War is *failure*," I say, louder than necessary. "You support a revolution from within. You don't invade, you *never* invade. You wanna be a catalyst, not a bully." I pause and take a breath. Why am I playing Erik? I don't give a fuck about Iraq, really.

"I like your theory. Tatiana tells me you're Greek. Were you in the army?"

Bitch. He had me there. "Twice. Once in Greece and once here."

He does his timid smile again, mixed with *I'll-let-you-off-the-hook-now*. What's up with the charity?

"Do you want another drink?" I offer. "She may take a few."

"Sure. So I guess we are going to meet her mother."

"I guess so."

"She's beautiful," Ray says, playing with his empty glass. "She has, like . . . two Oscars?"

"One. But I think Tati's father has two."

Ray looks confused. "Tatiana's father is also an actor?" he asks.

"He's a musician, and a director or screenwriter, or something."

He rolls his eyes. "I know he's a *musician*, ha! I hear they're suing each other. Her parents, I mean."

"Don't know, maybe." I turn and pig out on a crazy forkful of pasta. "Ask your client," I say with linguine hanging from my mouth onto my chin. Red specks hit my tie.

"Copyrights and defama——" Ray stops midsentence, as Tatiana is already behind him, messing with his hair. A quick throw-up, apparently.

"Okay, she's the dumbest person in the world, but she's still my mom." Tatiana sits and undoes my already loose, sauced tie. She rolls it up and puts it in her bag and starts to fiddle with my collar, caringly. "My godmother is here too, who's *insane*! Stathis, my angel, will you pay for me? I have no cash and I forgot my PIN," Tatiana says, worriedly, and answers her phone. "Are you wearing your iguana belt?" she asks as she picks up.

A waiter passes, and I hand him my credit card.

Ray goes through his jeans pockets.

"I got this one," I say.

"No, here." He slides two twenties across the table.

I don't touch the bills. Tension builds as the cash lies between us. I pretend to eavesdrop on Tatiana's babble while I think of Erik, the times I passed him cash under the table. The vet glances at the forty. I don't wanna take the goddamn bills. I look at the cover of the magazine under Tatiana's bag—an actor in his briefs says, "I learned how to grow up."

"For drinks," Tatiana whispers, and stuffs the cash in her bag. Then, on her phone, "No, I'm listening. Samsung for girls, BlackBerry for boys. Got it."

NEWSSTAND PICTURES OFTEN LIE, BUT Tatiana is her mother's clone. We find her sitting in the lotus position on a rooftop bed by the Soho House pool, playing with the cross pendant she wears over a T-shirt that says "Don't Talk to Me." She's surrounded by women whose body language appears to harbor her.

Tatiana jumps into the harem and kisses her mother, basically makes out with her. "This is Teresa, my *mom*!" Tatiana says, and they kiss again on the lips before Tatiana moves on to an old woman who has gold hair and more wrinkles than Yoda, and then to two identical well-built redheads.

"I'm Tatiana's mom," Teresa says, flirting with her daughter, who's now resting her head on her mother's lap.

I pick a satellite chair.

Ray sits by the old lady. She wears a massive bejeweled skull on her ring finger. Her T-shirt, matching Teresa's, says "Fast Fuck."

"I'm Tatiana's godmother and I'm from Spain," the old lady says without a trace of accent. She already looks bored with our invasion as she taps Teresa's hand. "I don't want you to be onstage looking all costumed. It's Madison Square Garden," she tells her.

"It's a gold jacket," Teresa says, combing her daughter's hair. "Think Michael Jackson, but the white years."

"It's embroidered," the old lady argues. "This is New York. We should go svelte, black. Something oxidized or sci-fashion."

"I've done ghoulish. It's not me," Teresa pushes back.

"Hey, movie star," Tatiana says to her mother, sitting up. "You look sexy no matter what you wear." She turns to Ray: "I hate her fucking body."

"You have my body," her mother tells her, calmly.

"Which marine division?" I hear one of the redheads ask Ray.

"Oh, don't be jealous. You're still our favorite tomboy," says the godmother, hugging Tatiana.

Tatiana pulls her mother into a three-way hug. "This is God!" Tatiana says, and kisses her godmother. "And this is Mother Teresa!" She kisses her mom. Mild laughter goes around.

"I had a friend in Mossad," Ray tells the redhead.

"Show me your tattoo," God orders him. "Tattoo is the new couture," she explains to Teresa.

Ray lifts his sleeve all the way to his shoulder. "It's an oceanic whitetip, my favorite shark," he says, feeling his own arm.

"Why?" Teresa asks him.

"He's a loner. He patrols the oceans. He doesn't care about the reefs. The most independent, unpredictable shark."

"He?"

"Have you seen one?"

"I swam with one in the Gulf of Aden during military exercises. It's a thick fish with long, rounded fins. I thought a plane was coming toward me. Sharks will circle you from fifty feet away before they come to check you out. He came straight up to us. Fearless."

"I like your face," God tells Ray. "Come by the studio to have some portraits taken."

"Thank you, ma'am."

"Have you killed a man?"

"No, ma'am."

"Have you seen people die?"

"I have."

"And how do you feel about all this happening because of Monica?" God asks him.

"Monica?"

"Monica Lewinsky!" she says, and coughs like a barking dog.

"I *like* Monica," Tatiana shouts.

"Monica's a historic *figure*," God squawks.

Is God high? Just weird? What is it about wealth and fame, or whatever she's selling, that makes it impossible to give up? Stop yakking, move to Florida, and be a grandmother, for God's sake . . .

The cell phone next to Teresa cheeps "The Killing Moon." Teresa throws a glance at it and ignores it. "Lapsang souchong," she says to a passing waiter. "With candied ginger. No sugar. And a drop of cream."

"You put milk in your herbal?" Tatiana pouts.

You put cocaine in your pussy.

"She's the reason Gore distanced himself from Clinton," God lectures us. "Which gave us Bush and Iraq, and a hundred thousand people dead."

"Ma'am, the fatalities—"

"*Listen!*" God raises her palm, and her skull ring creates a glowing comet's tail. "Clinton was riding his bike in the Oval Office during a tight race. 'I stand in front of you as my own man . . .' My *ass!*" God yells, coughs, and starts to shake, three feet from the pool. One of the redheads stands up, but God shrugs her off. "Look where *that* got us. And that embryo he picked to run with him, just because he had bitched about Monica."

"Who's Gore? Who the fuck is Clinton?" Teresa murmurs.

I can't help but stare at her. She's a knockout. When I'm busted with a *thank-you-but-that's-enough* smile, I stretch back in my seat to browse the people at the bar. Surprise—Paul, my b-school mate, is doing shots with a couple of guys. I get up and slowly walk toward him.

"What about Elián González then?" someone yells, and I hear laughter coming from the harem. By the time I make it to the other side of the terrace, Paul's by himself.

"I have not seen you here before," Paul says calmly, but he looks at me perplexed, if not alarmed.

"I am not a member, Paul. You know that. And it's good to fuck you too."

We sort of hug.

"So, what they say is true," Paul says.

"What do they say?" I ask.

"That you're partying hard these days."

"I think that what I'm doing *these* days"—Paul's code for my being dumped—"is pretty boring," I say.

"Come on . . . palling around with movie stars . . ."

"Care to join us?" I ask unenthusiastically.

"No. Not yet. I know how things work."

"No clue what you're talking about," I say, which is not one hundred percent bull. His father was a prime minister. Don't these people have a right of passage? A secret code that allows them to acknowledge one another within their Division One?

"But we're all glamorous now," Paul whispers, looking behind me at Teresa and company. "Who's the model?"

"He's not a model. He's a vet," I say.

"In Chelsea?"

"No. He is a vet from Iraq," I explain.

"*Serious?*" Paul laughs and looks at me, excited. "Is he Teresa's new boy? Has she filed for bankruptcy yet?"

"No. I don't know her." I look around. The deck is getting rowdy. "Where did your friends go?"

"They are colleagues," Paul corrects me.

"Are they off to mail anthrax letters to Condé Nast, then?"

"Good one," Paul says, but his mind is elsewhere. He stops gawking at Teresa and looks at me. "Let's have a shot of tequila," he says, and I nod. He gestures the V sign to the bartender.

"So, how are you? Really?" Paul asks me.

I double nod.

"Right," Paul says. "How's work?"

"Work's work."

"That's a start," he says.

"And an end." I do my shot. Paul does the same.

"Stathis, mate . . ." His voice is off. "It's funny that I ran into you tonight."

"Why?" I ask.

"'Cause I'm meeting Erik," Paul says quickly, and I want to make sure that he's joking, but blood sprints to my stomach. "With Warren," Paul adds.

I have to fight to keep my cool. "What? He, here? . . . Why? Warren? Who? . . ."

"Stathis, brother, I'm—"

"I'm *not* your brother."

"Listen. I got in touch with Warren when we did that Middle East story, right after we launched AccostingDubya. He's a cable news anchor. Erik was working on something similar for *The Nation*. We only met a couple of times . . ."

Paul continues speaking, but I'm deaf. I remember seeing Erik chatting with the news guy at his brother's party the night we broke up, and my guts spin like a washing machine. I turn to look for Tatiana, but there are too many people between us.

"Are you doing a number on me?" I ask Paul.

"What?"

"You met Erik twice and you didn't tell me. Are you doing a number on me?"

"It was a work story—"

"That's *exactly* my point, Paul. There's *always* a story with you."

"Hey!" He grabs my arm.

"*Get . . . the fuck . . . off me*," I say under my breath. My teeth are grinding.

"Stathis!" Paul shouts, but I am already bounding back to my tinseled sense of security.

Tatiana is chatting with a sixteen-year-old girl who is sitting on Ray's lap.

"Oh my God!" the teenager screams. "At Disney our diet was sleep and watch movies. No popcorn." She laughs. "Hi," Minnie Mouse greets me. She looks familiar.

"I'm out of here," I tell Tatiana.

"What happened?" Tatiana stands up. "Baby, take it easy. Let's go to the playroom downstairs for a smoke."

Ray winks at me and pinches the Disney girl. She jumps off his lap, and the four of us walk to the roof elevator.

"I'll take the stairs," I say, scared silly of a face-to-face with Erik. That very moment the elevator doors slide open, and I instinctively look at my BlackBerry. I have two missed calls, one from Alkis and one from my sister. People are still getting out, so I keep browsing my phone. There's a text from Gawel: "Are you stopping by tonight?"

We are inside the elevator, and the damn doors don't want to close. I get cabin fever. Someone presses the wrong button, and different floor numbers light up. What if I bump into Erik as I exit? It's only a one-floor ride, but it takes forever. "Jerk off," I text back to Gawel.

I follow the three of them into a glass-sealed playroom that looks like a gas chamber. Somewhere in the cloud I see Paul's employees, playing pool, smoking. They check out the Disney girl. Ray starts rolling a joint and I tell Tatiana that Erik is coming. "Good!" Tatiana says, but I can't breathe right, I can't follow her. She kisses me quickly on the lips. "Good for you!" she repeats. "Don't worry, we'll make out when he shows up."

Sweat drips down my back. I look enviously at Ray next to me, in his white T-shirt and jeans. I bet my suit makes me look like an accountant. He passes me the joint. I inhale all I can, and I'm in a Baz Luhrmann video—Paul's dogs accosting me, the Gin Blossoms screaming "Hey Jealousy," and the buzz of Gawel calling my cell phone.

Teresa walks in with one of her reds in tow.

"Come to Bungalow with me," the Disney girl begs, putting her hands around Teresa's waist. The movie star makes a Cleopatra pose—nose up, hand above her head—which makes the girl laugh a silent laugh and Tatiana's face turn spiteful.

"Only if my daughter lets me," Teresa says, and after freeing herself of Disney, she walks over to Tatiana. Tatiana doesn't really acknowledge her mother, but Teresa spoons her anyway.

Paul comes out of the elevator with a group of guys behind him. Warren's pink face stands out as they charge into the lounge area. I see that sober, familiar walk next to him. I only see Erik from behind. I know that blue shirt. For a second Warren puts his hand on Erik's shoulder, leans in, and says something to him. Erik pauses and listens. And then they are gone, into the main room. Did I really see that? My mind refuses to accept it. The Gin Blossoms' yelling "'cause all I really want is to be with you" is maddening.

Ray offers Teresa the joint.

She looks at it. "I like thick fingers," she says.

Ray laughs. "I can't even text," he says, and places the joint between her lips.

Teresa peeks at the pool table and inhales. "Tatiana, why don't we all go to Bungalow?" she asks her daughter while studying Ray. Then Ray passes me the joint and I fucking finish it.

The panic is over; pain lunges in. It's one of those moments when you know that your life has changed, without needing to explain or admit to yourself why. But I do—I have to understand where I messed up. All the things I did and the things I didn't do, all the opportunities I had or did not have to be Warren, to be walking next to Erik in Soho House. All the times I didn't play my cards right. The years wasted. And for once I wish I were my father or Jeevan. Instead, here I am, too educated to be a fisherman, too Greek to be Warren, now throwing good time after bad, watching Tatiana being a stupid brat, alone. Suddenly all I want is to escape, to get fucked up and fuck away.

"I need a shirt," Tatiana tells Teresa. "Give me your room key."

"I'll come with you, sexy," her mother says.

"*No!*" Tatiana yells at her mother. "We'll meet you at Bungalow."

FIFTEEN MINUTES LATER RAY IS naked next to me on Teresa's bed. There's one more whitetip between his waist and his thigh, and coke all over his fingertips as he plays with Tatiana's pussy.

"I'm not in the vagina business," I tell Ray.

"Yo!" He laughs. "Fuck off! For *real*?"

Tatiana gets on all fours to do a line from her mother's nightstand. I see razor cuts on her inner thighs before I shove my tongue into a bag of coke. The bitter powder races in me, next to the lines from the Gin Blossoms: " . . . you were the best I'd ever had . . ." I kneel behind Ray and push my dusty tongue into his hole right as he starts to fuck Tatiana. He groans and pounds her silly.

TWELVE

October 2006

THERE ARE FOUR OF US around the conference-room table at Command's office in midtown Manhattan. Our squares of networked phones, our slides and laptops and flash drives are spread everywhere as we fine-tune my presentation to the CEO of a biotech company.

"I don't believe in numbers," the senior-senior Partner who sits three feet away from Andrea tells me. "I believe in ranges," he explains, provoking in me an urge to ask him what time it is, or in what conference room we are pitching BioProt. "I want some forward thinking, some real intellectual muscle," the senior-senior goes on, and I feel like I am at dinner with Tatiana's godmother, or at a quantum physics lecture at Stanford. What's wrong with him? Or is my hangover making me hear things?

"Easy!" Justin blurts, and Andrea fires him a *how*-dare-*you* look.

"For Stathis . . ." Justin manages, and the two partners, slowly, their eyes still surveying him, return to their laptops.

"What the fuck is wrong with you?" I instant-message him.

"ICE MC—'Easy,'" Justin types back.

"What???"

"Come on, boss . . . 'This shows real intellectual muscle. Easy' . . . ICE MC's lyrics u were dancing to w/ Tati at Bungalow last night."

"You should get fired!" I type, and close the window.

"Two hours till showtime," Andrea announces after consulting her watch. "Stathis, can you project the master deck from your laptop onto the big screen for me?"

I do.

She looks at the screen with narrowed eyes. She moves her pen in and out of her mouth. "Okay, go to Segmentation."

I do.

"Keep going, keep going . . . There! Stop. Now, can you make the colors in your boxes a bit brighter?"

"I used our color template," I tell Andrea while nodding in the senior-senior's direction.

"I know, I know." Andrea raises her hand, and her Rolex-bracelet combo rattles. "We may go a touch off our colors, but *trust* me, I know BioProt. They drive orange Lamborghinis in LA."

Why are you here, then?

The senior-senior studies the slide on the wall. "As long as we stay Command about it," he cautions.

"Easy," I say, avoiding Justin's face.

My eyes hurt; I don't think I can see the colors on my screen properly. I'm so hungover I don't even remember being at Bungalow last night. I go to Bookmarks and click on Accosting, a link I must have checked twenty times since yesterday, and the site's landing page comes up. I scroll down until I find a picture of Warren leaving a gym, with Erik behind him. It's hard to identify Erik, but I can. There are almost a dozen postings underneath their photo. "Who's that cute guy with Warren?" GiuseppeForever comments. Then Justin coughs artificially and I look up. He waggles his head to the big screen, which shows an almost life-size Warren in his shorts. I smash the power button on my laptop and a complaining shriek comes out.

Andrea jumps out of her seat. "What just *happened*?"

"My laptop crashed. It's very rare, really." I try to smile, but the bitch is delirious. She is raising hell, she wants a backup. Now!

"Justin, go to IT and get a machine in here. Go!" the senior-senior orders.

He tries to calm Andrea down. "We'll be fine," he says reassuringly, and gestures to her Zen position.

She is still upset when at last, and only hesitantly, she goes back to her typing, her face telling us that we are all incompetent and any further screwups will make her cosmetics-billionaire fiancé blacklist Command to a handful of clients.

I unplug the projector from my machine and press the Power button. I open PowerPoint, and then I go back to Accosting. I scroll down Paul's website until photos of Teresa with Ray, in matching sweatshirts, walking, dining, and kissing in the West Village, come up. In one of them, Tatiana and Kate walk behind them. In another, I recognize my back as I hail a cab. The last one shows Ray kissing Tatiana on the cheek as she jumps in the backseat with me. "Teresa, for the boys!" someone commented.

When Teresa started dating Ray a few weeks ago, nobody was surprised. Nobody among us talked about it. Not Tatiana, not once. The fact that Teresa instantly got serious with her twenty-five-year-old trainer, who used to fuck her daughter—and me—seemed part of some pervading momentum. It was as if I was living EBS paranoia again, but now, after Erik, I browse life like a movie that I don't care how it ends.

"Yes!" the senior-senior answers his phone. "No, we are actually good," he says, eyeballing me. "We are about to send it." He laughs. "Oh my God! Did I just reduce myself to a brand manager?" More laughs. "Okay, okay, what will Charles think if he gets the same e-mail as Carter? For fun, tell me . . . humor me . . ." His imbecilic prattle goes on for the ten minutes it takes these Commanders to guess and second-guess who to cc on the simplest e-mail. It's a company-wide sport masked as healthy downtime: who to include or who to bcc. Questions that feed Command's paranoid culture of everyone-suspecting-everyone-else. It's so intrinsic and bankrupt—it lacks a Big Brother centralized efficiency—that it's almost Soviet. I listen to the senior-senior's petty schemes and I can't tell if his problem is stupidity, insecurity, or just fat.

"Washington is here," he says after he hangs up. He puts on his jacket and grabs his papers and laptop. "Stathis, I know we'll have fun with this."

"That's a great three-piece on you," Andrea tells him.

"Mohair. Thank you. I like your necklace."

She gives him a naughty smile as he walks out of the room. "It's *estate*," she says, but the senior-senior is gone.

Andrea looks at me, chastened, and I look at my laptop. Gawel's instant message pops up on my screen. I right-click Unavailable, close Accosting, and go about LA-ing the colors in the segmentation boxes—Andrea loves "French, almost electric blue." But I hear her fingernails tapping on the table. "Stathis, may I bother you for a second?" Her voice sounds strangely attentive.

I look up.

"Have you presented to a CEO before?" she asks.

"Once," I tell her.

"That's what I thought." She exhales. "Stathis, you're obviously a good consultant—that's why we asked you to do the presentation—but do you know how to handle people with real power? I've met CEOs on different occasions—" She stops and starts again. "I mean, what I want to say is, I should give you a few pointers for when you get up there to present."

We are the only two left in the conference room, so I can stare at her as I try to sort her out. Too woman for Washington, too thirsty for Command, she fucks a CEO and wears jewelry to work. I'm actually quite taken by how blind she is to all the WASPiness around us. My hangover makes me charitable, and I want to cue her that we are both Command outliers. "Thank you," I say, and for once I mean it.

"First of all, you don't speak proper English," Andrea says. "You are not a native English speaker, so sometimes you use an informal tone. The other day you said: 'It's sunny in retail,' and 'Don't spend too many calories on licensing.'" She goes on and I nod along, pretending that I am interested, that I'm listening. What she doesn't get is that my Greekness is the one thing I have going for me. Clients listen to my accent, the imperfections of my grammar, my angst about finding the right word—"Is it *affect* or *effect?*" I asked a thrilled audience in Atlanta—and they think that if this communication stretch is happening, is real, and is given some slack, then my strange, "tavern," strategic choices just might work. They give me the benefit of the doubt as an aftermath to the colorful Greek state they are already in, while I, well, I keep sliding into darker habits.

"I need to use the bathroom," I say, and start for the door.

"You're walking *out* on me?" Andrea asks.

"Call of nature. I'll be right back," I yell from the hallway.

"I want to talk body language next. Stillness!" Andrea shouts over her jingling bangles.

Justin hangs over the restroom's sink. His head is tilted sideways with some kind of pot, which looks like a sake jar, up against one nostril. Water—what I hope is water—runs out the other one.

"What the hell you doing?" I ask, and Justin stands up straight.

"Nasal douching. Cleans whatever's left in there," he says. "I know it's disgusting, but it works."

"Fucking kidding me," I say, and walk to the urinals. I begin to pee and the smell of formalin hits me. I close my eyes and think of nothing. When Justin blows his nose, I wake up, still peeing.

"Wanna try?" Justin asks. I see him raising his jar in the mirror above my head. "It will open up your sinuses for the presentation. You did some serious snow with Tati last night."

"Will you shut *up*?" I yell at him while scanning the bathroom through the mirror. I piss everywhere.

"Boss, relax! No one's here. I already checked."

"Thanks, I'll pass."

"Suit yourself," Justin says, and rinses his nose some more.

I get that quiver down the spine as my bladder finally empties. I shake, zip up, and flush.

"Ray gave me the nasal rinser," Justin brags when his head is up again. "Teresa can tell if he's done blow from his sinuses."

"What's Ray gonna do now that you got his kit?" I ask.

"Don't know," Justin says seriously, missing my sarcasm. "I guess he had to give it up since he moved in with her at Soho House."

"You hang out with Ray and Teresa?" I say.

"No more than you do," he says, defensively. "Ray and I work out together. Hey, boss, I almost forgot. Alkis messaged me. He said that he'll totally stop over if we can get him backstage at Teresa's show at Madison Square Garden tomorrow. I'm sure he called you . . ."

He didn't, but I nod my head, pretending I know what Justin is talking about.

"Gawel wants to come too," Justin adds. "Can you ask Tatiana for backstage passes? She doesn't pick up, and Ray is maxed out to his army buds."

"Gawel?" I ask, surprised but casual.

"He called me."

"How come?" I try not to look suspicious.

Justin shrugs.

"Gawel knows that you hang out with Teresa's daughter?"

"I may have mentioned it," Justin says. "What's the matter, boss?" He looks at me, concerned.

"Nothing," I say. "I'll see what I can do."

I wash my hands and linger by the mirror, shocked at how crappy I look. My eyes are red and puffy. I don't believe they'll let me pitch to a prospective client like this.

"Hey, thanks for the projector," I tell Justin.

"Of course. But what were you doing?"

"Oh," I try to downplay things. "A b-school friend of mine founded Accosting. It's a stupid site, but he asked me to take a look."

"No *shit*! That's the first thing I read every day. Has everything that happened downtown the night before. I'm on Accosting more than I am on *Bloomberg*."

His frat excitement's killing me. "Of course you are," I say, and feel the mucus in my coke-railed nostrils. I gotta move out of Tatiana's loft if I wanna make it to Christmas.

"Fuck it. Fix me up," I say.

"Bend your head sideways," says the kid with the toy. "Breathe from your mouth."

"WE ARE HERE TODAY BECAUSE you set some kick-ass goals for 2010," I begin my presentation in the jammed conference room.

"My big fat Greek capitalist!" BioProt's CEO roars, and a tsunami of laughter sweeps the room.

"But he's so thin!" Andrea screams, and she leans her head back the Alkis way.

THREE HOURS LATER ANDREA AND I walk into Nello on Madison Avenue. She does her phony thing: "*Fegatini con balsamico, prosciutto e melone.* And a glass of champagne." And I do mine: "Dirty vodka, straight up."

"The BioProt team loved you," she tells me after the waiter leaves. "They want you in LA for a prelaunch meeting in December. So you're officially on the beach until then."

"I understand," I say.

She tries to swap pleasantries, but all I offer is a mild smile here and there. After a few minutes she gives up.

"I'm flying to the Dominican Republic this weekend," she declares. "So I'll be quick."

"I'm going to Banana Republic this weekend," I say.

She throws me a pitiful glance. "I am not going to accept another Stathis, Stathis. This is not going to be like Paris. Is that clear?" she asks.

"Paris?" I play dumb.

"BioProt will go Lifestyle," she announces. "That's what we are doing. Cosmeceuticals; weight and hormone aids. Got that? Is it clear in that smart, stubborn Greek head of yours?"

I'm far from shocked.

"Maybe," I say, blinking, wondering how much she is willing to risk to help her man take over BioProt. How far is she willing to go to trade up? "Suppose we do," I say, hesitantly. "Why not?" I shrug. Erik did. He traded my patio for Warren's brownstone, or penthouse, or wherever TV people live. Warren, the next-generation Stathis, someone better, part of the "machine," for Erik to fight with. Then again, Warren might be immune to criticism, falling in that blind spot within Erik's pick-and-choose portfolio of protests. Like Kevin's job, or his own indulgence in running marathons. My ex was a hypocrite whom I fell in love with. Someone who had perfected the art of signaling underperformance, in order to get noticed. A reverse snob, thus the ultimate snob, who drove me bloodied and bowed all the way to addiction.

A long-sleeping fear of *what-does-all-this-say-about-me* wakes up. "We feed on what we don't have," Alkis once told me. There. My excuse, explanation, and failure to get what I want. Now, bitter, I'm not sure which I hate more: the fact that Erik is still so much a part of me that I act out on Andrea, or the fact that I used corporate frameworks, Andrea's world, to interpret my relationship with him.

"Anything to keep you trading up," I tell Andrea with a wink.

"Spare me your nerdy crap," Andrea says furiously. "You're not that innocent, yourself. *Beautiful Mind*, my ass! You've got no idea whom you're messing with, Greek boy."

"I don't? I thought your man was on the cover of—"

"I've tolerated your work-and-play-hard song long enough. I know what you do. I could have you deported with one phone call. And we all know what's waiting for you back home in Greece . . ."

I can't believe I'm not recording this.

She further raises her already-raised eyebrows, and I see Ray's whitetip coming right up to me. It's not the Greek Army that worries me; it's her insider meddling, once again, that scares the hell out of me. I can see my ass thrown in jail before the Greek Army has its way with it.

"There was science behind *Beautiful Mind*," I say calmly. "Game theory works; you can use it to outsmart your client's competitors." I pause, choosing between Alkis's play-the-game and Erik's (the Erik I knew) nuke-the-fuckers. "Sure,

Beautiful Mind was a show, I'll give you that," I add. "But it still looked after the client's, *only* the client's, best interests. And go ahead, send me to the stupid Greek Army. You'll be doing me a favor."

Andrea leans forward. "*This* is going to be done my way."

A BLOCK FROM NELLO, I check my BlackBerry. It must be the fifteenth time today, an obsession this fall; I'm still hoping for that message from Erik that will fix everything. I delete "Guess who got promoted at Lehman," "Alkis and Cristina are parents!," and "Command CARES." Fuck 'em. Fuck EBS, babies, Alkis, Lehman, and all the success stories in the world. A text from Gawel reads: "Good luck at the presentation." I'm on the verge of collapsing, but like a cranky kid who doesn't wanna go to bed, I text him back: "Want to?" My phone vibrates as I hail a cab.

"East Village," I say to the driver, who's mumbling on his cell. "Tonight!" I slap the plastic window between us.

IT'S ONE OF THOSE SATURDAY mornings that fill you with hope and get you up early, ready to fix everything. Those rare times when you feel like you'll get a grip on things. I shower and dress at Tatiana's—indifferent to the bathroom smell and the guy passed out in the hall outside her bedroom—grab my wallet and cell, and flee Franklin Street for the West Village.

I wave down a cab, sensing this air of Saturday morning in Manhattan, this eagerness about the possibilities ahead. *I'll make something out of my weekend.*

The cab cruises up Sixth Avenue, and I crave my espresso and the *FT* I'll get on West Fourth. Today I have a plan. I am meeting with a broker to check out an apartment, finally working on my exit from Tatiana's loft. I'll have lunch with Alkis, I'll call my sister and catch up with my nephew. We'll talk iPod, or whatever he wants for Christmas. I'll book those tickets for all of us to meet in Paris. I'll hit the gym, buy a new book, and power-nap before Teresa's show. I might even call up Gawel and explain to him—carefully, caringly—that he deserves better. And what the hell, I'll drop a postcard to Jeevan in Bequia, the coolest person I've met in the last ten years. This will be the weekend of my mending.

We cross Canal Street, and the boxy shape of the Soho Grand distracts me. I scan its windows for the room I lived in a year ago. I spot it three floors from the roof, its curtains two-thirds down; it's idling, clean and empty inside. I get a glimpse of Café Noir, my late-night hangout with Erik. "Fuck nostalgia," I whisper. I turn to the screen in my cab, which is showing clips of Warren in Afghanistan. No warning, nothing. No Internet Zeus hacking my screen to protect me. I go for the Exit icon, but the driver hits the brakes, I'm suddenly thrown forward, I double-touch the screen, and Warren's up again, playing with children in a refugee camp. I'm not trained to deal with this.

"I'll walk," I tell the driver, but he doesn't hear me. "Here's fine!" I shout.

He looks at me in the mirror and shakes his head.

"Carsick," I say.

I walk up West Fourth to Sant Ambroeus on Perry. I get an espresso and a brioche, open their copy of the *FT*. I go straight for the Life & Arts section, which has Jay-Z's picture on the cover: "Show Me What You Got, FBI." I flip the page to a caricature of Warren, who had "Lunch with the *FT*." I throw the fucking paper aside and ask for the check.

"IT'S THE NEIGHBORHOOD YOU WANT to be in," the broker says in a thick New York accent. A cloud of perfume mixed with sweat surrounds me as I follow her through the dark corridor that apparently leads to the "one-and-a-*half*-bedroom" on Bank Street that she is talking up to me.

The living room is surprisingly sunny. Its bumpy white walls—nails and cables buried by dozens of sloppy paint jobs—look anaglyphic and whole, like the stone walls on a Greek island. I smile at the idea of my two villages, Trikeri and Greenwich, with comparably patched walls but little else in common.

"Does it come with roommates?" I point to a few pages of the *Daily News* spread on the floor, covered with rat droppings and a fresh glue trap.

"Honey, this is New York," the broker replies. "It's a rent-stabilized building. In this neighborhood, who cares? You're a block from Magnolia Bakery and above Marc Jacobs. Literally!"

"Have you *seen* Marc Jacobs?" I mumble, walking into the half bedroom, or whatever this tiny second room is supposed to be.

"Once!" she shouts, dismissing my irony. "I was at Pastis with my girlfriends. Just five minutes from here. I'm telling you, this neighborhood . . . The unit is not available till December, but it's worth the wait," she adds, trying to read my reaction.

"I'm not sure I can wait that long," I say.

"Honey, do you know what I call these apartments?"

I really don't.

"I call them investment rentals!" she says proudly.

Erik hates the West Village. "Too pretty, too brunch, too nasal," he used to say, in the same voice he used to express his indifference to Paris or Prague. "Overdecorated Ohio wet dreams," he called them. I would grant him a pass on what's wrong with Ohio and listen to him talk up São Paulo and Caracas. "Cities! Think west-west Thirties. It's all about capacity. No bullshit West Village four-table restaurants. Got it?"

I did. That's why I'm all about the bullshit now. The more bullshit, the more "Tatiana" the restaurant, the better. Two months of sleeping in her loft, having thrown myself into her life, and I'm still shocked by how opposite yet similar those two are, were. Erik was Erik. He was anti-everything, while Tatiana is game-all: art, money, love, fashion, MySpace, the full monty. She flaunts her background. "I got my mom's looks and stamina, and my father's brains and self-destruction," she advertises. "And everything in between," which is plenty: affairs, awards, arrests, a Braque, a UN ambassadorship, bankruptcy. There's no discretion in her world; nothing's off-limits. Tatiana is a superlative, the reason people like Andrea move to New York.

But look just under the surface, and you run into an Erik-Tatiana sameness. Both are always poor and procrastinating—chasing the right people, never money—but at the eleventh hour, doors magically open. They both crack down on the so-called norm with such juvenile militancy, with such terrorism, that people around them want more. Tatiana is the strongman we follow to the Blue Ribbon (her Pakistani kitchen) to talk about whatever *she* wants to talk about. My Erik replacement, clearly. My new stalling in living, only this time it comes in black: between the two of us we cover most conditions and pharmacopoeias. I have insomnia and sleeping pills, Tatiana has coke and bulimia. We share alcohol, but she's also a cutter—"managed" by Paxil and Adderall—which makes her more fucked up, thus more entertaining, and makes me a selfish enabler. Do I have guilt? Sure. But I need distraction, which right now is the only way I can see surviving.

"And this is the bedroom!" The broker startles me. "Not bad for West Village."

There's another glue trap under a skull-stenciled window.

"Why do I see skulls everywhere?" I murmur.

"What, honey?"

Suddenly I have a premonition, an appalling hunch that Erik is changing. His new pals and hangouts . . . it is not that hard to see, really. He is going mainstream, upscale even, while I—just training, not good enough, now thrown away— grow more and more Tatiana-dependent, surrounded by drugs and Gotham glitter.

Fuck *your* skull, Erik! I'll take brunch and sleaziness, Nasal Village and Marc Jacobs. "Got an application form?" I ask.

TEN HOURS LATER I'M ON a barstool in Teresa's red-walled dressing room on Forty-Second Street. God and Justin, behind the bar, make vodka–Red Bulls. Doors open and close in this postconcert backstage gathering turned celebration. Some are sober, others drunk, a few in headphones.

Teresa wears a long knitted cardigan, sits cross-legged on a sofa, and talks with fans whom Security escorts in and presents to her in groups of four or five. "Did you like the show?" she asks the fans. "Do you know who's over there?" She points at Tatiana.

"Tatiana!" the fans, most of them underage Latinos, correctly answer.

Two sofas away from Teresa, Tatiana is busy curling Alkis's thick black hair. "Are you a genius like Stathis?" she asks him.

"No one is as smart as Stathis. He just needs a real job," Alkis says, and looks my way. "What do you do?" he asks Tatiana.

"I collect gift bags," Tatiana answers, and Alkis laughs.

Ray consumes stuff in and out of the suite, in the bathroom, while on the phone, talking to Security, to Wardrobe . . . Every few minutes he sails over to Teresa to kiss her, but his jaw clasps from cheap cocaine or something, and she's standoffish.

"Do you want a drink?" Tatiana turns and asks Alkis as she walks to the bar.

"Sure," Alkis says, and stares at Teresa, who is signing autographs.

Justin offers Tatiana a vodka-Bull. She takes a sip and makes a sour face. "If you give my mom's boyfriend your stuff, I'm gonna fucking kill you," she tells Justin, but he shakes a glass with ice and vodka violently, pretending he can't hear her.

"Tell him!" Tatiana orders me.

"Justin, don't give her mom's boyfriend your stuff," I repeat, but I can't keep a straight face.

"Don't laugh! Don't laugh!" she tells me, soberly. "You know that Ray has a coke problem."

"Right," I say, and do laugh. She can be protecting or projecting, or just desperate to be part of her mother's life—

envying her for Ray, or not. She's an addict; she can say anything.

A media mogul walks into the dressing room with his wife, a Teresa lookalike, the Asian version, and three bodyguards. The suite's main door closes behind them, and immediately things slow down as the big fish cuts across the room. Teresa stands up, and the couple kiss her. Then the three of them talk quietly.

" . . . I would close my eyes to get lost in your singing . . . but then I had to open them because I wanted to look at you . . ." I overhear the seventy-year-old billionaire saying while his wife rests her head on his shoulder.

"*So* don't wanna be famous," Tatiana whispers to me while staring at them.

"You want to stay half-famous then?" I say, and she gives me a *fuck-off* look.

Teresa points to Tatiana. "She's my passion," she tells the couple.

"No, *performing* is your passion!" Tatiana yells back to her mother, throwing the suite's temperature to an evening low.

Teresa gazes stoically at her daughter. She's either used to this or a good actress indeed.

"When are you going back to Los Angeles?" the trophy wife asks Teresa.

"First thing in the morning. *Depressed in Paris* goes into production next week."

"Where's Kate?" Ray shouts as he bursts through the bathroom door, sniffing and spitting. It's embarrassing to see him—his jaw is practically displaced—running into sofas in front of Teresa.

Tatiana fires Ray a look and snaps at Justin: "*Fuck* you. I asked you for one thing. What the hell is wrong with you?"

"We should go. Teresa needs to rest," the trophy wife says, and the billionaire kisses Teresa again. "Call us!" The couple leave and people in headphones start running around again, but faster, like making up for lost time.

Tatiana goes back to Alkis and brushes his thigh. "Will you be my angel? Will you take me downtown?"

Alkis gets up and spreads his hands in the surrender position as Tatiana pulls him by his belt. "Call 911 . . ." he says, and they exit.

"I need a break," Teresa tells Security. She sits back on her sofa and waves at me. "Stathis, can you come here for a second?"

I'm not sure exactly what's going on, but I don't feel good about this.

"Speechless," I say, half-kneeling in front of her, leveraging all the body-language respect I can, hoping to make this as brief as possible. "I had never seen you perform live before."

"Thank you. Now, can I ask you something?"

"Of course."

"Did Ray do coke? Look me in the eyes and tell me the truth."

I take a glimpse at Ray, who's popping back one vodka shot after another. Is she blind? It's comical to see how they tolerate him.

"If he did, it wasn't with me," I reply.

"If you're going to be like this, you——" Teresa lashes out at him, but she suddenly chokes. "You . . ." she coughs, " . . . you should find a place to spend the night."

Ray freezes, and sweat runs down from his hair to his cheeks. Even in this ridiculous state, he still holds the quiet innocence of a ten-year-old. "But I'll be lonely," says the man-child.

"One has to occasionally," God says, wiping Ray's forehead with a Kleenex. "Why don't we all go to my place?"

Teresa starts to choke again, her neck veins pulse, and a redhead nears us. I take out my BlackBerry and walk cautiously toward the door. E-mail, text, and voice mail alerts remind me of the dozen people I haven't called today, or this month, but Tatiana's number flashes and I pick up, relieved by the distraction.

"I'm going home with Alkis," Tatiana says over the phone before I get to speak. "Kate's already there. Come. Just don't bring Justin. I can't stand him."

"Sounds good," I say.

"I love you," Tatiana says in a sad voice, and hangs up.

"I'm not going *anywhere* with him like this," Teresa shouts.

Ray slams his glass on the bar and walks out the door. Exiting, he pinches my back, and right then I want to hang out with him.

"I'm not packing your stuff!" Teresa cries after him.

Ten minutes later, I'm in a cab with Justin and Ray.

"Who's that Alkis dude?" Ray asks.

"A guy Stathis used to work with," Justin says, shifting in his seat, reaching for something in his pocket. "He's cool."

"Does he have a master's like Stathis?" Ray smirks.

"I think Alkis has two, right, boss?" Justin says.

"I have two guns." Ray winks at me.

"I've seen your gun, Ray," I say, trying to make him shut up.

Ray laughs. "Does Alkis make lots of money, like you?"

"Alkis makes more," Justin says eagerly, holding a key under Ray's nose.

I take out my BlackBerry to wall them out, but halfway through my sister's voice mail, the dumb cokehead next to me gets loud and I can't hear a thing. I try to press 9—I do, really—but I press 7 instead. I have three missed calls, all from Gawel.

"Did you speak with Gawel?" I ask Justin.

"I told him I'd text him after the concert."

"I don't want him around," I say.

"Why? Gawel's down. He doesn't care."

"Is there anyone who's not down with *anything*, Justin?" I raise my voice. "And where the hell are we going?"

"Beatrice Inn," Ray says. "Before LA!"

"What are you going to do in LA?" Justin asks him breathlessly.

"Party all the time, party all the time, paaarty all the tiiime . . ." Ray sings.

"Really," Justin insists.

"I'm training Teresa's cast for her next movie," Ray says, and offers me a bump.

I stare at the key with the white powder on its edge that he holds close to my face. I'm still new at this, I'm not like these guys, so I'm totally in control. I can go either way.

"P-U-S-S . . ." Ray spells, and I take it.

"Stathis will be in LA in a couple of weeks too," Justin says.

"You're kidding me," Ray says, helping himself to a hit. "My brother . . ." He sniffs and offers me another. "Seconds, then?"

WALKING DOWN THE STEPS INTO the Beatrice Inn, I already feel a spooky vibration. Twenty-year-olds smoke on worn sofas that look as if they've been rotting there since a Cold War evacuation drill. After only seconds in this parlor, I know that something I'm supposed to find out will show up in this ridiculously low-ceilinged basement. I light up as Ray walks over to the Disney girl from Soho House. She throws her head back, the Andrea-Alkis way, before they kiss.

"Buying a round, boss. Wanna give me a hand?" Justin motions to the next room, and I follow him into a crowded bar that is tiled all in white, like a public bathroom.

"Put it out," a security giant says, squeezing by me, so I lower my cigarette.

Bob Dylan is barely audible, which is both a tease and an excuse for more blow. I spot a line of people belting the wall next to the bar. At the front of the line, people fuss outside a tiny wooden door. When it opens, three come out and four go in.

"How about a trip over there?" I ask Justin, nodding to the line by the bathroom.

"Oh, you don't need to wait in line." Justin smiles at me. "Unless you want to cut, of course. Here." He takes out his small plastic bag, sticks in his key, and does a bump. "These guys are bringing back New York!" Justin sniffs. Then he sticks the key back into the bag and offers it to me. I look around. People seem to know one another. There's an easygo-ingness of sorts, a hip-person-gone-bad-but-keeping-it-down-to-earth vibe. I take the bump, and Justin elbows us through the crowd to the bartender.

"Two tequila shots and three vodka tonics," Justin orders. The shots are gone at once. "Grab your drink. We're going upstairs," Justin yells, picking up the vodkas as they appear. "Best music in the city. We were dancing with Teresa till four the other night."

We walk through an open coat check, where the Disney girl is pulling Ray out of his sheepskin jacket. "I remember you!" She tosses her hair back. I nod, hand Ray his drink, and debate leaving my coat, but "Like a Rolling Stone" hits me like a bullet, drumming up the coke in me, and I sprint upstairs.

People dance and shout in the same low-ceilinged grime under a cheap disco ball, surrounded by red sofas and low-tech orange lights. The air is thick, suffocating, but no one seems to care. I spot a prop bar by the deejay and do one more tequila shot, and suddenly a pounding glee takes over me. It's 2006, but I Dylan-hum like I am at my high school's island party until a young British actress talking to Warren halts my drums. In the supernatural moment that follows, I see Erik behind him with a tennis player. My heart's beating fast, but it needs to go faster.

"Give me your stuff," I tell Justin.

I turn away and snort as much as I can.

"I wanna dance," I shout to the Disney girl, who sweeps Ray and me onto the dance floor, spilling my vodka all over her cowboy shirt. Ray gets on his knees to dry her, licks her belly, and for a minute I think I have built some firewall between Erik and me. Nothing can hurt me. Then Joy Division comes on: " . . . taking different roads, / then love, love will tear us apart again . . ." The very same song that played over and over on the radio in Bequia, and my adrenaline red-lines to a trance-valve that dumps everything. I look directly at Erik. He says something in Warren's ear. Warren glares my way and smiles. "Come on," I read his lips telling my ex, and Warren walks up to me. This is happening to someone else.

"Hi, I'm Warren," Warren shouts in my ear. He gives me his hand.

"Stathis." I nod.

"I've heard lots about you, Stathis." He's too close. He blocks Erik. I don't know what to do.

"Likewise." What the fuck am I saying?

"Oh, I have the worst reputation," Warren yells, again closer than necessary. Our faces touch.

"That's an Erik line," I say.

"It is, isn't it?" Warren laughs and pulls a few inches back. His eyes are penetrating, but they are a distraction right now. I'm near a touchdown. Then Warren turns and kisses the Disney girl. Erik's hand, Erik's fingers, touch my ear.

"How are my plants?" Erik shouts.

I look at the disco ball like it's going to tell me what to say. "Squirrels," I say.

"Your teeth are grinding, Feta. Are you going to bathrooms now?"

I meet his eyes. "When did you hear this song last?" I ask.

A suspicious face. "What is this?" Erik asks.

"Joy Division."

"Is this a trick question?" He smiles, and I see his wrinkles. *Speculate! Lie! Why are you so fucking casual? Why're you even here?* I need more blow to sort things out.

"Let's go downstairs." Someone taps my shoulder, and I instantly turn and follow Ray, who's leading the group with Warren. Walking down the six steps—I count—I know that Erik's behind me. I just do.

The Disney girl kisses a guy outside the bathroom and the door magically opens. Six, seven, eight of us cut the line and cram into a dark square room, the only light a dying low-hanging bulb above a ratty table by the sink. I'm in Abu Ghraib.

Ray and the tennis player push the table against the door. They take out two plastic bags and start cutting lines. Justin makes two twenty-dollar straws. I look at Erik, who looks at Warren, who's checking me out. Justin gives the Disney girl a straw and holds her hair as she goes through two big ones. Then everybody jumps in. There must be fifteen lines on the table, getting picked up fast. People snort and pass the straw. I stay on the edge of the group, and once again I look at Erik, who looks at Warren bending over the table. He picks up a couple and passes me the straw, and I freeze.

"Open the bloody door! It's legal now!" someone yells, pounding from outside. The table rattles and messes up the lines.

Warren puts some powder on his fist, on the spot between his thumb and his pointer. "Here," he offers, and I snort from his hand.

"You like the game?" he asks, sliding the leftovers onto my lips with his thumb.

A score-settling excitement explodes in me, and I lick what's left, looking at Erik, who looks at Warren, mad that he made a pass at me, at anyone. I could have been anyone. Then Warren turns and cups Erik's neck from behind, pulls him closer, and shoves his tongue into his mouth.

I kick the table, open the door, and spurt out.

"*Dick!*" someone shouts at me as I bump through people toward the exit. Two short twin blondes stare at me, and I push one of them out of my way. It's too fucking noisy.

"Brother, what's going on?" Ray grabs my shoulder. "Calm down, it's all good."

It's not. I want to fucking punch him.

"Stathis!" Justin gets hold of us. "Gawel's outside. He can't get in." He yells on his phone: "Gawel, Gawel! Can you get out of Andrea's ass and call back!"

I slap Justin on the back of his head, and his cell phone flies over the twins' heads. I sprint up the steps and dash out.

"Stathis! Stathis!" Gawel shouts from the crowd in front of the bouncers. I look down and make a sharp right. I can hear him running after me. There's a thrash, and from the corner of my eye I see Gawel flat on the cobblestone street. A bouncer zips his jacket and begins to walk slowly toward where he lies, and I bolt left on Eighth Avenue.

THIRTEEN

November 2006

YESTERDAY MORNING I GOT A text from Erik asking me to lunch this weekend, and I haven't been able to write a single bullet point since. I gesture along in conference rooms, getting more and more consumed in my speculations about what exactly he could want out of this: friendship—my ultimate fear? Sex? And what do I want? Explanations? Respect? Justice? My mind turns into a labyrinth of convoluted paths, an endlessly expanding Excel model ready either to crash or to yield "spectacular shareholder value," as Andrea says from across the table. And I nod like I am following her, but I've no clue what she's talking about.

Finally I go for a run by the Hudson River that morning, Saturday. I cross the West Side Highway and hit dog joggers, baby strollers, runners in bank-sponsored marathon gear holding Starbucks cups. I zigzag between them till I'm in the clear. I gain speed, and the wind off the river hits my face. The more I run, the more confident I get. I can do this, no matter where Erik stands on the bourgeois-bohemian scale. I start rehearsing jokes I'll tell over the empty plates and glasses of tap water—Cheney and Rufus Wainwright are on a plane to Dubai . . . —to show Erik how clever I am, to make him fall for me again, or for the first time, really. I feel firm in front of uncertainty, something I haven't felt since I ran in Fontainebleau in France. I'm back in the game, ready to shine over a plate of noodles.

At the loft I do push-ups, shower, towel off, and overdose on Tatiana's hair gel. I try to fix my hair, sculpt it the way she does, but I'm no Tatiana, and she's still sleeping. I look at Erik's X-Men joke in the mirror, and I'm back in the shower.

I throw on some clothes and step outside to get breakfast rolls. I feel like I'm running in circles.

"COME AND HAVE BREAKFAST WITH me," Tatiana says, spreading butter on the toasted bread lying right on the kitchen counter. "I made a pineapple omelet," she continues. "Do you want tahini, honey, or jam on your roll?"

There must be at least six jars of spreads open around her. Why does everything always have to be to the max with her? Aren't addicts supposed to get tired? Give up? Her mouth is sticky.

"I already had a roll," I say, sitting on the stool next to her.

She's in one of my shirts under the cashmere blanket she wraps herself in to move around the loft. She looks happy.

"What should I wear?" I throw a Command at her, a serious question played as a joke. "For fun, tell me."

No matter the drugs, the crashers, and all the other beastliness around the loft, outfits remain a stronghold, a topic of precision. Tatiana guards her sense of style (and everyone's around her) with strict rules. When I join her at Mr. Chow, it's her job to loosen my tie. For Sunday brunch at Sant Ambroeus I'm ordered into one of her father's cashmere turtlenecks.

Now her eyes ease, something that worries me, exposing my obvious panic. "I *love* Erik," she whines.

"You haven't met him," I say, tasting her eggy pineapple thing. I can't eat anything.

"That's correct. But now I have an excuse to take you shopping." She sips her coffee. "We don't want to scare the proletariat, so why don't we give your Wall Street coat a rest?"

I've long ago given up trying to explain to her the difference between corporate finance and management consulting—for her, every white-collar job is a Wall Street job—but today my stress makes me snap at her. "For the hundredth time, Tati, I don't work on Wall Street. I'm in management consulting."

"No, seriously." She is talking clothes; her face shines. "Why don't we get you *the* leather jacket? Your wardrobe will never be the same."

"Fine." I smile. "What the hell. You cooked breakfast, how can I say no."

She puts her slice down and touches her tummy. "God, I'm curvy." I can tell she's ready to cry.

"You're beautiful, no matter what they say," I hum, and Tatiana turns to the screen behind her, where Christina Aguilera sings in mute.

"Ha!" She leans and kisses me on the lips—jam, crumbs, and butter. "I'm so in *love* with you," she yells. "Speaking of food, I'm having brunch with Alkis uptown."

"Where are you guys going?"

"Oh, I'm not sure," she says, dismissively. "I'm meeting him at the Four Seasons."

"Isn't this the third weekend that he's come over?" I ask, glad for the digression.

"Fourth."

"Things are heating up," I say, carefully.

"You are ruining our breakfast, silly. And since when are you offering advice on relationships?"

"I don't want to be the bad guy here, but we both know that Alkis still lives with Cristina in London. They just had a baby together."

"I'm smitten," Tatiana says, faking shyness—she's not a good actress.

I love her and hate her. I want to protect her, but also lay bare her game of using Alkis for his wallet, of treating him like a bet with Kate, of fucking him up and then dumping him. But she's an addict, and Alkis is an adult. And who am I? An extra who lives through others.

IN THE MEATPACKING DISTRICT, TATIANA picks out a biker jacket for me.

"Try this on," she orders.

"Are you sure this is age-appropriate?" I ask.

"Belstaff has no age. If anything, you're too young for it," Tatiana lies, but I'm not used to being tended to. The last person who dressed me up was my sister. She bought me new pants and ironed my shirt before my interview for a high school in Athens. I check the price tag on the jacket, and I calculate the weeks, the months, that my father would have had to work in order to buy this ridiculously overpocketed Bel-shit—fashion always worshipped crap. Still, I see it through Erik's eyes. Could it be over-the-top? A joke? There he is again, snatching up my memories and wallet.

"*Stathis?*" Tatiana yells. "What do you think?"

"Mm?"

"George Clooney wears one. It's perfect for clandestine brunches like yours," she says.

"Did you just say clandestine? Do you read books?" I ask her.

"It's from Teresa's new movie, don't get too excited. Save it for your Niçoise."

"We're going Chinese," I say awkwardly, as if Erik's choice of a restaurant said something about my place in his new life. "Do you think I'm too old for this?"

Tatiana stops flipping through cashmere sweaters. "Yes." She smiles; we are not talking about the jacket.

It's too late for doubts. I'm doing this.

"What about my pants?" I ask.

"They'll do fine," Tatiana says. "Just pull your shirt out."

I give my credit card to the saleswoman. She removes the security tag, and I put the jacket back on. Tatiana yanks my shirt out. "The leisure way," she murmurs. I'm not Greek anymore; I'm just an actor with an accent.

We hail a cab and Tatiana gives me a kiss, and I decide I'd rather walk.

"Changed our minds," I tell the cabdriver who pulled up next to us.

"*Malaka!*" the driver yells, and tears off.

Not a good sign. "I'm just around the corner, really," I tell Tatiana.

"I adore you. Fuck him," she whispers into my ear. She waves good-bye. My old coat is in her hands.

I wave back and switch off my cell phone.

ERIK IS READING THE *NEW YORKER* at a window table in the large Chinese restaurant on Hudson and West Eleventh. It's past lunchtime; there's hardly anyone in the empty-walled room. I walk among barren tables like I've been summoned to a corporate cafeteria for an off-hours, off-the-record one-on-one with Andrea.

"Where's the bike?" Erik laughs in his old North Face jacket.

He's still Erik, though his black hair looks wavier. His skin is cleaner, whiter—if that's possible.

"Want a ride?" I ask.

"Still sharp, I see," Erik says.

"Takes one." I realize that he's not going to get up to hug, shake hands, or whatever exes are supposed to do, so I sit down. Now I stare at the wrapped chopsticks, the two bottles of soy sauce, and the veins on the backs of Erik's hands, which look exactly as they had when he worked on the tomatoes on my patio; a declaration that life goes on, perfectly unaltered. I can hear my breathing.

"I'm glad you said yes to lunch," Erik says, cautiously. "We left things . . ." He makes one of his involuntary half smiles. "You know. You were there. I needed some time to myself."

"Right," I say. "And Warren's helping you with that?"

Erik clears his throat. "Let's not go there. I'm sure you needed perspective too. Whatever that means in your case."

My case? He can't judge; he has no right. Plus, wasn't he in the same bathroom? I'm sweating in this stupid un-broken-in jacket. What if the tag's still on? Why do I ever listen to her?

"What did you do with my voice mails?" I ask.

"Excuse me?"

"What did you do with my messages?" I repeat as casually as I can. "Did you save them or delete them?"

Erik frowns, so I immediately backtrack: "It's a trivia question. My roommate and I have a bet about saved voice mails, that's all," I say, trying to conceal my nervousness.

It's a ludicrous lie and he sees right through it. I'm in the dentist's chair.

"Tell me about your roommate," Erik says with made-up interest, like he's letting me off the hook.

I'm afraid of him, but I can't stand his pity. "Are we going to be friends now?" I ask.

"If we choose to."

"Oh, *thank* you." I return his fake interest.

"For what?" he asks seriously.

"For not saying: 'We always were.'"

"Stathis, I'm not here to have old debates."

"Why are you here, then? Why are *we* here?"

"I want to talk to you as someone who cares," he says, and looks out the window, which is not very Erik. "And I know you care too."

"Yes. I *care* too," I echo, and laugh nervously.

"Something bad happened," Erik goes on.

"If you're talking about the Beatrice, I wasn't the one who—"

"Zemar's gone missing."

Fuck *me*. What about *me* missing? What about *my* pain, *my* burning eyes from not sleeping last night?

"Isn't Zemar always missing?" I try to keep my cool.

"This time is different. He may have been kidnapped."

"Where?" I ask.

"Somewhere in the Middle East," Erik answers, and once more he gazes out the window.

I'm so immaterial to him I want to laugh. "After four years together, you tell me: 'somewhere in the Middle East'? Somewhere in the *fucking* Middle East? Did you promise Paul confidentiality, or is this a Warren exclusive that you can't leak?"

"I know you're bigger than that, Stathis."

"Don't patronize me, and don't bet on it."

"Listen, I know you and Zemar had a connection. Maybe it was the Greek thing, whatever. But right now, you could make a difference if you share any information you have."

"Such as?"

"Such as those postcards Zemar sent you."

"This is why we're here, isn't it?" I feel robbed.

Erik says nothing. Then, "Not just that. Seeing you the other night. I worry about you, Stathis. You were—"

"Shut up," I say. "Stop marketing. Marketing's my job. Is this Warren? Some extra drama for his latest story? Some postcards from hell? Or are you the *conventional* rebel now? Okay with handing over Zemar's cards to the mercenaries in Iraq?"

"Is that a no, Stathis?"

"Stop saying 'Stathis' every time you say anything to me!" I shout. I breathe. "I only got three cards from Zemar," I say. "You've seen them. One-way cards. There's no return address on them."

"Anything could help. Remember the night you met him in LA? We ended up at the Chateau. When I woke up—"

"*The Chateau?*" I ask. "When did the Chateau Marmont become *the Chateau?*"

He shakes his head, ignoring me. "When I woke up, Zemar was gone. But you saw him, you guys hung out. You never told me what you talked about."

"You never *asked*," I say, pleased.

"Tell me now," Erik says uncomfortably, and I realize I still have a little sway over him. His hero, who liked me and bonded with me, gives me negotiating power. The tiny influence I may have on Zemar's future might be leverage for a quick fix with Erik. It's tempting, even if the consequences could be life or death, even if it turns me into *The English Patient*, a selfish prick who knows that in the end some punishing wrath might descend upon me.

"Well?" Erik insists.

"Zemar said that life is full of circles," I say. "That people reach some kind of threshold and then they change. He changed. He said that you would change too."

"Interesting," Erik says. "What else?"

"He said that unlike your brother, you are tough but vulnerable."

Erik looks at me curiously.

"Why?" I shrug. "Was he wrong?"

"Know what?" Erik says.

But I go on. "He said that your brother is obsessed with you."

"I don't believe that Zemar said that."

"Zemar was doing *heroin*," I shout in mad panic. "He showed up with two syringes, two passports, two everything. He was a fucking ghost. Why *wouldn't* he say that? Why do you *always* have to question me?"

"I'm not going to fight with you. What else did you see in his bag?"

Fuck you. "Is this why Warren put a move on me?"

He gets up.

"I'll give you the cards," I say, and Erik stops. "If we fuck one more time."

Erik leans over me. "Go *fuck* yourself," he whispers. "Does that work for you?"

A waiter approaches. "I need more time!" I yell, and grab Erik's hand. "Why are you with Warren and not with me?"

I see Erik processing his anger into mercy. "'Cause Warren comes from money, like me. Isn't that what you want to hear, Stathis? Wasn't that always the case with you?"

I WATCH ERIK'S NORTH FACE jacket vanish down Hudson Street. The waiter comes back to take my order. I drop a ten on the table and walk to the exit, but the waiter is trailing me. I open the door as he says something in Chinese to the girl behind the register. She chuckles and puts her hand over her mouth. I stop, struck by how steady she looks behind her cash register and how shaky my hands, and my life, are right now.

I walk like a zombie among West Village nannies and babies, somehow grasping that my world has been reduced to a series of traumatic episodes that I will have to learn to deal with faster and faster. I am getting better at switching from obsession to apathy to anger to depression. I am getting better at erasing feelings, at slowly killing myself.

By the time I text Gawel "140 franklin apt 2b," my shock has already turned into hatred.

I enter the loft, needing coke violently.

"Fucking *Tatiana!*" I yell, after I trip over a casserole that has been stuck to the floor for two weeks—a cooking night turned blackout.

I hobble to the coffee table, grab a large wooden box, and turn it upside down. Papers, photos, and junk shower everything. No little plastic bags, though. This is scary. This is unacceptable.

"*Tatiana!*" I yell again to no one.

I tramp to the kitchen counter and look under the meat slicer. Nothing makes sense in this fucking loft. I empty the bread box of minibar bottles and bracelets. A Formula One invitation folder looks strangely thick. I see two plastic bags inside and catch my breath.

Three lines later, I lie down on the sofa and start jerking off. I'm buck naked when the doorman calls. "Send him up," I answer, and cross the loft to unlock the door when I notice a woman from the building across the street staring at me. I shake my dick at her. "I'm gonna fucking kill you," I try to mouth to her, but my jaw is clamped shut. I leave the door slightly open and walk back to the sofa, where perverts can't see me.

"Stathis!" Gawel yells. He's all red cheeks and smiles. "Should I lock the door?" he asks.

"Mind the casserole," I say, and go on beating my meat.

"I guess we're all alone."

"Come here," I say.

Gawel walks timidly toward the sofa. "Finally, I see where you live. What is this? An artist's studio?"

I point at two lines on the coffee table. "Take them."

"Oh, no, thanks. I don't do that stuff." He takes his jacket off and sits next to me.

I grab his neck and push his head to the coffee table. "Come on, do them! You can do this. You'll like it more."

He snorts half a line and turns to look at me. Then he stares at the ceiling, where there is mixed footage of Bukowski, and Tatiana's mother landing a 747.

"Do it!" I yell, and Gawel finishes the line. "Did you feel that? Now do the other." I pull his jeans down. "One more. Take it." I put my thumb in my mouth and then I push it against his crack. He does the line as I thumb him.

"Are you going to fuck me now?" he asks, trembling.

I push him on the rug and bend him on all fours. I shove the head of my dick inside him.

"Wait!" Gawel yells.

"Fucking analyst!" I push my dick in farther. "Swallow my dick with your ass!"

"Wait! Stathis!"

"Polish shit!" I thrust my hand over his mouth and fuck him. He pushes my hand away and I grab his neck, choking him. He spins sideways and punches me on the chest, crying, which only makes me fuck harder. When he punches me again, I come.

FOURTEEN

December 2006

MY MOOD IS FROZEN, LIKE the New York weather.

"Get a life!" I yell to a tour guide who is helping women take photos of the brownstone where Carrie lived in *Sex and the City*. The women turn and look at me, smoking outside Sant Ambroeus, two blocks from my new apartment on Bank Street.

"What?" I shout, itching for a fight, but they say nothing.

Justin helped me move out of Tatiana's loft and into the place on Bank. I threw out the gas stove (pilot lights freak me out), got an old but fancy mattress from Kate, and hired Tatiana to furnish my "one-and-a-half-, *half*"—she got a kick out of repeating the "half"—bedroom.

"Constraints allow for interesting solutions," Tatiana said at one point, referring to my pad. "Then again, you're in your thirties and you have no furniture. Which is amazing. Gives me free rein."

Fine by me. Gloss it up, trash it down, bring bedbugs, as far as I'm concerned. Since I'm officially "on the beach" till BioProt kicks off, I "live" at Sant Ambroeus. I'm there every day, sitting uselessly on my barstool for breakfast, lunch, and dinner. I haven't been to the office for almost three weeks. I have managed to steer clear of Gawel, who hasn't texted me since I raped him, and Andrea and all the other Command silliness. Not that long ago, I would justify my whereabouts; now, I just don't care anymore.

The other regulars at Sant Ambroeus want no part of me. They smile at my bed head and roll their eyes when I smoke with the AA folks from next door. They make sure I know I'm breaching some rule of West Village etiquette. When I lived with Tatiana, everything was on fast-forward. People were in and out of town, in and out of rooms. Drugs and burgers were delivered at four in the morning, and I was surprisingly okay with all that. Now, I'm doing all right with my new neighborhood's stillness. I guess I'm pretty flexible. Tom, my next-door neighbor, has been here for forty-five years. The same AA faces hang out on the street; they just sit there, waiting for something to happen. At three every afternoon Louise complains about the weather, sitting at Sant Ambroeus's pink marble bar, which has become my new kitchen, desk, and living room. Fllanza, the barista, is my new "roommate," and Eddy, a homeless guy on West Fourth Street, my self-appointed "neighborhood doorman."

"I don't like these cows." Eddy points at the *Sex and the City* group. "I sleep outside two seventy-eight and they step on my stuff."

"Do you want a croissant, Eddy?" I offer.

My phone vibrates with an incoming text.

"Lunch with Tatiana. Now. Alkis."

"Perry and West 4," I respond.

Half an hour later Alkis, in a gray suit and a tie with puppies playing with balls, walks into the restaurant. He looks at me like I'm from another planet.

"Why are you wearing Birkenstocks at Sant Ambroeus?" he asks. It's the dead of winter and I have no socks on, but Alkis is worried that I'm wearing Birkenstocks at Sant Ambroeus. "And why are you in your coat inside the restaurant? Are you chain-smoking?" he says, annoyed.

"What did you do with my wife?" I ask, saving both of us some name-calling.

"Tati will be late. She's with Kate, picking up some things for your pad," Alkis says.

Todd, the waiter, greets Alkis by his first name—which is odd, given that Alkis lives in London, but I don't care to ask how come, or how many times Tatiana has already brought Alkis here.

We sit at the table three feet from the bar.

"We call this the kitchen table." Todd smiles, showing off his über-white teeth. "We keep it for the regulars." He winks at Alkis.

"Oh my God!" Fllanza screams from behind the bar. "Stathis, that is my *favorite* table. Enjoy!"

"Is everybody retarded here?" Alkis mumbles, getting comfortable in his seat.

"You're not in Knightsbridge anymore."

Alkis gives me a contemptuous look. "When was the last time you shaved? EBS recruiting?" He picks up his leather-bound menu.

"Do you still sign your e-mails 'Come-to-Lehman'? Because I may have a CV crunched up in my back pocket for you."

"Okay." Alkis smiles. "Let's start over." He puts down the menu. "How are you? How are things?" he asks. "When are you off to LA?"

"Next week," I say. "If everything goes as planned."

"What did you say you'd be doing for BioProt out there?"

"The usual," I reply, bored. "Portfolio management, pipeline and licensing prioritization. They added some bells and whistles, but nothing sexy."

"Who's the account owner?"

"A senior-senior from Washington, plus Andrea," I say.

Alkis punches the table. "Don't get me started on that bitch!" he yells. "Did I tell you that I e-mailed her husband's CFO, cc'ing her, after she told me she'd spoken to him? The guy had no clue who I was."

"I don't think they're married," I say.

"Wait, it gets better. Three e-mails later, the cunt doesn't even bother to explain to him who I am. Can you imagine?"

I can.

Alkis shakes his head.

"Relax," I say.

"Relax? Stathis, her guy is going biotech. I mean, okay,

Goldman is close to him, but I know I can help there." All of a sudden he looks at me suspiciously. I can see him processing. "He's not buying BioProt, is he?" Alkis blurts with a shit-eating grin on his face.

I stare at the happy puppies on his tie. The more I look at them, the more they look like rabbits, and I ask myself in which parallel universe I would ever wear such a thing. I wonder why I haven't explained Andrea's plot, and why I know I won't. It's not the rabbits, nor my growing distance from Alkis—Tatiana is the only reason we are having lunch today—that stops me from spilling the beans about Andrea and BioProt. It's the fact that I'm neither intrigued nor scared by work schemes anymore. It's the fact that my phone vibrates and although I'm already bored with Alkis, I don't pick up. The fact that I haven't spoken to my family for more than a month and that the idea of doing so, the idea of talking about myself, nauseates me. The fact that I've lost touch with everyone pre-Tatiana, and I like it that way. Tatiana is my family now, has became my family in that New York sense of the word. Sure, a fucked-up family, but one that accepts me as is, no questions asked.

"Buying BioProt? Don't know. I guess he could." I shrug. "Are those puppies or rabbits?" I point at his tie.

"It's Hermès, so it doesn't matter. And I'm not buying your shrug," Alkis says.

"Fine, he's buying BioProt." I say it so trivially that he has to let it go. "Do you think I care?" Alkis just looks at me. "Are you hungry? 'Cause I'm starving."

We order some pasta and a bottle of red.

"You and Tatiana have been glued together," I say. "Does Cristina know?"

"Cristina's cool," Alkis says, checking out Fllanza.

"Aren't you supposed to spend your weekends with your daughter?"

"It's all good."

"So everybody is clear on where things stand," I say.

"We're working things out. Listen . . ." Alkis breathes. I can tell we are about to have a dear-diary moment. "You know Tatiana, she is different," he says, trying to stay cool, but his excitement is breaking through. He grabs my arm, brotherly. "Slobs like us from Bayswater or Greece, we like the streets. Tatiana is *so* street. Good *God*, is she ever street." All pretense at hiding his enthusiasm vanishes.

"She can be," I say.

"She's the first girl I've gone out with who drinks like me, parties like me, pigs out like me. She even *fucks* like me, man. And here is the best part: she's also so *not* street."

"She can be confusing," I say.

"You see, I *like* that," Alkis says. "I think it's hysterical that she's always broke but so comfortable around money. It's like she was born with a taste for it, an ease with it. There's an haute provincialism in her pussy that drives my dick crazy."

I smile. Both Tatiana and Alkis are predators. Maybe there's something there. "Did you just say 'haute provincialism'? What if your mates from Bayswater heard you?"

"Stathis, I'm with Lehman now." Alkis actually says that.

"Tatiana is crazy," I say seriously. "You have to be careful. She's the promise that's never delivered."

Alkis leans closer. "No, she is *not*."

"Okay, she is not."

"She's inconsistent, but she's not unpredictable," Alkis says. "She opened up to me. She told me that she was a fat kid, which made her body-conscious and gave her that love-hate thing with her mother. She told me they filed for bankruptcy."

"She talks to her mother like a lover," I say. "She's competing with her."

"She talks to her father like a cheated-on mistress. So *what*? You need the context. They are artists. That's their thing, Stathis. The whole thing's an act."

Fllanza poses behind the bar. "I guess that's the premium today, isn't it?" I murmur.

"What?" Alkis asks, confused.

"Everything is an act, a fucking stage. That's how we get our highs, in food, sex, apartments. Everything. 'Normalcy is failure.' Didn't you teach that to the clients in France?"

"And what's wrong with that? What's wrong with *you*?"

"Nothing. I'm just tired," I say, and get up. "I'm stepping out for a smoke."

"Accountant!" Alkis whispers.

Outside, Eddy waves to me for a cigarette. I give him one, but he sticks it behind his ear, then checks his reflection in the side mirror of the all-black SUV parked next to us. The driver inside, watching something on the console screen, looks up and waves familiarly to Eddy. If you weren't born and raised here, I don't think there's anything that can prepare you for New York; the contradictions are staggering. When Henry Kravis eats at the far table at Sant Ambroeus, the "good" table, only a hundred-year-old wall separates him from the AA meeting room next door. He sips his Valpolicella, hearing—like I do—people cheer their sobriety anniversaries.

Eddy motions for another cigarette, and I give him a funny look. I light both of us and check my phone. There are two missed calls from Andrea, one from Paul, and one from an unknown number. I speed-dial my voice mail. "I've lost you" is all my sister left, and for a moment I think of how my life would have been had I never left Greece, something I rarely do anymore—had I never gotten that scholarship to study abroad. Maybe I'd live in Athens, that cementopolis, and work for the National Bank of Greece, anticipating my week in Mykonos every summer. Other times I imagine myself in Trikeri with just a bathing suit and a Buck knife to my name, fishing and playing backgammon, fucking goats in the winter and maybe a tourist in the summer. No, screw Greece. I'm here. That's that.

I take a long drag and scrape up whatever courage is left in my dirty lungs. Then I go through my cell contacts till I reach "Melissa Cabdriver." Her phone rings twice, but I hang up. I take another drag and study her contact stored in my cell. I never saved her last name; I don't think I ever asked her what it was. She was "Melissa" the "Cabdriver." Isn't that interesting? Maybe Erik was right. What would he have said had he gone through my contacts in those days? But Erik never snooped. Unlike me, he was not the suspicious kind.

I type: "Melissa, Stathis here. How are you? It's been forever. I'm heading to LA next week. Can you take me to the airport?" I read the draft twice before I delete "Can you" and type "Care to" instead. Nah, go real. I delete "Care to" and retype "Can you." I add "Hi" before "Melissa." What if she forwards my note to Erik with a ☺ at the end? What if she doesn't text at all? "When we fall for someone, we fall for everything about them," Tatiana once said, referring to Ray and her mother, the only time she spoke about them. "We fall for their neighbors, friends, groceries, addictions," Tatiana said. I breathe and press Send.

Inside, Alkis is eating. "The pasta was getting cold," he apologizes with a full mouth.

"No worries, mate," I say, still on a high from texting Melissa, my last bridge left to Erik. I peek at my watch. "Are you taking the afternoon off?" I ask Alkis.

He nods, eating. "A Partner has a weekend holiday thing in Southampton," he says. "He invited foreigners and 'orphans.' I told Tatiana that you guys should come, but . . ." he waves "blah-blah" with his hand. "Are you going to her godmother's for the holidays?"

"Yes. Maybe. I don't know."

"So." Alkis looks self-conscious as he swigs from his red. "What's Tati's story on me?"

I shake my head. "Not my style."

"*Ballpark*, Stathis. Ballpark. The headlines."

"Headlines don't matter," I say, and smile back. "They rarely translate to the bottom line. You used to say that shit, remember?"

"Did you just do *crack* outside?"

"What happened to: 'Delivery is for Division Two, for the Tokyo office.' *You* preached that. Why do you think Tatiana will bother with keeping promises?"

His face gets angry. "Will you stop jerking off for *once*? This is serious."

"So what if she says she's smitten! Are you *fifteen*? Tatiana's an addict. You can glamorize her as much as you like, but that doesn't change the fact that she's a mess."

"Hey!" He points his fork at me. "I've no problem with partying, never did, but you're supposed to be her friend, you quant-fuck! Or do you just tag along so you can get into the subMercer and the Bungalow?"

"I'm with her 'cause she gives me a home, whatever that means in New York. I love her, but that doesn't mean she doesn't need help," I say, and pause a second. "And maybe I do too," I add. It's the first time I've said that out loud.

Tatiana walks in, looking all miserable.

"I'm not through with you," Alkis says under his breath, his fork still pointing at me.

"Go close a fucking deal so you can buy her more dresses," I whisper rapidly.

"Hi," Tatiana exhales, without looking at either of us.

Alkis's face relaxes. "Hey, baby."

"Hi," Tatiana repeats. She sits down, barely letting Alkis touch her. "I'm starving. Nice tie, by the way," she says, searching through her bag.

"Thank you!" He is clueless about her scorn. "Let's get you some food."

Alkis calls over Todd.

"I'll just have what these guys have," Tatiana tells Todd.

"Would you like the penne or the linguine?" Todd asks.

"*Both?*" she says, as if Todd asked her something ridiculous. "And a negroni."

Todd leaves, and Tatiana gets back to her bag. She presents a piece of paper, of sorts. It's been folded three or four times and is practically shredded.

"What is this?" I say.

"Isn't this what you were searching for?" Tatiana hands me Zemar's card. "I keep forgetting to bring it to you."

"Shit," I murmur. "It's one of them. Where *was* it? I looked for them everywhere."

"Stuck under the projector for balance. I found it when Justin dropped a joint and burned it. Yes, that all-you-can-eat-sushi piece of shit burned my projector!"

Alkis zooms to the card. "What are you talking about?"

"Nothing," I say, putting the card in my coat pocket. "Just a note from a Greek friend."

Alkis turns to Tatiana: "How is Stathis's place coming along?"

"It's stressing me out. I want it perfect," Tatiana replies.

"Now, now. It's just a job, baby," Alkis says, comforting her.

"Alkis, my *life's* my job!"

"I'm the Greek. I'm the rude one," I say flatly, and Tatiana smiles. For a second.

"What style are you going for?" Alkis presses on. "Bachelor minimal?" He's hopeless.

"I'm going Mario Savio, Berkeley," Tatiana throws out absentmindedly.

"Is Mario . . . Mario . . . from the Beatrice Inn?" I've never seen Alkis scared before. "Is he a designer?"

"Mario *Savio*!" Tatiana vents. "From Berkeley *in the sixties*! Dammit, Alkis! Do you know *anything* about the free-speech movement? The guy's dead, for Christ's sake. My father's writing a script about him."

I make a *what-do-we-know* shrug. "She wants a library in my kitchen and books in my fridge. She's going for the leftish poet, revolutionary look."

"Don't forget *Osama bin Laden*!" Alkis says, throws his napkin on the table, and stands up.

"Come on," I say. "Let's finish the wine."

"E-mails came in," Alkis gripes, and reaches into his pocket.

"Leave it," I say, and he does.

"I'll call you from Long Island," he tells Tatiana.

She nods, eager for him to disappear.

Alkis gives me a dirty look and storms out.

"Have I missed something?" I ask, leaning back in my seat.

"I'm pregnant," Tatiana says, but I can tell by the cast in her eyes that there's more. "And it's Ray's."

I feel Zemar's scrunched-up card coming unfolded in my coat pocket. "I think I raped someone. And I feel nothing about it."

"So what happens next?" Tatiana asks.

FIFTEEN

WHEN YOU DO DRUGS, THINGS change. You acquire a tolerance for the fact that almost nothing turns out as planned. I see Tatiana's big eyes, and I don't have to ask what she needs from me or why. A ghost, she roams around my half-furnished apartment in gypsy-glam clothes, trying to feed me mashed broccoli while decorating my place. I'm her "case study," she says. She seeks to set-dress my barren studio with the "sophisticated frivolity" of "yesteryear." She wants to "bottle nomad seduction, a leftish spirit, but have it be *today*."

Do these concepts make any sense? Did they ever?

She presents me with monochrome posters of fat children, her mother in a Pirelli calendar, Philip Morris's blurry new logo, a portrait of Hunter S. Thompson, and an ad from the eighties that says, "If you were flying the Concorde tomorrow, you'd wear a Rolex."

I don't get it, but I smile anyway.

"What have we got in there?" Tatiana says, pointing at my Starving Students box.

"My textbooks from EBS," I say, a bit embarrassed.

"Looks like they've been sealed up for years. Why do you keep them?" she asks.

I have a hard time answering. "I can't let go. Believe it or not, I used those books to try to understand Erik."

"It's nostalgia. Stop doing that."

"No, seriously," I say tenderly. "I thought that business algorithms would help me optimize a relationship. I can't believe I'm actually saying that."

"Stop it," Tatiana says again and holds my hand.

She looks sick enough to be admitted to St. Vincent's, yet she's still lovely. I sit on the floor by the box and pull her next to me. "I have. I am," I say.

She takes her keys out and slits the box open. "So are we going to be able to get rid of these books?" she asks.

"I don't care about them anymore. I've no use for them. After Erik, I don't think I even care about work."

"Why?"

"I pushed hard at Command to impress him, at a time when he was unimpressible," I shrug. "Now he is impressed, just not with me." In the box I see my Decision Traps and Tools textbook. "I guess I picked the wrong problem to solve, at the wrong time," I say. "Or something like that."

"When did you know what was in store for you?" Tatiana asks.

"I went on for years choosing not to hear what Erik was saying, and hearing what Erik was *not* saying. During one of our fights he stopped to suck a cut on his thumb. He was so casual about it, like he was telling me he'd already checked out, or that he'd never been there in the first place."

Tatiana's grip on my hand tightens. "I am here," she says, so I kiss her.

"When did you know what was in store for you?" I ask.

"It's not the same." She buries her head in my shoulder. "She can have Ray. The guy's a user."

"Beside the point, Tati. Rejection is always rejection. It can hurt."

"I'm not infected by specialism. I'm not Teresa. I can handle it," Tatiana says.

I feel her tears down my neck. I look at the stuff she put up on my walls, all sorts of junk and shit. There's a collage showing Moby eating a steak, next to a poster of Robin Byrd in *Debbie Does Dallas*. All this crap doesn't add up, but it's okay in some weird way.

"You're good with contradictions," I say, and kiss the dirty tears on her face.

"The fact that people die in Java doesn't make my suffering any less," Tatiana sobs.

"When was the last time you called her *mom*?"

"*You* are my family now." She takes my hand and walks us to Kate's old mattress. We lie down next to a paper plate with a bunch of carrots and a bag of coke.

"Pain is good. It makes you forget things," Tatiana says, takes a bump, and rests her head on my arm.

We stay there. It's so quiet that I can hear a blend of her breathing and her watch ticking. Then she trembles, so I spoon her.

"Keep your hands on my tummy," Tatiana says.

I do.

"I'm leaving for LA soon," I whisper in her ear, and try to feel her pregnancy on my palms. I try to keep her warm. "I may be there for a while."

"Don't."

I kiss her hair and ear. "I'll protect you," I say, but I am not sure how.

SIXTEEN

West Hollywood

I HAVE NEVER BEEN TO A city more lethargic than Los Angeles, nor lived in a hotel more narcotic than the Chateau Marmont. There is an off-season air to the place that makes loneliness feel like a natural state. Weekends, I lie on my sofa smoking with an ashtray on my chest, watching the dust float in the rays of sun coming through the drapes. I count the pastel tiles above the kitchen sink and mellow out in my idleness. Everything seems slower in LA, sedated, more tolerable, especially my perception of myself. I left New York a coke-addled, sex-hungry zombie, and I still am, but here I look the part less. By switching from West Village bathrooms to LA cottages, I see everything through a veil, happening behind a fence or a pool house. I like it. Fading out of sight is a privilege in the hills.

I moved into the Chateau's main building the way a hyena hovers near lions, distressingly close to the cottage where I told Erik I loved him but far enough away to stare at the memory from a distance. Josh, at the front desk, gave me a junior suite on the third floor. "A quiet floor, far from—" he looked back at his screen—"cottage 88, where you stayed the last time you were with us."

Three weeks in, I still have not done that 88 walk yet. I'm not ready to face the stoop where for a moment I thought I had Erik.

"He moved into Warren's brownstone in Brooklyn," Melissa told me during our ride to JFK, smelling of baba ghanoush. She spotted them with Parker, "their son," at the Macy's Thanksgiving Day Parade. "Warren's son," she corrected when I stared at her in the rearview mirror. Was I in touch? Would I be back for Parker's birthday party? "Yes, maybe. Here." I handed her Zemar's postcard. I didn't have Erik's new address, so there. Melissa was now the custodian for the two-word note from the Bora-Bora kid turned Tora Bora phantom.

It's after midnight and the only sound in my suite is the drone, the never-ending throb that, nightly, mesmerizes me in the Hollywood Hills. Close to two, I leave for the pool. People start showing up from the gardens, like ghosts: " . . . my quasi-girlfriend . . . ," I overhear, " . . . enough blow to kill a small animal . . ." Things play out. There's an interface in the hills that helps one come to terms with life, or at least become resigned to it.

"I'M AT THE CHATEAU FOR twenty-four, pushing on some other BioProt front," I read in Andrea's e-mail. "Tomorrow I'm off to Silicon Valley. I'll be back next week, of course, but can we connect while I'm checking out in the morning?"

"Works," I respond.

THE NEXT MORNING AROUND NINE o'clock, Andrea is in her metal-leather sunglasses at the front desk.

"I hear good things about your work," she greets me. "As always."

"This is LA," I say.

"Yes, right." She reads from her BlackBerry with her shades on. "People love you or hate you."

"So, what's the client's status?" she asks.

"We are about to launch a screening marathon for them. We'll be looking at bio, genomics, and academic institutes for alliances or acquisitions."

"You can charge me," Andrea tells Josh, behind the desk. She presents a credit card from an ostrich-skin wallet. "Stathis, remember that we are not here to solve world hunger. We are here to help them make a difference for the handful of stakeholders involved." She turns to Josh: "I don't need to see the printed bill. I need to sign. Now."

"Of course," Josh says.

"I'm in a hurry," she explains to me. "Where were we?"

"Their stakeholders," I offer.

"Right. Which means that we need to prioritize. And, Stathis, I'm done with innovation. I want to see value via diversification. No excuses, no exceptions." She spreads her signature across the credit card invoice; she practically graffitis the desk. "I know you'll do an outstanding job," she says, and starts walking toward the elevator.

"About that," I cry after her.

She turns and slides off her sunglasses. She looks at me, alarmed.

"I'm not sure that we're a hundred percent aligned with BioProt management as far as the diversification strategy," I say.

Her eyes turn suspicious. "Carry on."

"I don't think they're comfortable with us favoring short-term returns, investments outside their core science," I say calmly.

Her expression turns icy. "Core science? Diversified biotechs are still biotechs."

"Lifestyle is pushing it, Andrea. Really."

"Stathis, sometimes we have to recognize that clients may not see things quite the same way we do, but that doesn't mean that they or we see things poorly." Andrea-isms follow: " . . . ill fitted versus ill suited . . . slender victories still victories . . . painfully shy clients . . ."

I look down. Her heels are made of the same bird as her wallet.

"I'm not sure that you understand their competencies," I say. "We are about to fill their pipeline with moisturizers." There.

"Stathis, Stathis . . ." She has the air of a schoolmistress. "Honestly, I wouldn't worry about it. Let's keep communication open. I'm glad you're on the team," she lies baldly, and presses the elevator button.

That was way too easy. "The bitch got someone on the client side," I murmur after the doors shut behind her.

THE MARQUISE-SHAPED CLOCK IN TERESA'S Maserati says two, but the sun begins to set as Ray and I drive up the hills. Ray gives the sky a wary look as it begins to rain. I turn and lean over, and through the back window I see red rays of sunlight spilling through the clouds as we enter God's private road.

"This is a De Tomaso," I say, touching the redwood dashboard. "They don't make the Quattroporte like this anymore."

"It's a fucking toilet," Ray slurs. "I had to get it towed to Costa Mesa last week to have the transmission replaced."

"We used to jerk off to pictures of cars like this where I grew up. Do I get to drive her to BioProt?"

Ray gives me a *you're-kiddin'-me* look. "What's in it for me?"

"Tell Charlie to deliver to the Chateau," I say, and his cowboy-angelic smile springs up. "Just this week that Teresa's in town," I add, to save face while I try to connect myself with his coke dealer.

"You got it." Ray hits the clutch hard as we start up the hill toward God's pergola parking lot. The Maserati complains and spins.

"*Watch it!*" I shout. Chickens cluck and flap their wings as they scatter. "God has chickens in LA?" I laugh.

"Crazy old bitch."

We park next to God's Alfa Romeo. Ray reaches into the glove compartment and takes out a .45 Glock.

"Brother, do you *have* to carry that everywhere we go?" I ask.

"I need to protect kids like you from the cougars in the hills," Ray says, and steps out of the car. He seems almost Greek, which gives me a blind spot. I can't see him as dangerous, even when he mixes guns with drugs.

I get out of the car and stretch my arms, transfixed by the nonstop view from downtown LA all the way to Santa Monica and the ocean. I've seen rainy sunsets before, but never this apocalyptic: skyscrapers, smog, chickens, sun through the rain—they all blend into an end-of-the-world scene, like in a movie.

I step out from under the pergola, and the rain hits my face. A few feet onto the lawn and I'm surrounded by hundreds of anthills, perfect little cones, getting pounded by water. On my left is God's house, a glass-walled hangar-like creation projecting hedonism and consent. Its wave-shaped roof cascades to three gentle boulders that touch the glass skin of the house. One of them is split between the terrace and the living room, penetrating the house. The other two flank a curved Noguchi swimming pool.

"Move your ass!" Ray yells, and he bolts downhill in the opposite direction from the house, toward a geodesic dome–like pavilion that blisters from the soil.

"What's in the ball?" I shout.

"A little wet here!" Ray waves me toward the dome. "Come!" He looks excited; it has to be drugs.

The dome is a library. Books upon books, on circular shelves holding on to the dome's belly. And yet there's nothing conducive to reading. There are no chairs or sofas, no ladder that I can find to reach the high shelves. It's as though one is supposed to magically take down a book and then leave, or not be there at all. I walk across the empty space nervously, like I am trespassing on an unfinished art installation, or on a giant framework's guts—HAL 9000's memory made up of hundreds of colored book spines, processing me. When I reach the other side, I try to break into the designer's mind. Edmund Hillary next to *The Art of Draping* by urban planning. What *is* this?

"The *hell* are we doing here?" I ask, but Ray shushes me. He drops a book on the floor and reaches into his pocket.

We share four fat lines on top of *How Proust Can Change Your Life* and then start the walk uphill. It is the first time that I have my own bag in my pocket, and I feel terribly muscular, like I could stand a direct hit by a two-hundred-pound Warren bomb. A heavy-metal version of "Careless Whisper" comes from God's house, and I feel Ray's hand on my arm. "Not a word to Teresa."

I nod.

Stepping into Tatiana's mother ship, I lock eyes on its plaster pseudo-ceiling and then scan up to a Nagasaki Fat Man roof.

"Saddam! Osama!" Ray yells at God's poodles, who are jumping on him. "Sit! Sit! Where's Bush? Where's your toy?"

Osama takes a quick sniff of me and goes back to Ray, who feeds him mints, or coke. Saddam dances around as we start to walk through this concrete nothing—no furniture, save two built-in rectangular ashtrays sprouting straight up from the floor, the only geometric references within a perfectly organic space. The music grows louder, and at the rear of this hangar space we see faces in a MasterCard-logo-shaped sunken living room, like an old drained pool in the middle of an auditorium.

"What does God do again?" I ask under my breath.

"She married a few times," Ray answers.

We go down the steps to the first of the two round mosaic-slated living rooms, which are separated from each other by metal-mesh draperies falling thirty feet from the ceiling. Teresa, in a "Fiat" sweatshirt, gets up from a round sofa and kisses me on the lips.

"I love her," she whispers in my ear.

I look into her eyes to see, confirm, that she knows what she knows, but Teresa turns to the eight or so loungers: "It's a script about real actors who play nonactors in a reality show."

"There's tequila and wine," God tells Ray. "And some vodka in the other room." She points to the metal-mesh drapes. She wears a poncho made of loosely knit-together square-end neckties. She smells like cigarettes.

"I saw your chickens jump around your Carabo," I say to God.

"My *beauties*," God chants.

"Do you have a rooster too?" I ask.

"Oh, I did. But a coyote killed him, with all my Brahmas. Horrible, *horrible!*" She jerks her hands away, and through her loose neckties I see her wrinkled breasts. "He didn't kill my Houdans, because they are black and scary." She turns to Ray: "We are out of gin."

"I grew up with a rooster," I say.

"He was my pasha."

"Stupid people think chickens aren't smart," I coke-talk.

Her bloodshot eyes rest on me; God is stoned. "I only care for the overlooked. Even if it is bad."

"How bad?" I ask.

"Genocide," God says.

"She is talking fashion genocide," Teresa yells from the sofa. "She's shooting Taliban fighters in Burberry checks."

"How did you talk the Taliban into Burberry-ing up?" I ask God.

"I see beauty and art where you don't," God says. "I see art in *Hello!* magazine and in the Taliban. I can show people how to kill brands by association, not by bombing malls."

"So you are decadent," I tell God.

"You confuse art with education because you are Greek. Greeks obsess with the peak. I'm interested in maturity. That's why they call me *God*."

I snatch a tequila shot, but God's not done with me. "Maturity is sexy too," she says. "Post-postmodernism, derivatives . . . they are the new peaks. My husband was a hedge-fund manager; he taught me that. That's why I've made Tatiana so convertible. She knows how to arbitrage through life. Stay still or next when she sees a rise. I'm turning her into the new Bruce Chatwin."

Next? Has God been talking to Alkis? "Who's Bruce Chatwin?" I ask.

"You should read him. He was buried in Greece," God says, before dropping a couple more names that I'm supposed to know but don't.

"I need vodka," I lie, and I walk through the metal draperies to the other side of MasterCard for a hit. No one is there. Two large square marbles, with ancient Greek anatomies on their sides, are used as coffee tables on a *flokati* rug. They are belted by another semicircular sofa, this one with a built-in console at its end that operates a screen that covers most of the room's curved wall and that shows Fischer and Spassky in some Cold War chess final. The silent tension on their foreheads spooks me. One of the console's buttons says "Roof," so I look up to a motorized part of the ceiling, half-open onto a wind sock–shaped glass, sparkling from the rain hitting this bachelor-space-age-capsule living room.

I sit on the rug and take out my little plastic bag. Before I cut, I peek through the metal drapes into the twin living room: Teresa's "Fiat" zipper has gotten caught in Ray's Herd-wick ram-skull buckle, and they are fighting.

"Grab Bush! Grab Bush!" God yells, and then, "Good boy, good boy."

I am in the middle of shaping beautiful lines on the Greek marbles when I suddenly realize that Ray is standing above me, his abashed smile gone.

"What the hell're you doing?" he asks. "Teresa will kick your ass all the way to Sunset if she sees you."

I nod my head slowly and offer my rolled-up twenty to him.

"I'm running out to get smokes and gin. You get it together."

I do my lines, and now the conversation from the other room seems louder, or I'm just more alert. I catch pieces here and there: " . . . it's not that cut-and-dried . . . I don't like this . . . I don't want guns in my house, end of story . . . People get angry, so take away the guns. People have sex, so give them condoms. People get pregnant, so give them the pill. It's quite simple, really . . . Have you talked to Tatiana? . . . What did you tell her to do? . . . Who am I to tell anyone how to live? Things happen, we'll deal with it . . . Have you told Ray? . . . No, not yet . . . Does the Greek know? . . . Stathis knows . . . Can we get *him* pregnant? . . . I love him . . . How do you say hard-on in Arabic? . . ."

Tatiana's number flashes on my cell phone, and I pick up. "Hey!"

"Hey yourself," Tatiana yells. "What the hell are you doing with my family?" I can hear Justin laughing in the background.

"I thought *I* was your family," I say.

"Aren't you supposed to be working?" Tatiana asks.

"Not on the weekends. How are you? How you feeling?"

"Stop asking me that."

"Trouble in Beatriceland?" I say.

"*Fuck* me, Stathis. I don't want you hanging out with Ray."

"Ray's a friend. You're family."

"Cut it out. If you dare tell him that I'm pregnant . . ."

"Relax!" I yell. Since we're probably both on coke, I need to stay calm for both of us. "Have I ever let you down?" I say calmly. "Did Kate speak to her doctor? Did you make an appointment?"

"I'm dealing with it. Kate cares. She didn't leave me."

Osama jumps onto the sofa, with a helpless Bush doll dangling from his jaw.

"I think you should call your godmother *Allah*," I say.

"I don't want you around Ray," Tatiana insists. "He's an underearning scum."

"I don't look at tax returns," I sneer. "Can we move on now?"

"Oh . . . 'cause Stathis is so humble."

"What's wrong with being humble but confident?"

"That's *exactly* what's wrong with you, Stathis. It's humble *and* confident. Not *but*! You're not doing us a fucking *favor*. You're not *Erik*!"

"No, *you*'re Erik. Getting bored and moving on, fucking everyone over. You made Alkis break up with his fiancée, the mother of his child, and then you dumped him."

"*Rapist! Middle class!*"

"I'm fucking *working* class!" I yell, reaching for my plastic bag. "Born and raised. Have you ever heard the word *job*?"

"I know your job—to hang out with me because my parents are famous."

"Fuck off and die," I say, and take a bump. "You use them as your props. 'Boohoo, I'm so scared . . .' Go fucking kill them, *both*, so maybe you'll get a life."

"Fine by me." Tatiana sniffles. "Teresa taught me how to throw up."

Saddam comes through the drapes with a heavy-metal jeweled skull on his collar. Osama jumps on him. "Why do I see skulls everywhere?" I mumble.

"Lee started it. It's an epidemic."

"Lee?"

"McQueen," Tatiana says. "It's his signature."

"Freak . . . When are you going to see a doctor?"

"I'm working on it."

I laugh. "Which means? Should I be worried?"

"I'm making up my mind."

"What . . . What the fuck. You're not ready for this. You're not *sober* for this. You hate Ray. You're in a revenge trip 'cause she stole your boyfriend."

"He was never my boyfriend, you *asshole*!"

"Whatever. You felt bypassed, humiliated. I love you, but you're a twenty-year-old drunk, pregnant bulimic." I sniff. "And so am I, at thirty-one."

She took a second. "Well, you're not pregnant."

"True," I say. "But I got a schizophrenic thing with my home too."

"I want to go to France for a while. I want to spend some time with my father." Her breathing is getting choppy. She sniffs cocaine, or cries, or both. "I want my mom."

"Baby . . . she's right here."

"Don't you *fucking* dare! Right now, you're the most important person in my life. I'll take the morning flight out to LA. Don't tell Teresa," she sobs, and hangs up.

I light a cigarette and slouch back on the sofa. The screen shows George Hamilton singing to Imelda Marcos. She applauds, laughs, and bends her head back the Andrea way. Then performers in glittering red costumes chant in absurd synchronicity to the Ceaușescus in a large stadium, followed by footage of Persian army replicas parading in front of the shah. I look for an ashtray, trying to figure out the scenes on the screen, the parties, whether there's a theme. Two hollowed Greek stones are next to an ancient amphora vase in the living room. I open the vase and see watermelon scraps, used tea bags, and nutshells. God's composting, and I get it: Tatiana blurs trash and art by living in both. She panfries next to a Warhol. She's indifferent to the unique. God cooks in a Picasso pot, *eats* the extinct.

I take one of God's hollowed stones, *my* stone, and shove it in my pants. But it hurts my dick, so I pull it out again.

"How's my daughter doing?" Teresa says, her eyes freezing on my unbelted crotch.

"She's sorting it out," I say, and Teresa smiles.

Are people proud of their children even when they totally fuck up? Could I ever go back to Greece? "And how are you?" I ask her.

"I am where I want to be," Teresa replies.

SEVENTEEN

THE POOL AT THE CHATEAU is a simple oval surrounded by trees. I'm about to fall asleep on my chaise longue, but Tatiana's sudden strokes make me open my eyes. She reaches the deep end, puts one arm on the rim, and waves to me.

"Jump in," she yells.

I glance at my watch; it's one a.m. The lights inside the pool, the only lights around, give her skin a healthy glow that it doesn't have in New York. "I'm not wearing any underwear," I yell back.

"Pussy," she says softly, yet loud enough for me to hear.

It's a large garden, but we are the only ones in it. I throw off my T-shirt and jeans and go for it.

We float for a while, talking nonsense, waiting for Ray's dealer to call back. I keep hearing my cell phone ringing when it really isn't. After the third false alarm, Tatiana tears her flannel bikini top off and throws it to the side of the pool.

"It's only fair," she says, getting rid of her bottom too. "Plus, swimming naked is infinitely better. You are Greek, you should know that."

"That's correct," I say, absorbed by two butterflies near her spruced-up breasts. "These are new." I touch them.

"Kate got them too," Tatiana says with enthusiasm.

"They are beautiful."

Her face goes all business. "What are you up to, really?"

"What do you mean?"

"Here. This. LA. Stathis, you've been moving from one city to another for years. What's the endgame?"

It's been a while since I've explained what passes as my life. I'd always been able to justify my running around the world—whether it was leaving Trikeri or chasing Erik. But now, naked, confronted, I'm stripped of excuses for my journey, and of my faith in it, and instead what comes to mind is all the time I've wasted. I see myself roaming, like Ray's lonely oceanic whitetip.

"Tu parles?" I ask Tatiana.

"Have some balls."

I look down. "They shrink in water," I say with a smile.

"Talk to me," Tatiana says. She comes closer and kisses me lightly on the lips.

"Fine," I say. "I just don't know how it all ends."

"That's not necessarily bad," she says, fixing my wet hair. "I can sort things out for you. Tell me about your village. How was it, growing up?"

She is a pregnant addict, she is sick, and I'm humoring her: "What do you want to know?"

"When did you fall in love for the first time?" she asks.

"That must have been my dog, Argan."

Tatiana laughs, and so do I.

"Hey, honestly," I say. "He was supersmart, the best dog in Trikeri, in the world. Okay?" I laugh again. "No. I mean, that's all you get there, love for dogs—there are no people. Either you turn into a saint, or you go mad. You masturbate a lot, you build fish traps, you go to church, you repair boats and nets, your knuckles get knobby and swollen. And if you leave and find love, you're so repressed that you fall unconditionally."

"I want to go there," Tatiana says. She takes my left palm in her hand and, poor thing, kisses it. "I love having sex by myself," she adds.

"Me too." I shrug, smiling. "Who do you think of when you masturbate?" I ask, a question I never dared ask Erik.

"Anyone. Kate, you, my mother . . . Does that bother you?"

"That you think of me? Or that you think of your mother?"

"Either. It's so natural."

"I care about you," I say, looking into her eyes. "I want you to be happy." I touch her tummy. "You need to fix this."

"I will, in France. My father is waiting for me. You'll like him. He's a genius, just like you."

She puts her hands around my neck and wraps her legs around my waist. I look up to the trees as she gets comfortable on me. She's fit for a cokehead.

"I love you," she whispers into my ear. "Please don't tell anyone I'm here. Please don't let me down."

"Have I ever?" I keep one hand on the rim of the pool, the other treading water, keeping both of us afloat. She buries her head on my neck as her ass bumps on my dick. "What are you up to now?" I ask.

"Nobody can know I stayed with you," she repeats nervously.

"I thought we settled that."

"I need a clean break from them. I can't stand it anymore. I want to change."

Naked in the pool, holding the daughter of a movie star who fucks herself thinking of her mother, and who, right now, makes my dick hard, I pretend I believe her. She wants to change, she says. She can't pay for a cup of coffee and flounces back from cattle calls like she's hot shit, and yet she's got it in her mind that she wants to change.

"They don't know you are here," I reassure her. "They'll never know."

"You are so handsome," Tatiana says, and I feel her breath on my neck. "So smart and subtle. When will you stop chasing this nothing? When will you stop hotel living?"

"I'm not sure," I say, and kiss her on the lips as she plays with my nipple. "Can I eat your ass out?" I ask.

"I want you to rape me, like you did that boy. But don't hurt me."

EIGHTEEN

March 2007

ALKIS, **IN A SHORT OVERCOAT,** drinks espresso by himself on the patio of the Chateau. He has no newspaper or handheld in sight.

"You live here, and you are still late," he says as I approach.

I had just woken up. "Welcome to Los Angeles. How is London?" I mumble, looking for a waiter so I avoid breathing on him. "How's your daughter?"

"Great," Alkis says, and from the corner of my eye I see him staring at me. "Don't worry, I will not torture you with pictures. You look roughed up enough."

I ignore him. "How is the fund-raising coming along?"

"Not swimmingly," Alkis says, tapping his hand on the table.

"I'm sorry to hear that," I say and finally look at him.

"Nah, it's all good. My boss ran into some of his Morgan mafia mates. They go all the way back to Boca Raton. They hooked us up with a big boy."

"That's good."

"One hopes," Alkis says. "You can take off your sunglasses now. How bad can it be?"

"What?"

"Whatever it is that you're doing. Everything," Alkis says. "Your Palm Springs shirt, to begin with. That coke look all over your face."

"I feel great," I lie, and peek at my shirt, Ray's shirt. "I try not to take myself too seriously," I mutter.

"You look like a sorry fuck. Have you been up all night?"

"Enough! Let's get some eggs or something."

We order a lamb sandwich, salmon, Bloody Marys, and a triple espresso for me.

"Coffee in LA is crap," Alkis says, and puts some sugar in his cup.

"I thought you liked this place. You were the one who brought me—" I stop.

"Christmas 2003," Alkis says with satisfaction.

I nod. "I know, I was here."

"So the Dubya is gone for good," Alkis says.

"Yes, Erik's gone. A hundred percent."

"Good. He was a phony."

"I've done worse. Let's not talk about him."

But Alkis is having fun. "Is Erik fighting the stem-cell war with his new boyfriend? From within the machine?"

"Don't know and don't care," I say, loud enough to feel my headache. LA's smoggy sun is approaching our table. This will be a long lunch.

Alkis gives me a condescending smile. "Really?"

"Really."

"Funny, that, 'cause I thought Erik was the reason you partied with Teresa . . ." Alkis shrugs. "One's got to match, right?"

He's an ass. He blames me for Tatiana, for his becoming her pet. For the fact that he broke up with Cristina for nothing. "I don't party with Teresa," I say.

"Oy, mate, last time you *bothered* to answer your cell phone you were at her place in Laurel Canyon. And you were hammered."

"Happens," I murmur. "And where were you calling me from? Tatiana's?"

He shakes his head, smiling. "Hillarical! You got me! Oh, you got me good."

The sun, my hangover; I want to throw up.

"By the way—" Alkis quickly checks the tables next to us. "Judging from the daughter, I can't *begin* to imagine how high maintenance Teresa must be."

"I don't know," I say. "She is overseas, shooting. She's not around."

Our food arrives.

"Eat!" I say. "Greeks are hungry."

"Don't get grumpy with me 'cause of your pals."

"I'm not grumpy."

"No, you're not grumpy, you're angry. You are angry because you can't afford them. If they stay up all night, they'll sleep in. If they drink their savings, people still ask them to go out. That's not your life. Never was."

I'm this close to telling him that I fucked his ex up the ass. "Is that why it didn't work out with you and Tatiana?"

Alkis gives me a pitying once-over. "Paul says you're neither blue- nor white-collar anymore. He says that you're *black*-collar, their clubbing entourage."

"Paul *talks*?" I say, and down half my espresso.

Alkis takes a deep breath. "He can, I suppose. Who would have thought Paul would be our success story?" he says seriously. "He's getting rich, on paper at least, and more famous than the people he stalks."

"Please, I'm eating . . ." I make a face. "And Tatiana's a friend. So let's drop it."

"She's a bipolar *prostitute!*"

I'm not sure where to start now. With the "haute provincialism" he used to smell in her pussy, or with her fucking him like a dog? But I don't know if he knows I've slept with her—one never knows whom Tati calls when she's wasted—which makes me slightly nervous. He could be sniffing me out, testing me to see if I'll come clean.

"What do you want from me?" I say calmly. "To write on a piece of paper that Tatiana is a whore? Is *that* what you want?"

"Pretty much," he says, and his face finally relaxes. "Do you know that if it wasn't for me, Paul would have 'lost' your number?"

"That's just Paul."

"That's *so* not Paul, mate. He sent you a postcard from Trikeri, from your bloody village, which he visited with his girlfriend. He and your father tried to call you. They were worried about you."

"Never got the postcard."

"He sent it to Command. I passed him your work address *myself* when he couldn't get online in Greece."

"Well, I've been on the road."

"You've been on the road going down. And it's a stupid way to go."

"What's a clever one?" I chug my Bloody Mary with a shrug, but Alkis's face stays serious.

"Just don't go. If someone fucks with you, like Erik did, or the way Tatiana fucked me over, maybe you don't have to fuck them back. And you *definitely* don't have to fuck yourself up. You learn and move on."

I don't need this right now. "Who wants an easy life?"

"Then toughen up. Smile and lie about it. Everything's a lie. Lie or die!"

"Like you do with work?" I throw back. I can't tell if I need more food or to get rid of some.

"You seriously think that you are better than me," Alkis says, almost laughing. "You go from one biotech to another, selling them the same shit. You only exist because pharmacos want to spy on one another. You're a delivery boy who makes way less money than I do. And look at you—I'm surprised you still have a job."

He thinks I still give a damn. "Well, they can't fire me," I mumble to myself, but Alkis picks up on it. His pitying expression is gone.

"Talk to me," he orders. I can tell by the sound of his voice that he smells blood.

"Andrea and some BioProt folks are devaluing the company," I concede, happy for the distraction. "So her man can do a takeover at a discount."

"I *knew* it!" Alkis exhales. "I fucking knew it." He leans toward me worriedly. "How deep are you in it?"

I say nothing.

He grabs me by my palm-tree shirt. "Listen to me. Now you *listen* to me. You'll be the first one to be subpoenaed if shit hits the fan. Andrea knows you're a cokehead and tolerates it. She may actually *like* it, 'cause you'll make the perfect ass to blame if they need one. Get a lawyer. *Today.* I can find some names for you in New York. This is no 'oops' with Tatiana anymore. Copy your hard drive—what am I saying, you can't do that. You have to 'lose' your laptop and ask for a new one. Get a prepaid phone and don't give the number to anyone but your lawyer. And stop e-mailing me. I'm *serious.*"

My brows furrow, and I nod my head in assent. All I really want to do is go back to my room.

"Stathis, I'm here for you. You're still my ace, mate," Alkis says, and his guy's-guy vulnerability comes through. I look at his broad shoulders; the kind they like to recruit to investment banking.

"And?" I shrug.

"And get the hell out of here. Finish the project and drop those leeches around you. You used to play rugby, for Christ's sake. You don't belong here! Andrea? Teresa? *Constantine?* The guy had to become a Muslim to measure up to his dad."

"You don't know him."

"Fuck him. I don't *wanna* know him. I know you. How about you transfer to London? Or get a new job there? I'm there, and you'll be closer to home. The Greek army was reduced. You can pay for part of your service."

"I'm not your EBS protégé anymore," I say, and stand up to him, literally. "May be a criminal, but I'm a man now."

NINETEEN

From: Andrea Farrugia <andreafarrugia@command.com>

To: Stathis Rakis <stathisrakis@command.com>

Date: Wed, Apr 4, 2007, 3:14 p.m.

Subject: BioProt video conf.

Statis, I believe our Strategic Alternatives are solid. Please set up one-on-ones with the steering committee to walk them through Strategy III (Cosmeceuticals).

Good client facilitation today, but you responded to my action items at 3 p.m. EST. THIS IS UNACCEPTABLE. I need turnarounds before noon my time. This is not negotiable!

Andrea Farrugia

Senior Vice President

Command Consulting

* I am in the business of impact *

From: Teresa BangBang <bangbang@yahoo.com>

To: Stathis Rakis <stathisrakis@command.com>

Date: Sun, Apr 8, 2007, 11:52 p.m.

Subject:

How are you, lover? I haven't spoken to Tati since I talked to you on the phone. She never picks up. She cut me out of her life after she moved to France, after she had the procedure . . . Her father, the asshole, doesn't pick up either. I'm in Paris shooting, and I can't concentrate, I can't perform. I know that you talk to her. PLEASE PLEASE tell her that I want to see her. Please, tell her to call me. Is Ray behaving back home?

I love you. Always.

Teresa.

From: Andrea Farrugia <andreafarrugia@command.com>

To: Stathis Rakis <stathisrakis@command.com>

Date: Thu, Apr 12, 2007, 1:12 a.m.

Subject: BOUZOUKIA

You looked like you arrived straight from a Greek bouzoukia at the video conference today. If you want to have impact, you should button your jacket when you walk into a meeting, and make sure the pink sticker from the dry cleaner is REMOVED from your shirt! Not looking after your looks is telling BioProt that you have no discipline, and that will hurt their appetite for risk.

I couldn't care less about "innovation fatigue." Impact, impact, impact!

Andrea Farrugia

Senior Vice President

Command Consulting

* I am in the business of impact *

From: Tatiana SmartFuck <tatfuckit@gmail.com>

To: Stathis Rakis <stathisrakis@command.com>

Date: Fri, Apr 13, 2007, 9:38 a.m.

Subject: Get to France.

My love, Aix is a paradise. The garden is amazing. I read books and go to the fruit market. I'm working on my relationship with my father. Come see us. Je t'adore. Emotionally and physically available, Tati.

From: Paul deBerg <paulDB@accosting.com>

To: Stathis Rakis <stathisrakis@command.com>

Date: Sat, Apr 14, 2007, 1:06 p.m.

Subject: AccostingTV Gallery opening invitation
A Game Changer—attached

From: Stathis Rakis <stathisrakis@command.com>

To: Paul deBerg <paulDB@accosting.com>

Date: Sat, Apr 14, 2007, 1:10 p.m.

Subject: RE: AccostingTV Gallery opening invitation
I never subscribed to your list.

From: Stathis Rakis <stathisrakis@command.com>

To: Andrea Farrugia <andreafarrugia@command.com>

Cc: Kirk Davies <kirkdavies@command.com>

Date: Fri, Apr 20, 2007, 3:14 p.m.

Subject: Rethink, redesign, redevelop
Andrea—
The majority of the metrics we picked favor Strategy III (Cosmeceuticals). What is the purpose of a full-blown portfolio exercise if our model is structured in a way that predetermines where to invest? It is conceptually messy and confusing to the client. We are about to transform Bio-Prot into a consumer products company. There's still time to rethink our approach.
Stathis.

From: Andrea Farrugia <andreafarrugia@command.com>

To: Stathis Rakis <stathisrakis@command.com>

Date: Sat, Apr 21, 2007, 1:12 a.m.

Subject: RE: Rethink, redesign, redevelop
REDRESS!!!
Andrea Farrugia
Senior Vice President
Command Consulting
* I am in the business of impact *

From: Kirk Davies <kirkdavies@command.com>

To: Stathis Rakis <stathisrakis@command.com>

Date: Sun, Apr 22, 2007, 10:08 p.m.

Subject: RE: Rethink, redesign, redevelop
Dear Stathis:
I celebrate our culture of debate. These are the types of
questions that we welcome. At Command everyone is
equal. We speak freely and we don't smooth out our differ-
ences.

Andrea loves merging science with commerce—she
loves hybrids. She lives in a condo hotel. How is that for
real (estate) options?

I hear that the BioProt people trust you, which is import-
ant. Yet your dress code has come to my attention. Andrea
is not asking you to wear a three-piece suit. Do what I do:
bespoke dress down when on the West Coast.
Regards,
Kirk C. Davies III
Senior Vice President
Command Consulting

TWENTY

BARELY SEE THE SUN IN LA. I live between BioProt conference rooms, tinted-windowed SUVs, and the hills at
dusk. They all contribute to a summer that makes everything seem surreally seamless—BioProt's cement campus
melds into God's hangar house, God's black sofas into Sunset
lounges where I hang out with Ray, and his oversize white
T-shirts into BioProt lab outfits. As work and play merge—I
manage biotech models and Teresa's bank accounts—God,
Ray, and Andrea become the different faces of a trinity. I
have to accept that either the world around me is mad or that
I am, and I choose the former, accusing LA of making me
manipulate science via commerce and cocaine via Xanax.

"How're you doing, man?" A forty-year-old guy in a skate-
boarder outfit taps my shoulder as I search for beer at a convenience store on Sunset. I've no idea who the dude is. Have
we partied? Fucked? Is he a client?

"I'm good," I say. "How are you?"

"Press on!" He smiles, and his crow's-feet turn upward.
"Do they still have you up there?"

"Up?" I say.

"At the Chateau."

"Basically," I say. I need a six-pack, and Ray is waiting outside in the car. I can barely stand up straight because of my insomnia, but this dude here in skate shorts won't stop chatting me up.

I look around for an excuse, anything. Middle-aged guys in Abercrombie & Fitch outfits browse the Raw–Organic–Vegan aisle. "Who am I to judge?" says Teresa from the cover of a tabloid on the bottom shelf, and I flash back to scoring in her garden, having three-ways with Ray in Tatiana's childhood bedroom, watching Ray peeing into the kitchen sink at the Chateau and on a nineteen-year-old, going to coke-for-sex parties in half-built houses, editing BioProt slides with God. So why shouldn't forty-year-olds resist aging? Why not the Andrea doctrine? What's the difference between God's celebrity-for-an-hour virtual-reality game and Andrea's Bio-Prot scheme for face-toning vibrating machines? If culture is driving science, then biotechs will become the new establishment, heading for the pharmacos' heyday of the nineties, oversaturated with cash, blockbusters, and denial about research and patent expirations. "I'd rather reinvent than invent," God says. What if we go Andrea, and give up on hard innovation? Let drug pipelines get acquired and then turn novelty to lifestyle and marketing instead. "You know that you're irrelevant, that you're extinct, when you follow the trend. And that's when it gets interesting," God taught me.

"I'm double-parked," I tell the dude. "Do you want to come to a formwork party?"

MY CELL PHONE IS RINGING nonstop, but some girl's torso blocks me from going for it. As I roll over, my hand gets wet from come or piss on Ray's shark. I see my phone under Teresa's kabbalah bendels on her nightstand.

"Hello," I groan.

"Are you sleeping?" Alkis asks.

"No. Sore throat."

"Right."

"What's up?" I hear office chaos in the background. I've no clue what time it is in London, or here.

"Listen, mate." Alkis sounds serious. He takes a second. "They found your Greek pal Constantine, I mean, Zemar, er, in Peshawar."

"What?" I rub my itching eyes. "Oh . . ."

"They don't know if it was an overdose or murder. It's news today. I mean, it's *part* of the news today. I thought you should know."

"What was it? Like . . . what did he take?"

"Heroin. They found him with a syringe in his arm. Channel Four said they'll do an autopsy in Pakistan. Hey, mate, everything's bananas today. BNP suspended withdrawals. They tell me they can't move their subprime bonds. I have to go. I'll talk to you later."

I pull myself out of bed, holding my phone tightly, and walk through Teresa's balcony door. I sit on the garden steps, and the mist that clouds Laurel Canyon sends a chill over my naked body. It's the first time that I feel cold in LA. There's too much in the garden, trees growing under trees, everything mishmashed to form a jungle just two miles from Sunset. The sound of the birds conflicts with the hum from the city. Nothing makes sense in Southern California. I dial my sister.

"Oh my God! Where are you?" she cries. "What time is it?" I can hear her sobbing.

"I want to come back," I say.

TWENTY-ONE

AT SOME POINT THIS FALL (though I never did figure out what fall meant in LA), my feelings of apathy soured into defeat. Constantine was dead at thirty-eight, Erik was long gone, Andrea had gotten her way with BioProt, and Tatiana was not picking up in France. A postcard I'd sent to Jeevan (addressed: "Jeevan, Moonhole, Bequia") was returned to the front desk at the Chateau.

The morning after our final presentation at BioProt, I'm up and packed before the sun rises. I want to catch the first flight to New York, as the prospect of traveling with Andrea later in the day is unbearable.

"I'm sorry that you are leaving us," Josh at the front desk tells me, handing me my final bill and the returned post-card.

"Thank you," I murmur, staring at the "Return to Sender" stamp from St. Vincent and the Grenadines. I look up and see Josh smiling. I'm thrown by how young he looks compared to how old I feel. "Thank you for everything you did for me," I say, and shake his hand.

On my ride to LAX, I keep telling myself that I need to text Ray; we never had a proper good-bye, not that we ever had a proper anything. But I can't get myself to type a single word. Flying back east, I try to understand this. I try to comprehend LA. The place where I gave up and stopped caring. Just like Ray, I got sucked into Hollywood culture and turned into a pig in the process, giving hand jobs to strangers and supporting Andrea. I ask for some vodka, hoping it will help me accept that no one can play the game without whoring themselves a bit. But the drink doesn't do it; I don't feel any better. I try to distract myself with *The Bourne Ultimatum*. I'm too tired to follow the plot, but I still get that Matt Damon is way conscientious. So I flip to *Ocean's Thirteen*, which seems closer to home.

BACK IN NEW YORK, I keep a low profile. I have to; I have no friends in the city anymore. I'm supposed to do some follow-up work for BioProt, but it's just support, remote work, and I don't need to be in the office. So I'm back to my old Sant Ambroeus habits. Once again I live and work on my barstool in the restaurant; once again regulars edge away from me at the bar; once again AAers and *Sex and the City* tourists roam around Perry and West Fourth; once again I try to ignore my phone. It's like I never left.

"Mate!" Alkis says when I pick up on his third try.

He's been in New York for a week, he says. He knows that I'm at Sant Ambroeus.

"I see" is all I say.

He is in town with Cristina. They are back together, sorting things out. Would I like to have dinner with them in the Village?

I have to think about this. We haven't spoken since LA except for a couple of generic messages—"Paul's e-trash empire made the *Huff Post*," "The Chinese to save Bear"— nothing on Tati, Erik, BioProt, or anything important whatsoever. Dinner with Cristina, before a proper catch-up, seems funny.

"Fine, here is the catch," Alkis says, after my long pause. "Kevin booked the table. I know he is Erik's brother, but he is the one who suggested I call you. Do we have a problem?"

"How come you are having dinner with Kevin?" I ask, thinking of Constantine, and I am grateful at the realization that Erik wasn't my first thought.

"We ran the London marathon together," Alkis says sarcastically. "You spent too much time in LA, mate. Think East Coast, think *smart*! The guy runs his own fund and we are on our third round of layoffs, with two fifty-points cuts this month. Our CFO's on the move. I *need* you tonight."

"Your CFO said the worst of the credit shit was over," I say, and Alkis hangs up on me.

I dial him back.

ALMOST FIVE YEARS TO THE day that I met Erik, I walk down my block to have dinner with his brother. I step into the low-ceilinged restaurant and pick up on a free-floating anxiety in its bar.

"This is Larry, the maître d'," Alkis says, introducing me to a man who's obsessing over a touch screen built into a podium. "Stathis is my favorite ex-colleague," Alkis adds.

Larry pivots his head between screens. He's cornered by a guy in a leather racing jacket and a Partner from McKinsey I've seen around the biopharma conference circuit. Alkis touches Larry's shoulder, and I understand the drama: everyone waiting is in desperate competition for a table.

Kevin, six-four, stands by the fireplace at the end of the bar. He has a martini in his hand and is talking to Helen, a brunette who's been hanging on to him since before I met him three years ago. His gray suit, his black turtleneck, and the circles under his eyes project success and unhappiness.

"I'll get us a drink," I tell Alkis, and make my way toward them.

"Captain Stathis!" Kevin tries to hug me, but Helen stops him and takes his martini out of his hand. The moment gone, we shake hands. He has Erik's curved-down eyes.

"Kevin!" I say. "You found your way downtown."

"For *you*, Captain, anywhere. You remember my girlfriend, Helen?"

Helen smiles coldly. I haven't seen her since Kevin's party, the night Erik and I broke up. She looks aged, in a forced, Stepford-wife way.

"Helen and I are old friends," I say, trying to break the ice.

She is in a printed horsehair suit, and her necklace looks like the Dow Jones Index of the last ten years, engraved on a bar of gold. Could I be seeing things? I haven't even had a drink yet.

"Alkis mentioned that you live in the neighborhood," Helen says.

"I live down the street," I say, still stupefied by her necklace. "But I've been out of town for quite a while. This is my first time at the Waverly Inn, actually."

"We love it," Helen says. "John is a genius. His food is so hearty, so winter! You'll become a regular."

"I'm sorry, but is your necklace, ah, what I think it is?" I ask.

"You better believe it!" Kevin jumps in. "US equities! Helen recently changed jobs. She is now the senior VP of public relations for—"

"*And* communications," Helen corrects him.

"And communications," Kevin echoes, "for a fashion house." He touches his gray suit. "Easy tailoring," he says, showing it off to me.

Helen rolls her eyes.

"What are you drinking?" Kevin asks me.

"Vodka dirty, up. And let's get Alkis whatever he was having."

Kevin turns to the bar.

"Are you celebrating Tuesday's rally?" I ask Helen, nodding at her necklace.

"Excuse me?" she says.

"Last Tuesday, we had the biggest market gain since 2002."

"Oh, no!" She laughs. "It's just conversation jewelry."

"It worked," I say, but she opens a malachite-embellished clutch and checks her cell phone.

Fuck you and your iPhone; we used to trade notes on the brothers.

The Disney girl walks in. She is flanked by two guys in rap-boxing outfits, and there's an androgynous creature behind her. She must have lost ten pounds since I last saw her. She's barely standing. Her lips, bigger, injected, match the color of her red-hooded dress. Larry takes them right into the main room.

"Stathis, here." Kevin hands me a martini.

"Thank you." I point at Alkis, who's now stalking the new person behind the podium. "I thought we had a reservation," I say.

"We do, but Alkis likes to drive," Kevin explains. "He's a New Yorker that way. Plus, I think he's been a bit jumpy since he's gotten back with Cristina."

"Where *is* Cristina?" I ask.

"Oh, she's on her way," Helen says with a dismissive gesture. "Something came up with the Four Seasons nanny."

"I never met Alkis's ex, but I've heard stories," Kevin says, raising his eyebrows. "She was a friend of yours, right?"

"Still is," I say, almost proudly. "Though I haven't seen her for a while. She moved to France."

"Alkis was pretty shaken by all that," Kevin continues. "She was a troublemaker."

"Who isn't?" I say, ready to bring up Constantine, but I see some connection in Kevin's eyes, and I let it slide. "She is just young," I say, and notice Alkis leading Cristina our way.

"Cristina!" Helen shouts.

"I don't believe we are here for a second time this week," Cristina complains. "I'm a vegetarian," she says, explaining herself, and kisses us. Same big smile and teeth. She still sounds, looks, and smells like Italy.

"Have you settled up at the bar?" Alkis asks Kevin.

Kevin nods and hands Alkis a whiskey, neat, and we follow the maître d' into the main room's glow. Candlelike lights reflect on fruit-red banquettes and an autumn-colored mural, filled with caricatures of bohemians turned household names. I recognize Dylan, Pollock, Kerouac, and Brando, all of them doing their signature unhealthy but sainted activities, drinking and writing or smoking and drawing. I'm fixated on them—they make me feel better about the coke I have with me—and I stumble on a table in the middle of the floor. A tall waiter grabs me before I land on a plate of truffled mac and cheese.

"Thank you, John," Alkis says.

"Thank you, John," I repeat, dazed.

People clap and cheer as John politely bows.

Our table is a room with a view—a banquette walled between the main room and the bathroom, with an internal window on the central tables. I sit at the edge of the bench, close to the bathroom, which is handy. Helen shares the far end with Cristina, Alkis sits next to me, and Kevin is directly across.

"Stathis, if this is your first time here you *must* try the tuna tartare," Helen says. "It's the strongest of the small plates."

I pick up the preview menu in front of me, which is odd; I'm pretty sure Alkis and Tatiana called me from here when I was in LA. "Preview? Didn't they open last year?" I ask Alkis.

"They opened in the 1920s," Alkis says, wolfing down a biscuit. He is stress-eating.

I browse the menu and waver between a line-appetizer-line combo and a quick entrée followed by a couple of lines. But the plates are described in pie-and-mash words—Amish chicken, clam chowder, lardons—which means large sizes, which means it could be tricky to choke it down fast.

"There is only one vegetarian plate . . ." Cristina sighs.

"How long have you been a vegetarian?" Helen asks her.

"Since I saw *War of the Worlds*," Cristina replies, and we all look at her oddly.

"Why?" Kevin asks.

"It made me aware of speciesism," Cristina says.

"Who wants wine?" Alkis asks, grabbing a second biscuit, but everybody stays with Cristina.

"What if aliens came to Earth and treated us like stock, like fuel?" Cristina says. "We would go: '*No!*'" She shakes a finger. "We would be like: 'You can't do that!' And the aliens would say: 'But we are only treating you the way you treat less intelligent species.' What if *that* happened?"

"Oh, totally," someone spurts, and I have bite my lip so I don't burst out laughing.

"Cristina is taking a class on voluntary social systems in London," Alkis says quickly, and people nod. "Where's the bloody sommelier?" he murmurs.

"John the Savior," I say to the waiter who spared me from the macaroni crash.

"My pleasure, sir," John says.

"Actually, it is the savior and the sinner from John," Kevin says contentedly.

What if I fucked you harder than I fucked your brother? Made you scream my name while I screamed: Fuck you, Erik.

"May I briefly interrupt to tell you about our specials tonight?" John says.

"I'm good to go, John. Tuna tartare and a burger. Medium rare," I say, getting up and heading to the men's room.

Ten minutes later, everyone is talking.

"This trend for compulsory fun at work is becoming *ridiculous*," Helen tells Alkis. "We are a step from having departments of fun."

"Paul's website says that people go from one inn to the other," Cristina says.

"Is there another Waverly Inn?" Kevin asks.

"Oh, no!" Cristina laughs. "They go from the Waverly Inn to the Beatrice Inn."

"I haven't been there," Kevin says. He turns to me and asks slyly, "Have you been to the Beatrice Inn, Stathis?"

I stare back and lie: "I have not."

Alkis gives me a knowing look. Whatever. I owe him nothing; I owe them nothing. I'm only here 'cause I fell for someone five years ago.

"So, what's up with you guys?" Kevin asks Alkis. "What's Lehman's story? What's up with O'Meara? Why is he moving to risk management?"

"It's just internal. Reshuffling. No blame game attached. If anything, it shows that we can deal with a storm," Alkis says, playing with his glass. "How are things on the buy side?"

"We're living in a Harry Potter movie. Don't say Voldemort. Don't say the R-word. *Recession!* Boo!" Kevin makes the stop sign with his hands. "It's a *joke*. You can bag a recession just by fetishizing it."

A bottle of red arrives, but I sip my second dirty martini— they come cloudy and strong. I look through our window to the main floor. The waiters, all men, attend editors, High Line heavyweights, writers, and painters seated in the central banquettes. They dine in tracksuits and pajamas, and scold their children for playing with their gadgets and food. People at peripheral tables do not gawk but are not oblivious to them either. Rather, they seem to have mastered the art of quick, semicontemptuous scans. Food here is an aside, an accessory. A woman in a man's tuxedo at the main banquette lights a cigarette. She sits under her very own image in the mural behind her: also portrayed in a tux smoking. I watch this weird person-mural, theater-Inn scene, and God's Ceaușescu footage pops into my mind: everyone dancing in a collective paranoia, transforming a whole country into an inane stage. "You know you're close to the end when theater becomes life," Demosthenes preached to the ancient Athenians.

" . . . because at the end of the day it's all about expectations management. Right, Stathis?" Kevin says.

"I'm sorry about your friend Constantine," I respond instead.

"What?" Kevin spits. "Well, yes. That was a shame." He is annoyed. He goes for his red.

"He spoke highly of you," I go on.

"I don't want to discuss it," Kevin says firmly.

"Fine. Let's talk about expectations management," I say. "Is that your brother? His take on management consulting's stupid jargon?"

"No more martinis for you," Alkis says, and moves my drink away.

I take out my smokes and light one.

"What the *hell* are you doing?" Alkis is mortified.

I point at the woman at the central banquette, smoking. But Alkis is furious: "That's the *owner's* table, Stathis! And we want to be able to make a reservation again. Go outside!"

I put it out. As I stand up, I notice myself trembling.

"Jesus!" Alkis shakes his head. "How do your clients put up with you?"

I'm fucking sick of everything about him. "Save it for Lehman," I say. "But maybe you won't have time to play smoking—witch hunt anymore."

I'm halfway through the main room when I hear a laugh I recognize. My jaw is shaking so much that I don't want to turn. But after Andrea shouts my name twice, I have no choice but to deal with her. Sitting pretty beside her fat man-friend–CEO, Andrea keeps waving me over. She stands up— she's wearing clothes she could have worn to work, though her jewelry is smaller—and introduces us. She does the grateful-Partner thing: I am "simply indispensable," a "committed consultant." And "Oh," they are waiting for "Carolina and Reinaldo," but I "*must*" have a glass with them.

John appears out of nowhere with a folding chair.

I give him an *are-you-stalking-me* look and sit down, but my legs won't stay still and I rattle the table; the wineglasses look like they're in an earthquake. I wonder how bad my jaw's shaking.

The CEO is in a black turtleneck that promotes his nipples. He looks younger than his age, the way very fat people often have no age. I notice his watchband, which is so tight on him, so ready to snap; if I stabbed his palm with a fork right now no blood would come out. I'm this close to laughing in the faces of the whale and the prostitute opposite me, but a string of questions crosses my mind: *Is he going for BioProt next quarter? Will he dump Andrea after the deal? Will they throw a BMW onto my bonus at the end of the year?*

Andrea wants to know if I'm enjoying my "much-deserved beach time after Los Angeles." She smiles as she stabs my knee with her nails so I'll stop rocking the table.

"Ouch!" I yell. "Er, well, it's good to be back in New York."

"Command would never have added so much value without Stathis," she tells the fatty. "Champagne!" She motions to John.

"It was a team effort," I say, and I begin to slowly rock their table again.

"Stathis has integrity," Andrea says.

"That is the most expensive virtue," the CEO adds.

"He is a purist," Andrea flirts, handing me a glass of champagne. "He believes that companies should focus on their core competencies," she says.

Blow is the only thing that keeps me from throwing up the very little tuna I touched.

"What about corporate evolution?" the CEO asks me.

"If it makes people happy, then I'm all for it," I respond.

I try to take a sip, but the champagne glass is a coupe—unreal in 2007—and I spill half of it on their buttermilk biscuits. People from the next table look at us.

"I'm sorry," I say, embarrassed.

John leans toward me attentively, but Andrea waves him away. "Stathis is a keeper," she says, dabbing at my mess with her napkin.

The CEO pushes the wet biscuits to the side. "Effective change can be uncomfortable, sometimes even disruptive." He checks for my reaction.

"Effective change, organic change, from within, has momentum," I say.

"What about just dipping in? People see opportunities, fall in love with ideas, and go for it," the CEO says, and touches Andrea's hand.

I look at his nipples again and try to fathom the companies, the weddings, the divorces, the children, the court fights that this orca must have been through, and I wonder why he is still throwing himself at the game. Why would he still cross lines and take all-or-nothing risks? Do people grow up, or do they just get fat while chasing their first high?—Which reminds me, I need to wrap this up and run home for a decent line.

"I thought that Andrea was a pure innovation gal, but I guess her interests have shifted. Oh well . . ." I say, and stand up.

"*Sit down!*" the fatty orders.

I do.

He lets go of Andrea's hand and points at me. "You are a consultant. All you do is look at drugs. But Andrea sees things holistically. She understands the patient experience. She knows that compliance is as important as efficacy. Women forget their cholesterol pill, but they never forget their moisturizer. Smart drugs will combine the two so they can control diseases better."

"Got any coke with vitamin C?" I wink in John's direction.

MINUTES LATER, I STUMBLE DOWN the street to my apartment. I walk in and try to turn on the lights, but my lamps are fancy

Italian things Tatiana picked out, and I can't find the switch-
es. I'm not sure why, but it's freezing in here. I'm ready for a
couple of lines to warm me up, but I hear voices in the corridor. I think they are calling my name. Could it be Alkis?
The CEO's bodyguards? Tom from next door? People might
knock on my door at any second, so I need to do my stuff and
escape to the Beatrice to pick someone up. I'm busy emptying
my little plastic bag when my phone vibrates with an incoming text.

"I hear crazy things about Tatiana. Please tell her to call
me!! Teresa."

I grab a book by Däniken that was lying under the Iridium
cell phone on the Museum of the Recent Past shelf that Tatiana curated, and cut two lines on its cover.

Finally, I feel that sweet bitterness going down my throat.
I'm better already.

I pick up my cell and type back: "for the tenth time T, ionly
speak with Tari when she calls. she nver picks up. will tel her."
I press Send and look around for my leather jacket, the one
Tati picked out for me, but I can't find it. So I put on my work
coat and leave for the Bea.

"Douche bag." Alkis's text stops me on my stoop.

"Send me the check," I text back, walking down Bank
Street.

"No worries. I'll keep your jacket," he responds.

"Looks like you might need it."

"Fuck you very much."

"No, fuck YOU."

I make a left onto West Fourth and another left onto Twelfth, which is empty. There's no one at the door at the Beatrice, it's not even eleven, and I can't think of anyone to call, so I keep walking to Hudson, and from there to Jane. I decide to hit Hudson Bar and Books, where I can do some quiet drinking and smoking, but the place is full of cocky first-year associates and their girlfriends. I order a cigar and two tequila shots and sit in a corner, where I start playing with the popcorn the bartender placed in front of me. The TV screen above the restroom shows Teresa pulling out a gun in a James Bond flick. Bond throws her onto a bed and kisses her, and I get this feeling that I might be too old to piss off powerful people or turn friends, like Alkis, into enemies. I look at the mirror behind the bar and see myself looking frantic and bloated. My forehead is sweating. I search my cell phone for the last "fuck you" that I traded with Alkis, but my hands have the shakes. I need one more line to find the Undo button on my phone, but the damn thing vibrates again.

"Whatudoin?"

"Who is this?" I text.

"I have your jacket."

This can't be . . . Fuck it. "What's your address, Kevin?" I type, and the idea that I might get one last shot in my five-year war with Erik sobers me up.

Something funny happens on my way to the Upper East Side. I don't think of Erik, or of the hoops I might have to jump through to sleep with Kevin. Instead I think of the tiny amount of blame I have for Constantine's death. It's like I am going to have to account for losing his postcards, for not sooner passing on to Erik the one I did rescue. I could have made a difference. Strangely enough, I can't even remember Constantine's face. I try to re-create his eyes and voice from when he talked with me, high, on the balcony of the cottage at the Chateau. Constantine is becoming a new memory. He looked up to Kevin: "He's smooth with girls, sports, everything," Constantine said. "Erik is Kevin's obsession. Kevin got the looks, Erik got the brains. They want to fuck each other." Constantine, a junkie, laughed.

KEVIN'S PENTHOUSE DOOR IS OPEN. He stands at the far end of his living room, looking out the window wall. I shut the door and he turns.

"Are you here to talk about Erik or Constantine?" he asks. "Or antiangiogenic agents?" he chuckles.

"Fuck you," I say.

"Where are we going to do that?"

TWENTY-TWO

November 2007

GREEKS SURE HAVE STAMINA," KEVIN says, and picks up the Amstel Light by his nightstand.

I reach for my jeans on the floor and grab my cigarettes.

"You can't smoke in here," he says.

I get up and throw my pants on.

"Go by the window. Make sure you blow the smoke out."

I light up and open the bedroom's balcony door. Two Labs orbit Buddha-shaped bushes on a lit-up roof across the street.

"When did you get those circles under your eyes?" I ask.

"What?" Kevin mumbles.

I turn, but I can barely see him in the dark. "When did you get those circles under your eyes?"

"None of your business," Kevin says. "None of my business. I don't know. Why?"

"Just things in common," I say. "One can be impressive on paper and a mess in real life."

"Thanks for saving me the therapy bill," Kevin says. He laces his fingers and turns his palms out, stretching his arms toward me. "Stick to your résumé, then. Stick to work."

"Kinda too late for that."

"Are you guys going through layoffs?" he asks sharply. He is more curious about or spooked by my job than he is by my come (his brother's ex's come) drying on his chin.

"Don't know," I say. "And don't really care."

He sits up. "How come? Do you have a better offer?"

"Nope. I'm just sick and tired of the bullshit I do for a living."

"Marketing drugs works. Marketing works," Kevin says, grabbing a Kleenex.

"I can't stand this up-or-out race anymore. I think I'm on my last legs at Command."

Kevin wipes my stuff off his torso and chin. "It looks like things are about to cool off a bit," he says. "This race that you're talking about won't be the end of us after all."

"It ended Constantine," I say, and try to read Kevin's reaction in the dark.

"It did not. Constantine was just stupid."

I take a long drag. "You are high on markets, he was high on breaking news. At the end of the day we are all high on something."

"The difference between me and Constantine was balance," Kevin says. "He didn't know where to stop. He was a danger junkie, among other things."

"That's what men do." I blow out my smoke.

"It was a dumb death. And keep your smoke out!" Kevin says. "When you do drugs or you're a war correspondent, you're hot stuff. But when you overdose, or you die trying to get footage, then you're an idiot."

"He knew the risks," I say.

"He thought he knew what his dealers gave him. He thought the Taliban would not fire at him because he was holding a camera. He had reached the point of no return. You met him; you know what I'm talking about. And I *said*, keep your smoke out."

I don't. I can't be the first smoker he has cheated on Helen with.

"Constantine looked up to you. He told me that you could always focus and do the right thing," I say.

"He was high even when we were kids in Hyannis. Of course I was the one who could focus."

I was intimidated by Constantine—by the idea of him— until I met him. Then I liked him. Now I wanted to defend him to this rich, closeted son of a bitch. "Extremes have appeal—they take balls. Your brother thought so," I say.

"My brother always fell for crap like that. He always put himself in the backseat. Behind Constantine, or Warren, or . . . or behind mean fuckers like you," Kevin says, and I see him smiling in the dark.

"But the backseat is not good enough for Hyannis now, is it?"

"If you say so." Kevin takes a good sip from his beer. "So, who's bigger?" He chuckles.

Bitch . . . "What are you talking about?" I play dumb.

"You're the only one who's slept with both of us."

"I haven't slept with Constantine," I say to gain time.

Kevin laughs. "Of course you haven't. I'm talking about Erik. So, who is bigger?"

I don't believe this. "You've never seen your brother hard?"

"We are not perverts, Greek boy."

It's my turn to laugh. "Right! What was I thinking?" I put out my cigarette on his door frame and flick it onto his balcony. "Hey, what're you doing for Thanksgiving?" I ask, but Kevin doesn't reply, and it's too bloody dark to see his face. "Are you *deaf*?" I shout.

"I might go to Boston," he finally says. "Or stay here. Erik and Warren are cooking."

"Do you need a date?" I ask with a shrug, and lean against the glass door. I'm beginning to enjoy this.

He lets out a nervous laugh. "No, thanks."

"'Cause it would be weird for Helen?" I smile. "Or Erik?" There. "We don't want people to get the right idea, do we?"

"Are you done?"

"What if I run into Helen in the lobby?" I ask.

"She's out of town."

"So I should get back to bed then," I say, and just the thought of it makes me ill.

"You can't spend the night here. I don't want any doormen talking."

"Don't flatter yourself. I fucked you because you look like your brother," I say. "What's your excuse? You fucked me because I fucked your brother?"

IT'S QUIET AT COMMAND. MOST people are either at clients' or gone for the day. I swap between Reuters and Bloomberg on my screen, wondering if Alkis will call after the e-mail I just sent him.

He does.

"Is this a joke?" is the first thing that comes out of his mouth. We have not spoken since the Waverly Inn. No e-mails, no texts. Nothing.

"How are you—" I pause—"mate?"

"Fine," Alkis says.

"I'm sorry about the Waverly Inn," I say, but Alkis doesn't respond. He might be distracted; I hear phones ringing in the background, someone yelling "*Fuck* them, we'll go with Deutsche on this one."

"I said I'm sorry," I repeat.

"Fuck the Waverly Inn," Alkis says quickly. "We're not in high school. Not today, anyway. Tell me you did not send that e-mail to Washington . . ."

"Did not."

"Good!" He exhales. "'Cause no one in his right mind would ever send such a thing. That is a termination e-mail. I mean, what *is* this? Are you blowing the whistle?"

"Call it whatever you want. Andrea changed BioProt's numbers, not me. She buried the analysis so her fat fuck could grab the company on the low. That is fraud."

"I *know* what she did. You told me at the Chateau. I read your e-mail. Trust me, you made it *very* clear."

"I don't want my name on her shit."

"Her shit *has* your name on it. You were the one who delivered her shit last September. What I don't get is why you suddenly want to be all by-the-book. Why are you outing Andrea now?"

"Because I wasn't given a choice? Because I'm done with her. With the whole thing."

"That whole thing made you who you are."

"Look where that got me," I say. "Your words."

"I'm talking about your savings account, for God's sake."

"Didn't you blast me and everything about me in LA?"

"Stathis, if you want to leave Command—and you should—this is *not* the way to do it. You need to grow up and be smart about this."

He's not listening to me. "Growing up *is* what I'm trying to do."

"Do you have a job lined up?"

"No."

"*What?*" Alkis blurts out to someone who is talking to him.

"I don't care what time it is over there, we are doing this *tonight*. Hold on a second, Stathis."

The on-hold tune on Alkis's phone, " . . . skies are sunny, bees make honey . . ." makes me smile, thinking about what would have happened if I'd told Erik about Lehman's "I'd Love to Change the World" sound track during our patio days. "You have your memories," Tatiana said to me the last time I saw her, in LA—as if I was supposed to be happy about them. I'm not, though; they haunt me. They make me ask *what if* about everything. What if Erik hadn't sucked the cut on his thumb when we fought? What if I'd never seen past Constantine's wrinkles? What if I hadn't sat down with him and listened to him telling me that both Erik and I would change? What if Alkis hadn't woken me up when Constantine died? What if I'd never woken up from LA myself? What if I hadn't fucked Erik's brother, in lust and disgust for Erik's world? What would have happened then? There are infinite possibilities; not all of them play out. But they start together. They've all been building on each other. Had I not gone to EBS, I would never have met Erik. Had I not met him, fucked him, and planned a week with him in Bequia, I would never have walked into the Command headquarters looking like I owned the place. Had Erik not told me that he cared for me—*cared*—I probably wouldn't have come up with my "Simplicity" shtick at work. Had he not fixed the patio, I might not have been promoted.

I am an addict now, but I can still change my life, just as Constantine said. I can hang up the phone and send the e-mail. Then I can walk down to Gawel's office and leave him a note about coffee, take responsibility, and have some closure before I leave for Paris to see my family. I can start my life all over again, I think as I look at the note on the three Olympic Air tickets on my desk: "Stathis, please check names and dates. I can FedEx the tickets to Greece tomorrow. You are booked at the Lancaster from 11/22 to 11/25."

After seven years, I am going to see my family.

"Sorry," Alkis says as he pops back on the phone. "We're trying to close a deal and things are turning into a colossal fuckfest. Where were we?"

"You were trying to scare me," I say, checking my watch; it's midnight in London.

"If you send that e-mail, you'll be cleaning out your desk by noon tomorrow."

"Perhaps. But she put pressure on me; I was following orders. She breached everything Command is supposed to—"

"Shut up!" Alkis cuts me off. "If you're trying to sue them, you picked the wrong month, mate. A year ago, *maybe*. Maybe you could have gotten a settlement that would've floated your ass for a bit. But not today; they have bigger worries. *You* should be worried. Clouds are everywhere. We're trying to wrap the simplest thing with Bear and we can't. Something spooky is going on. Could be nothing, could be everything."

"I'm not suing anyone. I just don't want this shit in my life anymore."

"Talk to your lawyer, 'cause you're playing against the house."

"Living in New York is playing against the house. You said this city is all wrong for me."

"Stathis . . ." He sighs. "I don't understand why every fucking lesson you learn, you need to learn in the hardest way possible."

I have no answer there.

"Do me a favor and sleep on it," Alkis says.

"I don't need to sleep on it. I need to *sleep*."

There is another pause. "Fine. How're you doing with money? How broke is your ass?"

"I've been on expenses for a while, I can bridge things," I say.

"Better make this the Golden Gate Bridge. *No one* will hire you if this blows up. People talk. On that note, scoop has it that you hit the ground running in New York, after LA, after I saw you. Paul told me you're all over town with—" he lets out a quick laugh—"Warren's brother-in-law. Sorry, Paul's text."

"Paul said *Warren's brother-in-law*?" I ask. "Really? He didn't say *Erik's brother*? Or *Kevin*?"

"Seriously, is that what upset you the most out of all the things I said? Okay, I can't babysit your ass anymore. Do whatever you need to do, I got problems of my own. Just one last thing. You've never been unemployed, you've never been without a business card. You send this e-mail and your life will change forever."

I look at the three Fiji bottles on my desk as I ask Alkis: "What do you think I'm doing with Kevin?" Then I open the draft of my e-mail to Washington.

"Listen to you . . ." Alkis says. "Schoolgirl. I don't give a toss what you do with Kevin, it's none of my fucking business. But Kevin drinks expensive red. If fucking your ex-brother-in-law will keep you from unemployment, so be it."

"Don't worry. They're not pulling me back in," I say, and press Send.

Now what, Constantine?

TWENTY-THREE

MY COMMAND E-MAILS HAVE GONE down by 80 percent. Firmwide invitations, Command CARES, and sale promotions make up page one of my in-box. "Accepted" work meetings are all of a sudden postponed or canceled. Although I have nothing to do, I still go to the office religiously, hoping to bring about the termination call from human resources. That, and to prepare myself to face Gawel.

So far, my preparation has amounted to aimlessly digging around in my desk. I examine unsubmitted receipts, key cards from hotels that I never threw out, old PowerPoint decks, and photographs that Paul sent to me at Command from Trikeri—one of him playing backgammon with my father, another of him showing off an octopus.

Then I think of Gawel again and hope that he manages rejection better than I do, that his anger and pain have diminished by now, and that after our talk, eventually, somehow, he'll forget how badly I treated him. I stand up, take a few breaths, and start the fifty-foot walk to his office. By the time I get there, I want to throw up.

Gawel is in a light-blue sweater, typing on his keyboard. He faces the window, so I knock at his open door.

He turns and stares at me. It's been a year. "Can I help you?" Gawel finally says, hesitantly.

"Hi. Yes. I wanted to talk to you for a moment. If that's okay."

The expression on his face is blank. "I'm listening," he says.

I motion toward the door.

"Leave it open," Gawel orders. "I don't have much time."

He is wearing reading glasses—he didn't use to—and his Tintin hair is a bit longer. I notice a framed photo on his desk, but I don't dare give it a good look while he is keeping me hanging there.

"Right," I say.

Gawel stands up. "I'm listening," he repeats.

"Right, right." I breathe. "I won't insult you by saying that I suddenly care about how you're doing, although I do. But I want you to know that *I know* that I was a bad manager. A shitty one. And all the things that went down, they had nothing to do with you."

"I know," Gawel says.

"You are a good guy and a solid analyst."

"Is that all? Because I don't care for an apology."

"Ignore it, ignore me. But if you ever want to know why things happened the way they did, I will tell you. That's all."

He nods. I nod back, and we stand there. Then I head to the door to leave.

"Why?" Gawel's voice stops me. "Why were you such an asshole?"

I have to turn and say this to his face; I owe him that much. "You were collateral damage."

I see a tiny pleasure in Gawel's eyes, the first sign of emotion since I walked into his office.

"I hope the rumor that you're about to get fired is true," he says. "Now fuck off."

I HAVE NO FRIENDS IN New York. I have no friends, period, and I don't mind it that way. I've stopped going to restaurants, even Sant Ambroeus. I'm happy to stay home and party by myself, staring at the crap that Tati put on my walls—a framed wad of bubblegum she spat out, a half-finished martini with Teresa's lipstick on the glass. I experience an adolescent excitement about my upcoming trip. I count the days until Paris, where I'll spend Thanksgiving with my sister and her children, even if I may be on drugs.

I have become obsessed with checking my cell phone. I need to make sure I haven't missed a call from human resources, or my sister, in case she needs something, but all I get is incoherent voice mails from Ray, and Paul's mass texts about "AccostingTV, a Game Changer."

With nothing better to do, I text Paul at his personal number: "Is hacking your next thing? 'Cause I have a bio billionaire for you."

"funny ur text. bio-hacking may be our next stop. really. rewind the mind through the body," Paul texts back.

I know he is not kidding, and the fact that what I now see as absurd is my friend's daily reality—even if he is Paul—makes me feel a touch left out. I have a moment of what-have-I-done doubt about my piss-off strategy. I think of replying some nonsense, but a second text from Paul comes in: "need to talk to alkis. he's not picking up. what's going on?"

Perfect. I type: "Bubble blues, Paul? Keep stalking and pimping, you'll make it through."

"Who is this?" Paul responds.

A couple of lines later, I am surprisingly calm. I think I see an end to all the crap I was supposed to want in life, and that gives me hope for some new freedom. I can't see myself getting off a plane in Athens and handing in my passport (that idea still gives me the creeps), but I can see myself on a fishing boat in Bequia, hanging out with Jeevan, probably the only person in my memory who seems authentic and real. I used to look down on him with pity, the way I did my father. Now I envy them both. What have I done better, anyway? Lived a decadelong fiesta that started with a scholarship and ended with me in Prada, chasing white powder. I gave it my all in conference rooms, when all I cared about was bagging some phony rebel. I didn't succeed at either. Now, calling it quits is all that's left to do.

"You stole my line," I text back to Paul's "Who is this?," and then I ring Tatiana to leave her a message—she never picks up—and tell her she's a cunt for disappearing, but she does pick up, and I'm stunned.

I am missed, I am in her thoughts all the time, I am handsome. She laughs. She is happy in France. Over there it's all about the everyday things, which are the *really* important things. Have I ever had a moment when everything made sense?

"How long will you stay there?" I ask her.

"Indefinitely," she replies, and I can see her playing with her hair, seducing whoever sits opposite her while she's talking to me on the phone.

"Get to France," Tatiana orders, and it hits me that between schools and jobs and running after Erik, I missed my chance to make real friends, or really care for the ones I had. When all is said and done, friendship is the love that we are most accountable to.

"I'm on my way," I tell Tatiana. "I am meeting my family in Paris this Thanksgiving. Finally."

She's ecstatic. "I want to meet them! We *have* to get together."

"I miss you too," I say, and sniff a bump, which makes Tatiana go silent. "Allergies," I say, but she doesn't react. "Tati? You there?"

"Baby, I worry about you," she says. "Justin told me that you don't go out, that you don't go to work . . . Are you partying by yourself? That's dangerous."

"No way."

"I'll tell Kate to put your name down for God's after-party tonight. I want you to go. Promise me."

"I promise."

"I can't wait to see you."

JUAN AT THE DOOR OF the Soho Grand hugs me.

"Juanito!" I say as Juan lifts me off my feet slightly. "Are you trying to flip me, bitch?" I laugh.

"You bet," says Juan.

"Not happening."

"Are you here for the screening party on the roof?" Juan asks.

"Free drinks . . ."

He elbows me into the outside lobby. "We've lost you since you moved to New York. You got to swing by more often, Stathis."

"Deal!" I say, and head to the elevators.

I exit into the penthouse's party roar.

"Stathis Rakis," I tell the tall girl with the list in her hand. She takes her time. I spell my name.

"You were a party of two . . ." she says.

"I'm by myself."

"Your friend has already checked in," she says briskly, and lets me in.

Neither Kate nor God is in sight, so I walk to the sponsor's bar to pick up an already-mixed vodka something. Then I head toward the balcony, but someone grabs my shoulder.

"You're my plus-one, boss!" Justin laughs.

"We're both Kate's plus-one, I guess," I say.

"Oh, Kate's gone," Justin says.

"Be real . . ."

"She jumped the bones of that short dude from *X-Men*," Justin says. "I was like, guys, get a suite . . ."

"Er, are you still doing Kate?" I ask.

Justin shrugs. "Never turned anyone down."

"Been there," I murmur.

"How're you doing, boss?" Justin looks at me with blood-shot eyes. "I don't see you at work. You don't text back." He seems concerned. Then he smiles. "Are you coming to the Beatrice later?"

I scan the smokers through the glass door. "Maybe. We'll see."

"Shit, boss! You'd be so proud of me. I was in Princeton and someone was telling Andrea how much he loved *Blink*, you know, Gladwell's book of anecdotes. So tonight at the Spotted Pig, I was explaining to my analyst how we'll turn our DCF into a decision analysis model, when guess who walks in?"

"Yes, that's interesting," I say, spotting God giving an interview at the other side of the penthouse.

"Who walks in?"

"Who walks in?" I repeat impatiently. What does he want from me?

"*Malcolm Gladwell!*" Justin shouts.

"Really?" I say, uninterested, but Justin does not read me.

"You can't miss him, the dude's Halloween." His jaw shakes, he talks and spits on me. "So I go: *fuck* decision analysis. We'll call our project *blicision* analysis!" Justin laughs, spilling vodka over his pink shirt. "I love you, boss!"

"Yes, so proud of you," I say, and try to walk away from him toward the balcony, but Justin grips my hand.

"*What?*" I yell. "Blicision analysis. I got it, Justin. I *invented* that shit. Let go."

Justin winks. "Come with me, boss."

My phone rings. It's a number I don't recognize, but I have my own stuff in my pocket, so I pick up to get rid of Justin. I raise my eyebrows while motioning to my phone and walk out to the balcony.

"Captain Stathis," Kevin says over the phone. The static is terrible.

"Where are you calling from?" I ask.

"Car phone," he says.

Didn't car phones die in the nineties? "What's up, Kevin?"

"Where are you?" he asks.

"At a party."

"Nice. Where's that?"

"Downtown . . . at the Soho Grand," I say. "What's up?" I try to sound busy.

"Nothing. I'm heading back to the city, from Greenwich, and I could use a drink."

I stay silent.

"Actually, I have a meeting down on Wall Street first thing tomorrow," Kevin says.

"Really?" I say, and think of the years when I used to cook up meetings so I could fly across the country to fuck his brother.

"Yeah, it's at seven thirty," Kevin says casually.

"The early bird . . ." Now *beg*, motherfucker.

"Come to think of it, I could check in at the Grand and skip the morning rush."

"I made up a business trip to Montreal once just to spend the night with someone. But we can't always get what we want, Kevin."

"Really? What is that like?" he says, and laughs.

Like snorting speed instead of coke by accident—appalling. "Let me make it simple for you," I say.

"Oh yeah?" he says with a *bring-it-on* tone.

"A friend of mine told me that when we fall for someone, we fall for everything about them, the whole package. So you were my fuck-you-Erik fuck; you were part of my closure. And by the way, thank you for that."

"Dude, who cares if—"

"*Wait*, there's more. I used to live at the Soho Grand. The people at the door know me. You wouldn't want them to take note of your pathetic little life, now, would you?"

He is silent.

"I'd stay away if I were you," I say, and hang up.

A bittersweet feeling comes over me.

This was the last link to Erik, now cut loose, and the sadness that was always part of not being able to possess him mixes with relief, an exciting freedom that has arrived with closure. For the first time in a while, anything seems possible. I want to stroll downtown, get lost on the Lower East Side, and watch passersby, or just bump into someone on the street. I rush inside and look for the elevators, but Justin comes out of the bathroom. "Boss!" he calls. His jaw tweaks, bad. "Kate put our names down at the VIP room. Let's go see what's shaking."

"I don't give a fuck," I say.

"Huh?"

"Justin! I'm checking out!" I say, and his face becomes as serious as it gets.

"So the scoop is true," Justin says. "I thought it was a rumor, but you are leaving Command."

"Yes, the scoop is true. I'm leaving."

"Fuck, boss. I'll miss you." Justin hugs me. He presses something into my hand.

"What is this?"

"A parting gift. Good stuff. Parting with a *y*! Got that?" Justin smirks.

"Yes, yes."

"With a *y* . . . That was good!" He laughs.

"I *got* it, Justin."

"What's next, boss? Got something bigger going down?"

"I don't know," I say. "I'll go see my family. Maybe I'll get a stove." I feel a chill. I am suddenly worried. I think of all the things I'll need to get by. Not now, but soon. "I'll get a job," I say. "Hopefully a real one. One where I get to ask real questions."

Justin puts his hand on my shoulder—I can't tell if he's reaching out or losing his balance.

"Boss, Alkis told me that after he left consulting he never felt that free again," Justin says. "You may never be this free again."

I feel like I'm running out of time, now that I'm a tired, middle-aged, practically unemployed man who has no country. It might be tricky to start over. Loneliness takes hold of me, and once again, I see Ray's whitetip patrolling the oceans. Well, it's too late to start feeling sorry for myself. There must be something out there that I'll want to call my own. I don't know what that is yet, but hopefully I will.

"I've been way free," I hear myself saying. "I want boring next. I want Jeevan."

"*What?*"

"Never mind."

"Boss, Alkis is talking recession."

"I *want* a fucking recession!" I yell, and people turn.

TWO DAYS BEFORE THANKSGIVING, I walk into Two Boots on Greenwich and Seventh Avenue for a slice of cheese. There's no one in line, so I'm done with lunch in ninety seconds. I step outside to light a cigarette, and the weather is unseasonably warm, so I shove my leather jacket into the plastic bag they gave me at the Apple store. I take a puff and glance at my watch. Six hours till my flight to Paris.

I am smoking away, imagining my nephew and niece running toward me at the airport, when I recognize a voice.

"You're still smoking!"

I see Erik hurrying toward me from Seventh.

I stiffen, bracing for a seismic shift in me, but it doesn't come.

"Hi?" Erik says.

He's swimming in an oversize Abercrombie & Fitch hoodie, and, if I still know him, that would account for his tentative greeting. He looks like what he used to sneer at. I could easily take him down.

"I'd be all, go for it," Erik says, pointing at my cigarette. "But I'm coming from there." He waves toward St. Vincent's Hospital across the street.

"Hi," I say. "What happened?"

"Warren's son cut himself at a birthday party and we brought him to the ER for a couple of stitches. Nothing serious. I stepped out to get him a soda."

"Parker cut his finger?" I ask lightly, surprised that I'm not surprised or even upset to see Erik playing dad.

He just nods.

"I hear they're closing the hospital down," I say, and blow my smoke away from his face.

"Yeah, bummer," Erik says.

"Mismanagement or real-estate something."

"New York . . ." Erik says, and leans back on the Two Boots window. His legs relax. He's a different Erik, not the one I remember, who was always ready to sprint. I notice him taking me in, as if I'm someone he just met, or someone he'd known for years and now unexpectedly sees in a different light. I sense tension as he waits for my next move.

"I'm sorry about Constantine," I say.

"Right," he says, and looks down at his yellow Puma shoes. I could easily take him down for those too, but what would it prove?

"I am sorry I lost the rest of Constantine's postcards. Do you think they would have made a difference?" I ask.

Erik looks across Seventh at the fence covered in 9/11 memorial tiles. "No. Not really," he says.

"That's what I thought." I nod.

A man rushes out of Two Boots and brushes my bag. Erik makes his half smile, and I have this image of the past, of him outside the hut at Montmelian, the first time he smiled at me that way. "Is that yours?" Erik asks, poking at the Apple logo.

"That's mine. But it's not *for* me."

"Still a techno snob."

"I'm meeting my family in a couple of days in Paris," I say, smiling.

"Greeks bearing gifts—" Erik stops, embarrassed, like he was catching himself slipping into an old habit. "Seriously, that's excellent," he adds soberly.

"Finally."

There is impatience on his face, and I have a hunch that he's about to bring up Kevin. He does.

"I hear you helped my brother with a due diligence," he says, so casually that I know he is overcompensating. He knows.

I look straight into his eyes. "Does it matter?" I ask.

"No. Not really," he says, once again avoiding me.

Another few dead seconds go by. Talking about Kevin makes me sad. I have a flight to catch, and I haven't finished packing. I put out my cigarette with my foot. "It was fun, Erik," I say, exhaling the last of the smoke.

"Yes, Stathis, it was." Erik gives me a full smile. And that is my sign-off.

Memories mutate; they overpower the truth. We keep what we wish to remember. It was fun and goddamn pain, all mixed together. We shake hands and Erik goes for that extra second, which I allow him because I don't need it.

"See you around," I say, and walk north on Greenwich. As I turn the corner onto Bank Street, my phone buzzes.

"I don't believe this," I answer.

"What?" Tatiana asks.

"Guess who I just ran into."

"Who?"

"Actually . . . it's not important. How are you?"

"Huh?"

"How *are* you?"

"I'm good. I'm just checking in on you," Tatiana says. "Make sure you don't miss your flight."

"Still watching over me."

Tati giggles. "Always."

"I can't wait to see Markos and Zoë," I say, sitting down on my brownstone's stoop. The trees on Bank Street have started to change. This might be my last fall in New York, and for the first time, I'm awake to how beautiful my block is.

"What did you get them?" Tatiana asks.

"Gadgets, iCrap . . ."

"Aww, I wish I were there with you to go shopping for gifts."

"We'll go shopping in France. At that fruit market in Aix you've been e-mailing me about."

"Oh my God, I'm such a good cook now. You'll gain five pounds in a *week*. Where are you guys staying in Paris? Hey!" Her voice turns dark. "I don't want you to see Teresa over there."

"I wasn't planning to, but—"

"*What?*"

"Tatiana, she's been worrying about you. She calls me all the time. Tati, listen, she really—"

"Stop!"

"Okay . . ."

"Are you still in touch with Ray?" she asks, calmer.

"No. He sends me a text once in a blue moon."

"Drop him."

"Don't worry about him," I say. "I have. I don't even understand his messages. I give him six months before he breaks up."

"Do you know that he got high and beat the shit out of my mother?" Tatiana asks. "He sent her to the fucking hospital."

"Shit. I did not know that. I'm sorry," I say. "Tatiana, listen. One more reason you should call her. She's probably depressed, she needs you."

"I'm working on it," Tatiana says softly. "I will."

"Good." I light a cigarette. "Better sooner rather than later."

"Things take the time they need to take," Tatiana says. "Are you still smoking?"

"Well . . . things take the time they need to take."

She laughs.

"Just because you moved to France doesn't mean you're the poster child of health," I say, and there's an awkward pause. "Okay, I should not have said that. I am impressed with what you did."

"What are you impressed with?" she asks suspiciously.

"You, leaving New York . . ."

"You don't know how I live here."

"No, I do not," I say. "But you sound happy, living with your father. I don't think I've ever heard you more together."

"My father is in Berkeley. I'm kind of alone."

"We are alone together," I say, and out of the blue I think of Jeevan. I remember Erik and me holding on tightly to his dinghy, heading south to Tobago Cays, at the far end of the Caribbean, when Jeevan spotted a tiny red boat out in the middle of nowhere. Instantly, he started racing toward it, ripping through open waves—no life jackets or radio on board. "What in the hell are you doing!" Erik screamed. "You're gonna get us drowned!"

"He's my friend," Jeevan said, pointing at the boat calmly and fearlessly. "I want to say hi to my friend."

"Come here after Thanksgiving. Stay with us for a bit," Tatiana says.

"Us?"

I process her silence while looking at my loafers, the loafers she picked out for me. "You never had the abortion, did you?"

"I've never been happier. Come."

"I'm not sober," I say.

"I know," she says.

"What's your son's name?"

"Stathis," Tatiana says.

ACKNOWLEDGMENTS

SPECIAL THANKS TO PETER ALEXANDROU, Jonathan Burnham, Alex Cannariato, Aris Constantinides, James Connolly, David Cobb Craig, Tanmoy Das Lala, Stefanos Economou, Jennifer Farrugia, Makis Gazis, Brian Gerrity, Ozerk Gogus, Lisa Goldenberg, Christina Haag, Brian Hamill, Barry Harbaugh, Jonathon Irpino, Peter Jeffreys, Sofia Karvela, Alexia Katsaounis, Maria Koundoura, Eric Lee, John Lyons, Mick Malisic, Constantine Manos, Scott McCormack, Sandra Mintz, Ian Olson, Heather O'Neill, Marco Pinter, Jonathan Procter, Seth and Lauren Redniss, Marjorie Reitman, Celia Roniotes, Jody Rosen, Ira Sachs, George Samoilis, Eric Schade, Aria Sloss, Christy Smith, Blair Steckler, Alexandra and Judith Stonehill, Mickey Sumner, Karim Tartoussieh, Joshua Tierney, Lycourgos Tsirakis, Grigori Vyssoulis, Christopher Westley, Sallie Wiggins, Mauricio Zacharias, and—the most important person—my mother.

ABOUT THE AUTHOR

IOANNIS PAPPOS IS A MANAGEMENT consultant and writer from Pelio, Greece. He is a graduate of Stanford University and INSEAD business school, and he has worked in both the US and Europe. *Hotel Living* is his first novel. He lives in New York City.